She was troubl[e]

But, Lord help him, he did love trouble.

And he loved the way she was wearing her hair, flowing wild to her shoulders. Yeah, she was a stunner, his Irish. And then he noticed her pink dress. A redhead in a pink dress?

His spine went rigid. It couldn't be. *Kerrie Muldoon* was his blind date? His gaze ran the length of the mirrored wall he was facing—and he realized the bar was crawling with cops. That waiter. That waitress. That couple.

And, of course, Kerrie herself.

Good. None of them had spotted him. So, by dumb luck alone Nick Diamond, a.k.a. Roman Donnello, had escaped their trap.

But then, Roman knew he could never really escape Kerrie—his one love, his Irish.

Dear Reader,

You've told us that stories about hidden identities are some of your favorites, so we're happy to bring you another such story in our HIDDEN IDENTITY promotion.

This month meet Nick Diamond, a.k.a. Roman Donnello, in Adrianne Lee's exciting new novel, *Alias: Daddy*. Seattle homicide cop Kerrie Muldoon is about to have her worst nightmare come true, when she runs into the mysterious father of her two secret twin girls....

Says the author, "I'm a Seattle area native, married to my high school sweetheart. I started out writing mysteries, but have always been a romantic at heart. It was only natural that I'd eventually combine my two loves. In 1991, the day after I'd given up writing for good, I sold my first book. It was seven years after I started writing seriously. So, let me 'intrigue' you—because I believe romance is best when it's spiced with suspense. I love hearing from readers. For an answer and autographed sticker, please enclose a SASE. Write to me at P.O. Box 3835, Sequim, WA 98392."

We hope you enjoy Adrianne's *Alias: Daddy*— and all the books that have come to you in HIDDEN IDENTITY.

Regards,

Debra Matteucci
Senior Editor & Editorial Coordinator
Harlequin Books
300 East 42nd Street
New York, New York 10017

Alias: Daddy
Adrianne Lee

Harlequin Books

TORONTO • NEW YORK • LONDON
AMSTERDAM • PARIS • SYDNEY • HAMBURG
STOCKHOLM • ATHENS • TOKYO • MILAN
MADRID • WARSAW • BUDAPEST • AUCKLAND

Special thanks to Carol Hurn, Mary Alice Mierz,
Nadine Miller, Judy Strege, Toni Bronson,
Gayle Webster, Susan Skaggs, Kelly McKillip,
Anne Martin, Barbara Bretton, Susan O'Boyle,
Tim Perry and my AOL loop sisters.

ISBN 0-373-22422-2

ALIAS: DADDY

Printed in U.S.A.

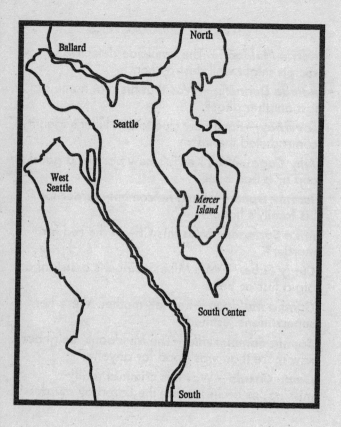

Ballard

North

Seattle

West
Seattle

*Mercer
Island*

South Center

South

CAST OF CHARACTERS

Kerrie Muldoon—The homicide detective's secrets might well destroy her.

Roman Donnello—Was that his real name or just another alias?

Loverboy—Each new clue to this killer's identity contradicted the last.

Tully Cage—Was Kerrie's new partner a good cop or a bad one?

Jeremy Dane—Would he commit murder for his family's honor?

Mike Springer—Was this CPA in the red for murder?

Cindy Faber—Was Mike Springer's assistant as big a liar as he?

Glynna Muldoon—Kerrie's mother. Were her superstitions justified?

Sophia Sommerville—The Muldoons' neighbor saw more than was good for anyone.

Dante Casale—Was this criminal really missing, or orchestrating the Loverboy murders?

Chapter One

Any minute now, the killer would walk through the door.

Kerrie Muldoon shifted on the restaurant seat. She was wired for sound, but feared the wire had come loose, that she couldn't be heard. It was one thing playing bait to catch a cold-blooded murderer; it was another to do so without backup. "Cage, can you hear me?"

"You're comin' in loud and clear, Muldoon." Cage's New Jersey accent tickled her ears. He'd been her partner since his transfer to Seattle six months ago, and she'd trust him with her life. *Was* trusting him with her life.

"He's late." Impatience nipped her. She shoved her fiery tangle of curls out of her eyes. The door joggled. Her instincts kicked to full alert and Kerrie sat straighter, her gaze riveted to the entrance of F. X. McRory's. The shape of a tall man filled the doorway. "Wait. Maybe this is h—"

She broke off, swearing as the man's face came into view, the greatest face God had ever created, a face she'd hoped never to see again...a face she remembered every day of her life.

His blue-black hair was longer now, grazing the tips of his ears and the collar of his London Fog coat, but his ebony brows still cut straight slashes above eyes the rich amber of the tequila gold shots he favored.

On another man, his bold nose would dominate, detract from his handsomeness, but on Nick Diamond it added strength, character. Too bad strength of character wasn't one of his attributes. Her eyes swept his brazen mouth, and her heart kicked up a beat. She forced her gaze to his jaw, reminding herself that it was as square as the man was crooked.

Self-preservation and fear collided inside Kerrie. She swore again.

"Hey, Muldoon, what's with the gutter mouth?" Cage's voice blared in her ear.

"Huh?" Kerrie hadn't realized she'd even spoken; one look at the man moving steadily toward her table had stripped her senses. What the hell was he doing here? Now? After three years?

"Hello, Irish." His deep voice caressed her ears like the sweet, mellow notes of a concert violin. "You know, I wondered."

Steeling her body, she glared at him, trying to ignore the impossible and completely unacceptable thundering of her heart. "What did you wonder, Diamond?"

"If this was still your favorite restaurant."

It had been *their* favorite restaurant. If Loverboy—as the press had dubbed the killer—hadn't made a practice of meeting his victims in this bar for a drink, she wouldn't be here now. "Old habits…"

"It looks the same." His gaze never left her face. Without an invitation, he pulled out the chair opposite Kerrie and, lifting a long, muscled leg over the back of it as though he were mounting a horse, sat. "But you…you look better than ever."

"Well, some things change and some don't. You're still spouting the same old blarney. Probably explains why you're alone, Nick."

"And every bit as sassy, too." His lazy gaze rolled over

her. "Why do you assume I'm not meeting someone here?"

Unwanted jealousy prodded her, and Kerrie jerked her chin a notch higher. What was the matter with her? This man was the biggest mistake she'd ever made—and she never made the same mistake twice. "What a coincidence. I'm meeting someone, too. So, make yourself scarce."

"Now, is that any way to greet an old friend?"

"We were never friends, Diamond."

A smoldering gleam warmed his golden eyes. Kerrie's breath snagged. He leaned toward her. "You're right, Irish, we were so very much more."

Fire burned a path through her belly at the memories he roused—memories she had never completely succeeded in burying, memories that could still haunt long, lonely nights. Damn the man. He would not turn her life upside down again.

Cage's voice sounded in her ear. "Muldoon, is this Nick Diamond guy our first suspect?"

"No." Heat spiked her cheeks. She'd forgotten they could be overheard.

But Nick thought the "No" was for him. His black brows arched and he reached across the table and grazed his knuckles along her jaw. "Don't deny it, Kerrie. That little heart-shaped birthmark of yours isn't exactly in a spot you'd likely show a casual acquaintance."

Cage whistled. "What little heart-shaped birthmark?"

Mortified, Kerrie batted Nick's hand away and reared back. One of the undercover officers acting as a waitress, witnessed the action and hurried over. "You ready to order?"

Kerrie shook her head. Double damn. Nick Diamond was about to screw up this stakeout. She had to get rid of him. "No. This is not the man I'm waiting for."

"Then...I should come back later?" the waitress asked uncertainly.

"Why don't you do that?" Nick said.

"No." Kerrie glared at him. "He needs a table of his own."

"We don't really have anything available right now. You could sit at the bar, sir." The waitress suggested.

"That's okay. I think I'll stay where I am."

The waitress glanced at Kerrie with renewed uncertainty. Kerrie feared she'd blow both their covers. She shrugged. "It's okay. I'll handle it."

The second they were alone again, before she could vent her rage, he said, "You see, you don't really want me to leave."

He was dead wrong about that. "I don't really want to cause a scene, but I will if you aren't out of that chair by the time I finish counting ten. One."

"I'll go...if you'll have dinner with me tomorrow."

"No. Two."

"Then you can count to ten a dozen times, I'm not budging until you agree to have dinner with me."

"Never. Three."

Cage cut in. "Accept, dammit, and get rid of this guy."

"I will not have dinner with you. Not now or ever. Four."

"Then lunch. Here." Nick's mouth curved in a wry, sensual grin as he rose slowly out of the chair, giving her the full effect of all that she'd been missing for three years. "Noon, Irish. Don't be late."

So help her, she couldn't stop her gaze from raking up his long, lean, completely masculine body. So help her, she couldn't stop the ache of yearning deep inside.

Cage's chuckling did that. Stopped it cold. "Whew! Are you sure that Diamond guy's not Loverboy?"

"Positive."

"Then who the hell is he?"

"None of your business. We have a murderer to catch. You worry about that." She wasn't going to concentrate on anything else. Certainly not on Nick Diamond.

From across the room she felt his eyes on her. She tried shaking off the sensation. She hadn't gotten to the rank of homicide detective with the Seattle PD at the young age of twenty-nine from lack of stamina and willpower. She was thorough, methodical, gutsy. She had been to the wall and back.

Her fierce pride would protect her. This time.

But she was still a woman. And right now, that feminine side felt more vulnerable than it had in a good long while. If she hadn't already set up three cocktail dates for this evening, she'd call off this stakeout and reschedule it for another night. But she was as stuck as a bug in thick jam.

WITH HIS BACK TO THE BAR, Roman Donnello settled his gaze on Kerrie Muldoon, the redheaded spitfire who'd tangled up his life but good three years ago. So, she still thought his name was Nick Diamond. He supposed it suited his purposes to let her go on thinking that for now. He circled the thick rim of the shot glass with his index finger, his eyes focused on Kerrie.

He'd been crazy about her…until he found out she was using him. That blow to his ego was almost as bad as the fact that she'd meant him real harm. He'd run as fast and as far from her as he could get and never looked back.

The crowd noise elevated, and Roman could swear someone had called him a liar, the word a whisper in his ear, a murmur in his head. Although he'd deny it with his dying breath, Kerrie Muldoon had stayed in his mind like a recurring fever, haunting at least half of his dreams every week of his life since.

He blew out an exasperated breath. She *would* have to

be here tonight. He should have tried meeting his "date"
somewhere else. Kerrie crossed her long legs beneath the
table, one foot bouncing with impatience. His mouth dried.
He gazed transfixed at the bouncing limb, remembering
how those legs felt wrapped around him. Trying not to
remember.

She was trouble.

Lord help him, he did love trouble.

And he loved the way she was wearing her hair, flowing
wild and free to her shoulders. It was usually braided,
pulled off her face, that damnably, unforgettable face with
its luminous emerald eyes, its long, straight, lightly freck-
led nose, and its sassy, pouty lips.

He ignored the wild thundering of his heart, the quick
hard pooling of lust in his groin. She was a stunner, his
Irish. She took his breath away. But he supposed that was
fair. He'd left *her* breathless on more than one occasion.
A grin tugged at the corners of his mouth as he savored
the memory.

Was the guy she was waiting for the man in her life
now? Oddly that thought rankled him. Well, the guy had
no class. Kerrie wasn't a woman to keep waiting.

He tossed back the shot of tequila, then clanked the
glass on the counter. It wasn't like her to put up with it,
either. She'd obviously dolled up for the creep—in that
scrap of a pink dress that was catching the eye of every
guy in the bar.

Pink dress?

A redhead in a pink dress?

It hit him like a jolt that the description his blind date
had given of herself fit Kerrie. His spine went rigid. *Kerrie*
was the woman he'd made the "date" with? His instincts
flashed on red alert. Not Kerrie. He'd have recognized her
voice anywhere. He'd spoken to someone else.

What was going on? This time, letting his natural an-

tennae operate, he glanced around the bar, blocking out
the clamorous buzz of conversations, sports TV and clat-
tering glassware.

"Well, I'll be damned," he muttered after a moment.

"You say something?" asked the man occupying the
stool beside him.

"Talking to myself. Bad habit." Roman spun toward
the counter, and signaled for another drink, then lifted his
gaze to the mirror that ran the length of the wall he was
facing. The bar was crawling with cops. That waiter. That
waitress. That couple.

By dumb luck alone, he'd escaped their trap. Self-
disgust tweaked him. He should have spotted the setup
immediately. In his business, that instinct had saved his
hide more often than he could count. Irish had distracted
him. Just like the last time.

Their gazes met in the mirror and he raised his shot glass
to her and winked. She glared and spun away from him.
He chuckled to himself. He didn't doubt she was still angry
at him for leaving without saying goodbye three years ago,
for screwing up her case, cursing him now for walking
back into her life.

Roman considered the exchange they'd shared earlier.
Whatever had been between them three years ago still
lived. He'd seen the fire in her emerald eyes. Felt it in
every fiber of his being. "Starting tomorrow, at lunch,
Irish, you're going to discover how it feels to be used."

KERRIE SQUIRMED on her chair. This had to be the longest
stakeout she'd ever suffered through. Not only did her first
date stand her up, but so did the second. All the while
she'd felt Nick Diamond's eyes on her. Nick Diamond.
She scowled in disgust. A slick name for a slick gangster.
She'd wanted so badly for one of her dates to be somebody
spectacular, a man Nick would hate seeing her with. She

hated herself for caring what he thought. Hated herself worse, for being aware that he, too, had been stood up.

He was the only person in the world she was genuinely afraid of and not just because of her attraction to him.

"I can hear your stomach growling, Muldoon. Maybe you should order an appetizer." Cage broke into her dark musing, but her usual good humor had deserted her. Probably Nick Diamond's fault. She could feel him watching her and didn't dare glance around.

"You're right, Cage. It's nearly ten. If date number three isn't here in five more minutes, I'm calling it a night."

At that moment, a man, tall and blond, with a self-possessed air came through the door. His three-piece navy blue suit fitted his lean body as if tailor-made. He glanced at his watch—probably a Rolex, Kerrie thought—then scanned the bar.

She squared her shoulders, but the guy waved at someone behind her and Kerrie let out a taut breath. She had better compose herself before the next date or she'd never manage to make it through the interview. Another man appeared in the doorway. Instinctively, Kerrie knew this one was the one she'd been waiting for.

It wasn't his appearance, but the way he managed to draw no attention to himself, despite the pristine white dress shirt he wore—its long sleeves rolled to the elbows revealing well-muscled forearms—and jeans, creases ironed down the center of each leg. He, too, scanned the bar. Spotting Kerrie, he straightened, seemingly adding another inch to his six-foot-plus frame. Kerrie whispered to Cage, "He's here."

The man had short brown hair, neatly combed, and cool blue eyes behind fastidious wire-rimmed glasses. He said, "Kerrie?"

His voice was soft, stirring nothing more in her than the

urge to ask him to speak up. "Yes. And you must be…"
Damn. The guy's name had gone right out of her head,
thanks to Nick Diamond.

"Ah, Jeremy Dane." He offered her a pink rose.

Kerrie smiled. He wasn't the Adonis she had prayed for,
but he would do. She thanked him for the rose and gestured for him to sit. Despite herself, she felt a smidgeon
of satisfaction. She sensed eyes boring into her back. Nick
Diamond, of course. She shivered, the satisfaction scur-
rying away as if it were a mackerel frightened by a shark.

"Is something wrong?" Jeremy asked, taking the seat
across from her.

Kerrie shook herself and forced her faltering smile up
at the corners. "No. Not really. It's just that…I've never
done this before."

"Done what?"

"Met someone through a classified ad."

"I see."

"Have you?"

He poked a finger at the bridge of his glasses, a leery
look entering his cool blue eyes. "Once or twice."

Kerrie waited for him to expand, but he didn't. She bit
back a frustrated sigh. "I guess it can't be too bad then if
you're willing to try again."

"No."

Cage's voice slipped into her ear. "This guy is some
conversationalist."

"Uh-huh," Kerrie responded without thinking.

"Pardon?" Jeremy leaned closer.

"Nothing." But her cheeks heated. She had to remember not to answer Cage.

The waitress came, took Jeremy's drink order and left.
He fingered the rose. "Why did you run the ad?"

"Oh." She laughed. "After a couple of disastrous blind
dates fixed up for me by friends, I decided the Classifieds

had to be better. I could list what appeals to me and maybe
have something in common with men responding to the
ad."

"You said you work for Computer City? Doing what?"
His eyes were hot behind the glasses, suggesting an intense
nature beneath his calm, fastidious exterior. Disquiet spun
through her and she glanced away from him. Jeremy
touched her hand with one clammy finger, and she jerked
back toward him.

"Talk to me," he demanded in his soft voice. His expression implied that her attention should belong to him
and no one else.

Her throat dried. She took a sip of her club soda.
"About?"

"Your job. Your life. Anything. Everything."

Usually adept at small talk, Kerrie could think of nothing to say. "I, uh—"

"Ask him about his job." Cage broke in.

Jeremy's drink arrived and by the time the waitress collected the money and left, Kerrie felt more in control of
herself. "Really, you know more about me than I do about
you. Why don't you tell me where you work?"

"Boeing. On the assembly line. Boring, repetitive
work..."

As Jeremy started asking her personal questions, Cage
fed Kerrie the false bio they'd worked up. Occasionally
she threw in a telling question or two. Always, Jeremy
skirted answering as if he had something to hide. As if he
might be Loverboy? His behavior sure put him near the
top of their suspect list.

They were an hour into the date when Jeremy touched
her hand again. "Let's go somewhere more private."

Kerrie's stomach knotted at the suggestion. "I'm sorry.
I like you, Jeremy, but I'm not ready to move that fast.

I'd like to get to know you better. Maybe...a second date?''

Wounded pride, anger and frustration passed in such rapid succession through his eyes that she'd almost thought she'd imagined them. Almost.

His gaze was steady now, controlled. "Sure. Here? Night after tomorrow? Dinner?''

"I'd like that.'' She'd hate that. This guy made her skin crawl. Maybe it was his eyes. Maybe it was his evasiveness. Maybe it was the way he tapped her hand when she glanced away from him. Maybe it was all three.

"Eight?''

"Great.'' Great, indeed. She'd made two dates tonight that she hadn't wanted to make. The one for dinner she would keep. The one for lunch she would not.

"May I escort you to your car?''

"No, thanks. Maybe another night.''

"A cautious lady. I can be patient.'' Jeremy kissed the back of her hand, said good evening and left.

Kerrie wiped her hand on her napkin beneath the table, muttering to Cage, giving him a description of Jeremy, "He's leaving now.''

"See you tomorrow, Irish.'' Nick's voice, close to her ear, sent a tingle shivering down her spine.

She recovered too slowly to respond. He was already at the door, following Jeremy outside.

"IRISH, HUH?'' Tully Cage laughed as she entered the undercover police van. Cage was a couple of years older than Kerrie. He had blond hair, crew cut, and teal blue eyes, with a scar that sliced through one eyebrow, giving him a mean look. In the past six months she had discovered that he could be mean when the situation called for it, a trait she admired at those times. But overall, she'd say she'd been lucky in the partner pool. Cage was a decent cop, as straight an arrow as ever flew through the Seattle PD.

"How come you never told me about that Diamond guy before?" he asked in his strongest New Jersey accent, an inflection he always played up whenever he teased her.

"There are a lot of things you don't know about me, Cage." She plopped onto the van's front passenger seat. "Let's keep it that way."

It was the wrong thing to say. She could see the interest it sparked in his eyes. But he didn't pursue the subject. "What did you think of Jeremy Dane?"

"He gave me the creeps. He's either a run of the mill sleazeball, or Loverboy."

"Well, we'll know his life story inside and out by morning."

Not that that gave her consolation. She was the one who had to meet him again. "I wonder why the first two dates never showed."

"Your guess is as good as mine. Let's file the report and go home."

At the station, Kerrie went to the locker room and changed into blue jeans and a white T-shirt. Feeling more like herself, she joined Cage at his desk. He looked up from a handheld recorder. "I called the *Introductions* line and retrieved the messages."

Kerrie perched a hip on the edge of his desk. *Introductions* was the newspaper column where they'd placed the classified ad. "Any new callers?"

"No. Two old callers. The two who stood you up tonight."

"Oh, yeah. What did they want?"

Cage punched the Play button. "Listen."

A scratchy voice came on. "This is Troy. I thought you were different from the others, Kerrie. You said you were looking for some*one* to call your own. I came into the bar tonight thinking that *one* was me. But you were with an-other man. I watched you from the shadows. He made your face light up. Liar. Don't you know how to be faithful to *one* man?''

Cage pushed the Stop button. ''Nice, huh?''

Glad she had missed meeting this guy, Kerrie shook her head. ''And I thought Jeremy Dane was a creep.''

Cage smirked. ''The second call is just as interesting.''

He started the tape again.

Kerrie's heart nearly stopped. The man didn't identify himself, but the voice sounded very much like Nick Dia-mond's.

''Am I mistaken?'' Cage asked. ''Or does that sound like the guy who calls you Irish?''

Nick Diamond...a murderer of young women? He was a dangerous man. If she was right about him, he was a smuggler. But a cold blooded killer? A psychopath? She couldn't bear the thought that she'd slept with such a man. And worse.

She hugged her stomach. Then again, hadn't she sus-pected his bosses of having connections to the mob? If she was honest, hadn't she had her share of nightmares where Diamond appeared as a mobster hitman? And hadn't he remained date-free the whole four hours he'd been at the bar?

''Well, do you think it's him, or not?''

''I don't know. Play it again.''

Listening three times to the man apologize for being unable to keep the date and asking to reschedule for an-other time, only made her three times more certain that the caller was Nick.

''I'll deal with this tomorrow,'' Kerrie said. ''Right now, I'm going to type up my report and go home.''

''I'll type it. You go on home now.''

''You sure? 'Cause I'm going to take you up on it.''

"I'm sure."

Twenty minutes later, Kerrie entered the three-bedroom house in West Settle that she shared with her widowed mother. A light was on in the living room, emphasizing the vivid ruby of the Victorian furniture that had once resided in her parents' huge house and was now crammed into the tight confines of the small space.

"Mom, what are you still doing up?"

"I wanted to make sure you got the message." A slender woman with vibrant red hair, Glynna Muldoon was curled on the sofa in a robe. Small and delicate, she usually looked ten years younger than her fifty-six years, but tonight there was undefined dread in her pale green eyes that gave away her true age. "Your lieutenant called. He wanted you to call him at home the moment you came in. I told him it was late, but he was very insistent."

A surge of apprehension surged in Kerrie. It wasn't like her boss to call her at home. She hoped Loverboy hadn't struck again.

Glynna followed Kerrie to the kitchen phone and stood to one side wringing her hands. Although it was after one in the morning, the lieutenant sounded wide-awake. "I just talked to Cage and I'm going to tell you exactly what I told him. The mayor climbed my frame tonight at the benefit dinner. He wants Loverboy caught. Now."

Kerrie let out a held breath. At least, there had been no new killing. As far as anyone knew anyway. "We're doing our best."

"Not good enough. I don't like having my frame climbed by the mayor or anyone else."

Kerrie didn't blame him. She didn't like it any better than he did. She curbed her rising temper. "We got a couple of leads tonight."

"Cage tells me you might know one of our suspects."

Kerrie tensed at the mention of Nick Diamond. "Cage told you about the messages?"

"Yes. Do you know the guy or not?"

"Maybe. I don't know. I'm not positive it's his voice." But she was positive.

"Well, we're not taking any chances. I don't want Loverboy killing anyone else."

Her heart hitched. "Neither do I."

"I'm glad you see it that way. I've already spoken to Cage about this. I don't want you taking any unnecessary chances, but I want you to keep the lunch date you made with that Diamond guy. In fact, I want you to stick to that man like glue. Make up excuses to be with him. Ask him out if you have to."

"But—"

"Don't 'but' me, Muldoon! Cage will be backing you up. Just do it!" The phone went dead.

Furious and shaken to her toes, she hung up.

"You're as pale as a ghost, Kerrie Carleen. I knew it. I've been expecting bad news all day—ever since that black cat crossed my path in front of Riley's Market this afternoon. I'm right, aren't I?"

"Yes, Mom, you are." Kerrie gazed down the hall at the closed bedroom door and shuddered. "The lieutenant just condemned me to hell."

Chapter Two

Kerrie was late, and F. X. McRory's bar was noisy with noontime patrons. But even in a crowd, Nick Diamond drew her attention like radar to an incoming enemy missile. Memories threatened to engulf her. He was seated at their old table. She shrugged out of her wet raincoat and tightened the band around her collapsed umbrella, holding the memories at bay with a new resolve she'd found sometime during the bleak hours before dawn. She'd be damned if she'd let him know he was getting to her. She'd be damned if he'd get to her.

Weaving between the occupied tables, she muttered, "He's here."

"And I'm here, too." Cage's voice filled her left ear, offering a double-edged reassurance: on the one hand, backup was only a shout away, on the other, her partner would hear every word she shared with the unpredictable Nick Diamond.

Forcing a pleasant expression, Kerrie shoved her thick curls back from her face and closed the distance separating her from Nick.

He was on his feet, his amber eyes lighting as if they were twin suns. "Irish…"

He didn't say he approved of her soft green sweater and hip-hugging plaid skirt; his eyes said it for him, rolling lazily, appreciatively over her. Heat skimmed her flesh and coiled in her belly. With sheer willpower, she held her amiable expression.

"I chose this table—" he dipped his head and a lock of his raven hair brushed his forehead, and the corners of his mouth tipped upward "—for old times' sake."

"Well, I'm not the sentimental type." She dropped her raincoat over the back of the chair facing his. "One table is the same as any other to me."

Was that disappointment or amusement flitting through his eyes? She couldn't discern before his grin widened and zapped her animosity, weakened her knees. Neither before nor since Nick, had a man so affected her. But why? How could her blood be heated to boiling by a man who might be a cold-blooded killer? Was there something missing in her moral fiber? Was it her innate love of danger that made Nick attractive?

Whatever the cause, she had to master these feelings and dispose of them. Otherwise, this man could strip her of everything she held dear.

Against her protests, he insisted on helping her ease her chair up to the table. His subtle aftershave settled around her, a bewitching fragrance that suited Nick and Nick alone, and made her pulse thrum.

He murmured near her right ear, "I like the new perfume."

"New perfume?" It was so close to what she'd been thinking about him that she flinched. "I'm wearing the same scent I've always worn."

He returned to his chair and sank into it with the grace of a dancer. He shook his head. "No…I remember your scent. This is different."

Kerrie caught a hint of vulnerability in his eyes. It confused her. She didn't want to know he could be vulnerable. Couldn't afford to think of him as human. "That just goes to show you how faulty memory can be. I haven't changed perfumes in five years.''

She could tell her lie had dented his ego, but he recovered quickly, his gaze caressing her face. "I was starting to think you were going to stand me up.''

"Would I do that?" But she would have. In the blink of an eye. In a heartbeat. In a New York minute. And yet standing up Nick Diamond would have been in defiance of her lieutenant's orders and netted her nothing more than a place on the unemployment line. A fate she could ill afford. "Your ego so fragile these days, Diamond, you couldn't bear being stood up by two women in as many days?"

It took him a second to realize she was referring to last night's no-show date. His expression sobered. His voice lowered. "If one of the women was you, Irish.''

Despite her best efforts at detachment, she felt his words steal through her, whispering across that secret place where she'd interred her tender feelings for him. Her body went rigid, and she grabbed the menu, hiding behind it, buying time.

This man had swept through her life as if he were a hurricane, devastating her, nearly destroying her. But now she was older. Wiser. Stronger. Even though she still felt an attraction to him, she had infinitely more to lose now. No. She would not succumb to his potent sex appeal. Or her own misguided memories.

A cocktail waitress strode to the table and began refilling Nick's coffee cup. She turned toward Kerrie. "Coffee or something stronger?''

"Coffee will be fine.''

As the waitress took their lunch orders, Cage murmured, "I've been reading the report on this Diamond guy. For all intents and purposes, he didn't exist before four years ago.''

Cage wasn't telling Kerrie anything new. She had conducted her own search for Nick Diamond three years ago and discovered exactly the same thing. She suspected he was Mafia. He had a dozen aliases.

The waitress left and they were alone again.

Nick said, "Aren't you going to ask what I've been doing for the past three years?"

"Sure, why not?" Kerrie laughed and shrugged, keeping her voice and expression neutral, even though that was exactly what she wanted to hear. "What have you been doing?"

"Nothing very interesting." He sipped his coffee, forcing her gaze to his sensuous mouth. "Did you miss me, Irish?"

"Not for a minute." The lie zinged off her tongue.

He covered his heart with his hand as if she'd wounded him. "Not one minute in three long years?"

"Not even thirty seconds." *Terrific. He'd rather flirt than talk.* Schooling her impatience, Kerrie added cream to her coffee. She needed a starting point, something that would get him to open up, but which of the things she "knew" about Nick were true?

Come to that, what had *she* ever told him that was true? "So, what are you doing in Seattle?"

Nick grinned. "I'm here as a favor to a friend."

"Nothing illegal, I hope." She sipped her coffee, feeling bolstered by the hot liquid.

"Illegal? Now, why would you ask that?" His amber eyes gleamed with feigned innocence. "Oh, of course, I forgot...because you're one of Seattle's finest."

Despite her best effort not to show her surprise, Kerrie's eyes widened. How long had he known she was a cop? For three years? Was that why he'd left Seattle so abruptly? Had she somehow blown her cover? Had she guessed she was investigating his company for smuggling?

Or had he run a check on her after he'd left Seattle? Either way, it didn't matter now. She set her cup down. "My occupation is hardly a secret."

"Then why did you tell me you worked for Seattle Lighting, selling light fixtures?"

Cage spoke before she could answer. "I don't like the direction this is going."

Kerrie wished she could reassure her partner, but he'd have to settle for letting her do what damage control she could. She arched a brow and leveled her gaze at Nick. "I suppose *you* were one hundred percent forthright with me?"

Nick reached across the table and grazed his knuckles along her jaw. "Every romance needs a little mystery."

"Romance?" Cage queried.

"Personally, I find honesty refreshing," Kerrie said in the coldest tone she could manage. "Why don't we try some now?"

"Sure. You start. Who were you trying to catch here last night? It wouldn't be that 'Loverboy' the local newspapers are full of lately, would it?"

Cage squawked and swore. "How did he know that?"

How had he known? Kerrie wanted to shout at her partner. *Nick was a hood! Hoods could smell a roomful of cops from a mile off.* Instead of shouting, she took a calming breath, willing herself not to be sidetracked by her partner's anxiety. "I can't account for your vivid imagination. The only thing I was doing here last night was having a pleasant date. I was most certainly not trying to catch anyone called Loveboy."

"Loverboy." Nick *tsked,* his devilish smile lighting his handsome face. "Did you know you blink when you lie?"

Cage swore again. "He knows we're on to him. He knows your true identity. I think you'd better terminate this interview."

Anxiety tightened Kerrie's stomach. Maybe now was a good time to start listening to her partner. She rose from her chair.

Nick followed suit. "Where are you going?"

"I forgot," she said coolly. "I've got another appointment and if I don't leave now, I'll be late."

"But you haven't eaten."

"I've lost my appetite." She started to reach into her purse for her wallet. "But I'll pay—"

"No. I invited you. Lunch with an old friend."

Kerrie shook her head. "I told you before...we were never friends."

"All right...lovers."

"Lovers?" Cage teased, his New Jersey roots traceable in his voice. "Is that why you didn't want to meet with this guy?"

After Nick Diamond's remark about her birthmark yesterday, Cage knew full well that was the reason. Fuming at both men, she retrieved her umbrella from the floor and shook it at Nick, speaking to him as well as her partner. "That's history. Let's keep it that way."

Nick reached across and, as gently as a baby's touch, nipped the sleeve of her sweater between his finger and thumb. "Are you sure that's what you want?"

She blew out a frustrated breath. "Positive!"

She pulled free, gathered her raincoat and began weaving her way between the empty tables. She mumbled, "I'm halfway across the restaurant."

Cage sighed. "Good."

Struggling into her coat as she moved, Kerrie rammed her hip against a table. Pain spiraled from her hipbone and pulled her up short. The person at the table jerked his head up. Beneath the brim of his felt hat, his sable brown eyes were hot and unfriendly. Kerrie blinked and stepped back, excusing herself.

But the man's odd expression replayed in her head as she hurried onto the sidewalk. He'd seemed startled and yet, the look in his eyes had been chilling as though he knew and...hated her. She shivered. Did she know the owner of that face?

The rain had let up, but the October wind gusted down the busy street, tossing leaves and debris along the gutters and sidewalks. Tension hurried Kerrie toward her five-year-old Mazda at the end of the block. She barely glanced at the unmarked Seattle PD van parked on the opposite side of the street. Just knowing Cage was there reassured her.

Footsteps sounded behind her, and the skin at her nape prickled, that odd sensation she got whenever she was being watched or followed. "Cage, can you see me?"

"Yes."

Fear flushed her skin as she envisioned again the eerie eyes of the man whose table she'd bumped in the bar. Her car was less than five feet away. "Is someone following me?"

"As a matter of fact...yes."

Her pulse wobbled. She reached into her purse and grasped her gun.

Cage chuckled. "It's your lunch date."

"What?" Furious, she closed the gap to her car, then wheeled around.

Four feet behind her, Nick reared to a stop. His black leather jacket hung open at his waist, and the wind ran fresh fingers through his ebony hair. He started to speak.

Kerrie cut him off, glaring at him. "I said goodbye."

One corner of his mouth quirked upward and a huge dimple dented his cheek. "Actually you didn't. You just left. Rather rudely, I thought."

"Then we're even. That's exactly the way you left the

last time I saw you.'' She turned her back on him, unlocked her car door and yanked it open.

"I knew you were still angry about that." Nick caught the door and held it as Kerrie climbed into the Mazda.

She peered up at him. "I'm not angry. You did me a favor by disappearing."

"A favor? Good. Then you owe me one. I'll collect now. I need a lift to my hotel."

With her patience thinning, she dug into her wallet, then withdrew a quarter and boldly tucked it into the coin pocket of his jeans. "Call a taxi."

Her gaze lifted in time for her to see the slight widening of his eyes. She bit her lip to keep from smiling and gestured for him to back up so she could shut the door.

Cage said, "Maybe you should give him a ride. Find out where he's staying. We could dust your car after for fingerprints."

Kerrie's brows lifted at her partner's sudden about-face. She swore under her breath and poked the key into the ignition, but didn't start the car.

Still holding the door, Nick leaned down until their faces were level. "You have to drive right past my hotel."

"I'm not going that way."

"I haven't told you where I'm staying." His breath feathered across her lips, smelling of mint and coffee.

She tensed. "I haven't told you where I'm going."

"Back to the station to write your report about our lunch, right?"

Fear shimmered through her. But was she afraid Nick was Loverboy or was she just afraid of Nick?

As if he'd read her mind, Cage said, "Don't worry, Muldoon, I'll be with you every block. And if we can pick up some prints, we might get a handle on this guy."

"It's getting downright cold out here." Nick shrugged

against the chilly wind, then glanced at the sky. "Was that a raindrop?"

She sighed and rolled her eyes. "Oh, all right. I'll take you under one condition—promise you won't talk about our past."

He nodded, then hurried around to the passenger side of her car. Surreptitiously, he glanced at the van across the street, recognizing it for what it was. "I'll be damned," he whispered as it dawned on him that Kerrie was wired for sound. That the police had been listening to their every word.

The full ramification hit him as he dropped onto the seat beside her. My God, she must think *he* was Loverboy. Anger seared his gut. Damn her. She was more cop than woman, and she was setting him up again.

If he weren't so angry, he might find it amusing. Here he'd been thinking himself so clever. That *he* was going to use *her* this time, and all the while she was making a fool out of him again. He heard the van's engine fire. Her "backup" would be following them. A vindictive thought crept through his mind, bringing a grin to his lips. With an effort, he suppressed it and he reached for the seat belt.

Kerrie started the engine and pulled into traffic, too aware of Nick's disturbing bulk beside her. She focused straight ahead, thanking the powers that be that he was finally quiet.

Rain began to fall, thundering against the roof of the car and causing the windows to fog. The wipers clacked and the defroster huffed—normal Seattle sounds that Kerrie found familiar and comforting in a world that too often was alien and disturbing. She started to relax.

"Don't worry, Irish." Nick's husky voice vibrated along her nerve endings, and Kerrie swore silently. Before she could tell him she wasn't worried about anything, he leaned close to her. Despite her best efforts to resist, she glanced into his amber eyes.

"I don't need to talk about our past," he murmured. "I can tell every time we're together that you're remembering it."

Cage chuckled.

Kerrie's temper snapped. She stomped on the brake, and with tires squealing, jerked the car to the curb. "Get out."

For once Cage seemed at a loss for words.

Nick looked out at the rain, then back at Kerrie. He made no move to comply to her command. She should have reached over and opened his door, but that would have meant touching him. Her jaw still tingled where his fingers had grazed it earlier and she didn't want to touch him, didn't want any other part of her to feel his warmth. "I said, get out."

His gaze fell on her mouth, puckered in anger. A sudden blood-heating hunger swept him. God, he wanted to kiss her; the force of it shocked him. But he could see if he tried she'd slap handcuffs on him so fast his wrists would rattle. He glanced out at the rain again, then back at Kerrie, his expression as repentant as his words. "Okay. That was uncalled for. I'll behave."

Behave? Kerrie's anger flared as if it were a reviving fire and she struggled to douse it. She doubted Nick even knew the meaning of the word "behave." She bit back the urge to tell him that. The best thing to do was accept his apology, rein in her temper and drop him off. Quickly.

"Muldoon?" Cage's voice issuing from her police radio—instead of directly into her ear—startled her. She glared at the radio. She was as angry at Cage for laughing at her as she was at Nick for creating the problem. She wasn't sure she wanted to hear anything from Cage. Pulling into traffic again, she glanced into the rearview mirror.

The van was still behind her. Still following. Whatever Cage wanted, he could say to her privately.

His voice issued from the radio again, sounding anxious. Why was he using the radio now? Perturbed, she grabbed the handheld microphone and answered. "Muldoon, here. What's up, Cage?"

"Your mother was in some kind of accident."

"What? When? Where is she? How is she?" The questions tumbled out of her with the speed of her accelerating heart as frightening scenarios leaped through her head.

There was a pause from Cage and then he said, "She's at Virginia Mason. No other details yet. I'll see what I can find out and call you right back."

Kerrie had already started up Pill Hill, the district above Seattle named for all the medical facilities located there. "Make it fast. I'll be at the hospital in two minutes."

Chapter Three

Tension in the Mazda zipped a notch higher. Roman watched Kerrie's knuckles turn white against the black steering wheel as she dodged through traffic with the daring and expertise of a professional race driver. So intent was her expression, he figured she had blocked out all else—including the fact that he still occupied the seat beside her.

Detachment was something most cops became adept at, usually sooner than later, but despite her profession, beneath it all, Kerrie was a daughter. He knew too well that her professional reserve flew out the window when family was threatened or injured.

He considered what he might say to calm her down and quickly rejected the hollow clichés that sprang to mind. In the course of her daily grind she'd likely offered worthless bromides more times than she could count to families of victims.

Kerrie swore. The car rammed to a stop, then almost instantly started forward again with a lurch, jerking Roman against the seat belt. Right now, there was only one thing that could truly ease the heart-thudding, pulse-jumping fear that was coursing through her veins: a doctor's assurance that her mother would survive and be as she was before whatever accident had befallen her.

Recklessly, Kerrie took a corner too fast, then slammed to a stop again at the entrance to a covered, six-story parking garage. Moments later, they were ascending through the narrow passageways at freeway speed. The Mazda's tires chirped in protest. Roman held on, his gaze sliding to Kerrie.

He wanted to ask about her mother. But in the six weeks he'd shared with Kerrie three years ago, she'd never mentioned her parents. Or siblings. Or aunts, or uncles, nephews or nieces. Hell, for all he knew there was a whole clan of Muldoons they'd never discussed.

Their conversations had centered on business, his business, or their pleasuring each other. More often, they hadn't talked at all. Erotic images filled his head. Roman swallowed hard and shoved them away. She, too, had family who could be hurt, perhaps killed; the pain of recent loss squeezed his heart, and like a train shifting on a track, realization jostled him.

He'd let Kerrie distract him, diverting his focus from his mission in Seattle. It was time he stopped playing games. Time he fixed on the task he'd come to perform.

Kerrie was out of the car and heading toward the stairs before he could disengage his seat belt. She didn't notice him chasing after her. Rain fell in sheets as she sprinted across the street and into the Virginia Mason Medical Center. The police van pulled to the curb. Roman ignored it. Wet and disgruntled, he followed Kerrie to the reception desk where she was inquiring about her mother.

But it wasn't until they were on the elevator that she glanced at him and a look of bewildered recognition, then annoyance registered in her eyes. "What are you doing?"

Roman grinned wryly, trying to diffuse the tension that issued from her like steam off a damp sidewalk. "I believe it's called 'riding in an elevator'."

Her face darkened with impatience. "What are you doing *here?*"

"I'd like to make certain your mother is okay."

"Why?"

The question brought him up short. He noticed a drop of rain on her forehead, but resisted the temptation to brush it aside. Why *did* he care about her mother? He'd never met the woman...never given her a thought before a few minutes ago. Reasons eluded him. He frowned hard. "I don't know...but I do."

"Well, get lost. I can't deal with you right now."

The elevator doors slid open, but before Kerrie scurried off, Roman caught her arm. "Irish, you're as pale as a ghost. Likely in shock. If your mother is awake...aware, do you want her to see you like this?" He loosened his grip, wishing the odd knot in his throat would loosen as well. "Wouldn't you rather take a minute to catch your breath?"

She bit her lower lip, her chest heaving. After a long moment, she nodded. Roman released her, and they stepped off the elevator. The doors clacked shut behind them. Kerrie closed her eyes and took two slow, deep breaths. He couldn't remember ever seeing her look so...so vulnerable. Nor could he recall a woman's vulnerability touching him more.

With an effort, Roman resisted the urge to pull her into a comforting embrace. She wouldn't welcome such a gesture...not at this moment...not from him.

She opened her eyes, their emerald depths clearing, the shock subsiding. "Better."

"Yes," he agreed. "Better. Which room is she in?"

Kerrie raised an eyebrow. He suspected she was about to question him again on the subject of his interest in her mother. Instead she planted her hands on her shapely little hips and ran her tongue along her delectable upper lip, the gestures drawing his attention to areas of her he was trying damned hard to ignore.

She said, "I appreciate what you just did for me, staving off a hysterical outburst, but you and my mother…gas and water. Please, just go."

Roman puzzled the gas and water analogy for half a second, until it hit him that she still thought he was Nick Diamond, not the sort of man any woman in her right mind would ever introduce to her mother. Maybe this wasn't the time or place to straighten her out. Maybe it was. "There's something I need to tell—"

"No, not now." Kerrie held up a hand to silence him. "One accident at a time is my limit." She spun on her heel and headed down the hall, promptly disappearing around a bend. Roman caught up with her just as Kerrie approached a uniformed cop, a Gold's Gym lifetime member from the size of him.

Roman sidled up to them and stopped. The patrolman's pale eyebrows lifted. Kerrie shook her head. "Never mind him, Erikssen, tell me what happened."

"There was a knifing."

All heat drained from Kerrie's face. "My mother?"

A handsome, silver-haired doctor emerged from the nearest room. A stethoscope draped his tanned neck and a white lab coat protected his expensive suit. Kerrie abandoned Erikssen. "Oh, Jon. How is she?"

The hard lines around Dr. Jon Vauter's dark eyes softened as he adapted a consoling expression. "Shaken, but otherwise—"

"Shaken?" Kerrie cut him off. "I don't understand. Erikssen said there had been a knifing."

Dr. Vauter nodded. "The other woman wasn't as lucky as Glynna."

"Other woman?" One of her mother's friends? Kerrie's heart hitched. "Who?"

Erikssen jumped in as if she'd asked him the question, giving her the name of a stranger. Kerrie drew a ragged breath, relief slipping through her. Her mother wasn't hurt. No one she knew had been stabbed. Guilt tainted her relief. *Someone* knew and loved the other woman. "What's her condition?"

"She was DOA," Erikssen answered.

Kerrie cast the patrolman a bewildered glance. "How was my mother involved in this?"

This time the doctor answered. "Glynna insists we let her tell you, Kerrie."

She shifted toward the doctor again. "And she's all right?"

"She had quite a shock, but otherwise she appears to be fine."

Relief threatened to drop her to her knees, but Kerrie resisted the urge with all her might. She would not embarrass herself with a show of feminine frailties. Not in front of Erikssen, who might carry the tale back to the station. Not in front of Nick Diamond, who knew too well how to use her weaknesses against her.

She squared her shoulders, and mentally pulled herself together. Her mother was fine. Not hurt, just rattled. "When can I take her home?"

"Well, I would like to keep her overnight—"

Kerrie cut him off. "But you said she was fine."

"Merely a precaution, Kerrie. Shock is always unpredictable."

Kerrie cast Jon Vauter a sidelong glance. He wasn't just their family doctor. A widower of five years, he was also her mother's frequent dinner companion and tennis partner; he'd even proposed marriage once or twice. She suspected his concern now was more personal than professional, a consideration that dissipated her tension another notch.

"Kerrie? Is that you?" Glynna's voice floated out to them.

For the first time in an hour, Kerrie grinned. "You'll have to excuse me, gentlemen, I'm being paged."

Against the stark white hospital sheets, Glynna Muldoon's vibrant hair stood out like a scarlet rose on freshly fallen snow. She looked relieved to see Kerrie. "I'm so glad you're here. Maybe you can talk some sense into that…that…doctor. I told him I was perfectly fine. All I need is to go home and be with my girls."

Glynna had recently combed her hair and applied makeup—both testaments to her well-being, which reenforced Kerrie's belief about Jon Vauter's motives in making her spend the night here. The last of Kerrie's stretched nerves relaxed. "You'll be home with us tomorrow."

"Don't tell me you're siding with Jon? Ye Gods, I'm not some feebleminded old fool downed by the ravages of one shocking incident." She tapped her chest in the general area of her heart, her neatly polished nails brilliant against the faded hospital gown. "This fifty-six-year-old ticker is as sound as any half its age."

"Nevertheless, you gave me quite a scare." Kerrie smiled at her and moved to the edge of the bed. "What exactly happened?"

Glynna sighed. As she leaned into the two pillows propped against her back, she clasped her right hand over Kerrie's. Her left hand was fisted against her side, as if she held something precious in her grasp.

"Well, it was my lucky day, I'll tell you that. I was downtown, shopping. Last minute Christmas items, you know." She flinched. "That reminds me. I don't know what became of my packages. Do check on that."

"Yes, ma'am." Glynna always began Christmas shopping the day after Memorial weekend. For her not to be finished this late in October was rare. But Christmas shopping was the last thing Kerrie wanted to talk about now. "Mom, tell me what happened?"

Glynna's gaze had settled on something above and behind Kerrie's shoulder. Kerrie glanced around. Nick Diamond. He stood near the door, the lower half of his face partially shaded from view. His ebony hair was still damp, giving it a provocative sheen and his seductive amber eyes were warm pools of concern. Her throat tightened with emotion. The fear she recognized and admitted, but the other emotion she would neither accept, nor acknowledge.

Roman strode toward them, stepping from the shadows into full light.

With a rustle of sheets, Kerrie's mother sat straight up in the bed, her soft green eyes wide with alarm. "Do I know you, young man?"

"No." Roman tipped his head to one side, supposing the fright he saw in the woman's eyes was from the scare she'd had earlier. "I'm here with Iri...Kerrie."

Kerrie sputtered, "Yes, ah, he's, er, a—"

"Roman Donnello," he said, having decided he could straighten Kerrie out about his name later. He ignored her surprised expression.

"Donnello?" Glynna shook her head. "No, that's not the right name..."

Her gaze drilled into him as if she were trying to place him, as if she thought she *did* know him. Why? They'd never met, and to his knowledge, Irish had no pictures of him.

"Ye Gods!" Glynna's gaze flicked sharply to her daughter and she drew in a sharp breath. "Kerrie Carleen, he looks just like Gab—"

"Mother!" There was an hysterical edge to Kerrie's voice. "I don't think Mr....Mr.—"

"Donnello," he stated again. What was the matter? What had caused the sudden uneasiness that permeated the room like an invisible, yet chilling, fog? Kerrie was shaking.

"Mom, Mr. Donnello, doesn't look like anyone we know." Her voice held a pointed edge, as though she was warning her mother about something. "Do you suppose we could get back to what happened to *you* today?"

Roman bit down his frustration as the two women exchanged an anxious glance. What the hell was going on?

Stiffly Glynna settled back against the pillows, her gaze riveted to Kerrie. "D-did I mention I'd been Christmas shopping?" Her voice quavered slightly.

Kerrie nodded, and pulled in an unsteady breath, too aware of Nick's presence and the danger it posed—now that her mother realized who he was.

"The streets were so crowded today," Glynna said. "Lunchtime and all. Anyway, a large group of us were gathered at the crosswalk, waiting for the light to change. Someone kept bumping against my backside, so I moved forward a step and that's when I felt it."

"The knife?" Roman asked.

She blinked at him. "My, no! A knife? Why would you think... Ye Gods, is that what—?"

"Yes." Kerrie frowned at Roman. "Please, go on. We'll try not to interrupt."

Glynna swallowed. "What I felt was something under my right shoe. I lifted my foot and there was a penny. *Find a penny, pick it up and all day long you'll have good luck.* The second I bent over to pick it up, the woman beside me let out an odd little gasp. I'd supposed I'd jostled her with my packages, or stepped on her foot or some such, so I grabbed the penny and straightened, intending to apologize and explain. But the woman's face was all contorted as if she were in agony. Reminded me of the day your father—"

Glynna broke off. She shuddered, remembering either

today's stabbing or her husband's death. "Before I could ask what the matter was, the woman grabbed me and started sliding toward the pavement. The light changed and people flooded around us. I thought the woman had fainted. I tried getting someone to help me, and that's when I noticed the blood on my hand, on the woman's coat. All over her side, a huge dark patch that just kept getting bigger and bigger. I must have screamed, because suddenly lots of people were offering assistance. I remember an ambulance, but not much else. It's all sort of hazy."

Roman's neck prickled. Something about this incident bothered him. He couldn't put his finger on it, but he'd felt this same gnawing in his gut before. When Wendy died. Did *this* stabbing have something to do with Lover-boy?

Kerrie caught a puzzling emotion in Nick's eyes, as though after hearing Glynna's account of the incident he were more concerned about her welfare than he'd been earlier. Nonsense. This day had her so rattled she was finding worries where none existed.

She smiled at her mother. "I'm just glad that you're all right."

Glynna lifted her left hand and slowly uncurled it. A penny lay in her palm. She stared at it. "Lucky is what I am."

Roman had always heard picking up a penny was bad luck. Real bad luck. The gnawing in his gut increased. Glynna Muldoon had been lucky. Today. But he had an awful feeling that her luck had about run out.

Irish needed to know.

But would she listen? Frustration flashed through him. She was one pigheaded woman. She might not listen just to spite him. He wanted to pull her out into the hallway, insist she go somewhere with him so they could talk in private. But she and her mother exchanged another anxious glance. He realized whatever was going on between them—whatever tension he'd unwittingly heightened—took precedence at this moment.

Without being asked, he excused himself and left the two women to hash out their problem. He stifled the urge to eavesdrop. As curious as he was, he needed to think, to figure out why he thought Glynna Muldoon, not the other woman, had been the intended victim of the stabbing.

Was it because something about this stabbing produced the same prickly feeling he'd had when Wendy was murdered?

He leaned against the wall and shut his eyes. Hell, he couldn't prove a case on feelings. Damn it all. He didn't know how this fit into the puzzle *he* was trying to solve. And yet every instinct he had told him it did.

He shoved away from the wall as Kerrie emerged into the hall. Spotting him, she rolled her eyes. "I was hoping you'd be gone."

"I still need a ride to my hotel."

"Get a cab." She hurried ahead of him to the elevators and punched the Down button.

"Are you going to put a guard on your mother's room?"

With a start, she lurched around, then issued an annoyed sigh. "Why would I do that? It was a random attack."

"Was it?"

She eyed him suspiciously. Did he know something she didn't? "Do you have proof to the contrary?"

"No, but..." How could he explain his gut instincts without sounding ridiculous?

She shook her head at him and punched the Down button again. "It's not your concern. Just stay out of it, okay?"

"I can't."

"Then maybe I should have you booked and investigated." She wheeled around, her eyes shooting daggers. "Believe me, nothing would give me greater pleasure."

"Really?" He tipped his head and a lock of his raven hair danced across his high forehead, highlighting the gleam in his amber eyes, the sensuous smile tugging at his irresistible mouth. "I could think of something that would give you far greater pleasure."

The visual filled her head before she could stop it, spilling heat into every part of her. She growled, spun away from the elevators and slammed into the stairwell.

Roman followed, his long legs easily overtaking her shorter ones on the lower landing. He grabbed her wrist and pinned her against the wall. "Dammit, will you listen to me?"

Kerrie's heart climbed her throat. Their gazes collided, locked. She couldn't look away, couldn't dodge the amber heat issuing from his raven-lashed eyes, couldn't douse the answering fire deep within her very being, couldn't breathe for want of him.

Roman lowered his head, all thoughts of explanations, of Loverboy and stabbings, forgotten in his sudden need to possess this woman, his woman, his Irish. He captured her mouth with his and passion exploded at the contact, fierce and rough, full of freed longing.

Kerrie reached up and grabbed his neck, her hands plowing into his thick hair as he pulled her close, fitting her hard body against his harder need. The awareness of his erection spurred her on, pulled a breathy moan from her. An answering groan burst deep in Roman's throat, resounding in her ears, her heart. His hand skimmed down her leg, grasped it at the back of the knee and lifted it to his hip. His strong fingers slipped under her tight green skirt toward her panties...

Dear God, the audio wire. Kerrie reared back, batting at his hands, shoving at his chest. "Don't. Stop!"

From somewhere below them, a door banged open and

voices echoed up the stairwell. Alarm joined the dismay on Kerrie's face. Straightening her clothing, she turned and fled down the stairs.

It took Roman a moment longer to get control of himself. Then he started after her. Hell, it felt like he'd spent most of this day chasing her.

Two floors down, he ran into a group of nurses and other hospital workers coming up. He lurched toward the wall, the women copied the move. Roman veered toward the stair railing, the women did the same. One of them laughed and shrugged, muttering something about a standoff. Roman grinned without humor, bit down his impatience and retreated back onto the landing, pressing himself against the wall while they passed.

He'd lost precious minutes, but by the time he had a clear pathway, he'd recovered his senses enough to realize that he'd let Kerrie take off without hearing him out, without hearing his concerns about her mother.

He charged down the remaining floors. How much time had passed? How much of a head start had Irish gotten? He emerged on the sidewalk and squinted against the rain. She was nowhere in sight. Neither was the police van.

Anxiously he sprinted across the road, into the parking garage and up to their floor, taking the stairs two at a time. The Mazda was gone. A squeal of brakes echoed through the belly of the building. Roman swore.

KERRIE WAS SHAKING all over. What had gotten into her? Letting Nick kiss her? The image of her response blocked out everything else and she knew it wasn't letting him kiss her that had her trembling. It was that she'd kissed him back with an abandon she'd only known one other time in her life. With Nick.

Had the attack on her mother robbed her of her senses? Or was it her mother's shock at realizing who Nick was that had stripped away her rationality? She merged with freeway traffic headed south. She had to be insane to still feel his lips, his groping fingers, his turgid need. Her own need tingled through her.

She swallowed hard, checked her rearview mirror and changed lanes. Thank heavens, she'd come to her senses. Remembered the wire. Otherwise...

No. Nothing would have happened. Nick had simply taken advantage of her in a vulnerable moment—as she'd known he would. She let out a derisive laugh. Honestly, using his so-called concern for her mother. She shook her head. The lengths he'd gone to—hinting the attack hadn't been random. She wanted to scream. Of course it had been random. Who would want to stab her mother?

The radio squawked, startling her out of her thoughts. Cage. She took a deep breath, then answered.

"How's your mom?" he asked.

"To quote her, 'lucky.'"

"Yeah, I heard. You headed in here?"

"No. I'm going home."

"Oh, yes. Obligations. I'll do my notes on your lunch date and you can type the report in the morning."

"Thanks." She turned the radio off and changed lanes again, steering onto the West Seattle freeway.

Good thing she didn't have to meet Jeremy Dane until tomorrow night. One encounter with a Loverboy-candidate a day was more than enough. The thought made the hair on her nape stand at attention, made Nick's words about the attack on her mother not being random jangle inside her head.

She reached for her cell phone, contacted headquarters and was put through to her boss. She explained the situation, then said, "Lieutenant, could you see about posting a guard on my mom's room?"

"Any reason?"

"Just call it a precaution."

He hesitated only a moment. "Considering the nature

of the case you're on, I think I can find the manpower to
guard a patient overnight."

She breathed a sigh of relief. "Thanks."

"No thanks necessary. I want you fresh in the morning,
concentrating on catching Loverboy, and you won't be if
you're worried about your mom. Now go home and un-
wind."

"I'll try." But instead of unwinding, Kerrie was more
tense by the time she pulled into her quiet neighborhood
in West Seattle. She steered down the alleyway and up
behind the redbrick house. The three-bedroom rambler
with a basement and detached garage was far from new,
but she loved it as much now as the first time she'd seen
it five years ago.

Pride of ownership, she supposed; it was her first major
purchase and she'd earned the down payment on her own,
which had emptied her savings. For a year, the only furniture she'd had was her bed, one old beanbag chair and
a secondhand TV.

Then her dad died, leaving Glynna lost and lonely in
their grand home in Redmond. They'd decided to sell it,
pool their assets and live together. It had turned out to be
a godsend for Kerrie. But after today, would the household
ever be the same again?

She parked in the garage, then headed three doors down
to her neighbor Sophia Sommerville's ancient, two-story
house. Sophia, who had a passion for purple, had painted
the place a bright lavender with grape trim.

After two knocks, Sophia opened the door. A slender
woman, Kerrie had often thought Sophia might be a real
beauty, but she down-played her best features, even wearing her iron gray hair permed unattractively close to her
head. She was drying her hands on her mauve apron. Her
fierce brown eyes widened in surprise. "Kerrie, I was expecting Glynna. She's running a might late. Is anything
the matter?"

"Yes. But she's all right." Kerrie quickly gave Sophia a hasty rundown. "She'll be home in the morning."

Sophia and Glynna had met at Riley's Market shortly after Sophia had moved into the neighborhood last year. Widowhood gave them common ground and they'd become friends.

Sophia pulled her inside the foyer. "My goodness, you've had quite a day."

If you only knew, Kerrie thought, drawing in a deep breath rife with the scents of lemon oil and freshly baked peanut butter cookies. Her empty stomach gurgled. "Are the girls ready?"

"Yep. Been little angels, as usual. They're in the den, playing."

Kerrie followed Sophia. A buzzing arose from the kitchen. "Oh, my cookies," Sophia exclaimed, excusing herself.

Kerrie stopped in the doorway to the den. Every time she came upon this sight her heart filled to bursting. Now was no exception. The twins were playing with giant plastic blocks, jabbering in a language only the two of them understood. Maureen noticed her first. "Mommy."

She scrambled up on her two-year-old legs and toddled toward Kerrie, arms outstretched. Her sister echoed Maureen's delighted squeal and followed her across the room.

Kerrie squatted and opened her arms to receive them. They were dressed alike in pale blue coveralls and long-sleeved white T-shirts, but her daughters were paternal twins.

Maureen resembled Glynna and Kerrie, her hair a tangle of fiery curls, her eyes a soft emerald. But from her glossy raven hair to her thick, ebony-lashed amber eyes, Gabriella was the image of the twins' father. Nick Diamond.

Chapter Four

Nick Diamond. Kerrie reared back from the peephole in her front door. How had he gotten her home address? What was he doing on her porch at nine o'clock at night? What was he doing on her porch—period? Had he somehow learned about the twins?

The thought brought her heart into her throat. Her pulse roared in her ears. Maybe if she was really quiet, he'd go away. She tiptoed backward...and slammed against Glynna's antique plant stand. Visions of the giant Boston fern smashing to the hardwood floor snapped her around. Too late.

The resulting crash could have awakened the dead. Had the twins heard? Kerrie's throat constricted. Inanely she stared at the mess, torn between scooping it up and checking on her sleeping children.

The doorbell pealed, instantly followed by Nick's voice. "Come on, Irish. Open the door. We need to talk."

Talk? Terror jangled through her as sharply as the pealing doorbell that echoed through the halls. If the shattering pot hadn't awakened the twins, the blasted bell soon would. Damn the man. She stepped over the mound of fern and dirt and broken ceramic pot, and yanked open the door.

The evening wind that blasted her face carried his subtle, mind-bending scent. She lifted her chin a notch higher. She would not respond to him, not to the way the breeze riffled his sleek raven hair, not to the way his damnably compelling eyes glowed as they caressed her face, not to that cocksure tilt of his head, nor that mischievous-little-boy grin dimpling his cheeks.

"Hi."

Hi? As if his being here were the most natural thing in the world. As if his being here could mean anything but disaster. She lashed out at him in fear more than anger. "What did you do—go back and harass my mother until she told you?"

"Told me what?" His raven brows tipped low, accentuating the amber of his eyes, and she saw genuine confusion in their heated depths. "I haven't been back to the hospital today."

He didn't know what she was talking about. Relief slithered through her. He didn't know about the twins. A man of his passion would demand the truth from her otherwise, not feign ignorance. "Then how did you know where I lived?"

He ignored the question. "Aren't you going to invite me in?"

Cold wind sliced through Kerrie. She glared up at him, hugging herself against the chill. Nick was wearing his body cleaving Levi's, cowboy boots and a heavy black leather jacket. But fresh from the shower, her hair still damp, she wore a threadbare old sweat suit and fuzzy slippers—neither of which offered protection against the stormy night. "Why should I invite you in?"

He grimaced, hunching into the collar of his coat. "Because it's cold and rainy out here and what I have to say may take a while."

Kerrie laughed derisively. "I don't want to hear anything you have to say."

Roman bit back a grin. God, she was breathtaking and beautiful…and as stubborn as an old mule. "Whether you want to or not, you *are* going to hear me out."

"Really." She laughed again. "You overestimate your powers of persuasion. What's it like having an ego the size of the Kingdome?"

She reached for the door.

Nick slapped his palm against the door and shoved inward. "I'd rather not have an audience for what I want to discuss with you, but if you insist, we will." He caught her by the wrist and pulled her out onto the porch.

"Stop it! Kidnapping is against the law. I'll have you arrested."

"Okay. You can call from McRory's."

"No!" She dug her heels in. "I can't leave."

"Why not?"

She floundered frantically for an excuse. "Be-because it's raining…and I'm not wearing a coat or shoes."

"I'll carry you." He bent as though to scoop her into his arms.

His scent surrounded her and memories of his embrace doubled her panic. Where was her gun when she needed it? She shoved him away. "No! I'm expecting a call from…from Mom."

Nick sprang past her and leaned against the door frame, effectively blocking her reentrance into the house. He folded his arms across his wide chest and arched a raven brow. "Then invite me in. We are going to talk and it is going to be now."

Kerrie blew out a breath as hot as the anger bubbling through her chest. "What don't you understand about the word no?"

"Nothing. But no isn't a word that's going to stop me, Irish. I can be as stubborn as you any given day. You are going to hear me out!"

Kerrie was breathing hard. "Why should I?"

"Because I'm after Loverboy, too."

Her eyes widened slightly and her mouth dipped open, but she quickly recovered. "A-after him?"

"Yes." Pain etched in the fine lines around his eyes and mouth. "His first victim, Wendy Waring, was as close as I'll ever come to having a kid sister."

His simple statement robbed the fight from her. An icy chill—the kind her mother would call someone walking over her grave—swept Kerrie. Loverboy's *second* victim had been her ex-partner's fiancée. She had suspected Loverboy might be one of many things Nick Diamond and she had in common, but not once had it occurred to her that *victims* would be the link.

"May I come in now and explain?"

She bit her lower lip. Kerrie Muldoon, mother and woman, feared this man more than any she'd ever met. What if the twins awoke? One look at Gabriella and...

Could she take the chance? Kerrie Muldoon, homicide detective, argued that she should. If Nick Diamond had vital information about Loverboy, even one small clue that could lead to the killer's identity, she had to take the risk; or another woman might die.

"Irish?"

Reluctantly she nodded, waited for him to move aside, then entered the house. Her gaze darted down the hall to the twins' closed door. *Please, God, let them sleep through the night as they usually do,* she prayed, bending and scooping up the spilled plant. She carried the fern to the kitchen, with Nick at her heels. Nearing the counter, she spotted Maureen's plastic bib gaily decorating the bottom of the sink, and once again her heart climbed her throat.

Quickly she plopped the plant on top of the bib. Had Nick seen it? She gathered the courage to turn and face him.

He smiled at her. "If you'll show me where you hide your broom, I'll sweep up the rest of that mess in the entry."

"I'll do it later." Kerrie exhaled painfully. He hadn't seen. "Right now, I'm only concerned about saving the plant."

She set to work making a pretext of saving the plant, covering the bib with more dirt. Her heart thundered at the near calamity, at the possibility that she'd left out something else of the babies'.

Roman watched Kerrie pick bits of colored clay from the dirt and the roots of the large plant, then glanced away, taking the moment to inspect her kitchen. He liked the effect, lots of oak and creamy tones with dabs of bright green, like her eyes. He drew a deep breath. "That coffee smells good. Mind if I help myself?"

Kerrie turned from the sink, giving the kitchen a rapid, surreptitious once-over. Was there less air in the room, or was she having an anxiety attack? Finding no telltale signs of the twins' existence, she breathed a little easier and gazed at Nick with returning confidence. "You won't be here long enough to drink any coffee."

His mouth quirked in humor. "As much as you'd like me to disappear—"

"Yes, I would." She wiped her hands on the dish towel she kept draped over the refrigerator handle. "Just like three years ago, but—"

"But I'm not going to." He helped himself to one of the mugs hanging from the cup rack and filled it with coffee. "In fact, what I have to say might last as long as it takes us to finish this pot."

"This conversation is going to start and end with Loverboy. Anything else you can keep to yourself. I'm not interested."

"I think you'll change your mind. Besides, this doesn't

start with Loverboy.'' He frowned. ''But it must tie in somehow.''

''Really, Nick—''

''No. My name's not Nick Diamond. That was an alias I was using three years ago.''

Kerrie rolled her eyes. ''Big surprise. How many have you used over the years?''

''Dozens.'' He filled a second cup with coffee and offered it to her.

Kerrie ignored the proffered cup. ''I guessed as much.''

''Yeah, but I'll bet you never guessed the correct reason why.''

''I'd take that bet.''

''You'd lose.'' He shoved the mug toward her again.

''I doubt it.'' Deciding the quickest way to get him out of her house was to humor him, she begrudgingly accepted the cup. ''So, what's your real name? Oh, let me guess, Roman Donnello.''

''That's right.''

''Sure, and I'm Garth Brooks.''

Roman chuckled. ''No offense to Garth, but he never looked as good as you.''

''Could we get back to Loverboy?''

''Eventually.'' He carried his cup to the antique dining table that seemed too formal for the room, too formal for Kerrie's tastes. Her mother's? He started to pull out a chair.

''No! Not there,'' Kerrie chirped in alarm. The second he pulled the chair away from the table, he'd see the child's booster seat. ''I'd prefer we did this in the living room.''

He lifted an eyebrow suggestively, seductively. ''Because a kitchen is too cozy?''

The air between them seemed to evaporate.

''Something like that.'' Letting out a painful breath, she

led him into her elegant, if overcrowded little living room, the one area of the house she'd straightened after dinner, the one area of the house she could swear contained no telltale sign of the twins.

Again, Roman guessed the straight-backed sofa and delicate tables, fussy lamps and somber colors were not of Kerrie's choosing. In fact, they reminded him of Philip Waring, Wendy's father. Philip's tastes ran along similar lines as these. He kept the thought to himself, set his mug on a glass panel of the coffee table and removed his jacket, tossing it casually over the back of the ruby Victorian sofa.

The heavy jacket looked graceless, as odd as he felt, perched on a sofa that was too dainty and rigid for his size and comfort.

Or was Irish the reason he couldn't quite relax?

She'd chosen one of the two chairs facing him, perching on the edge like a bird ready for flight. He wanted to kiss away her frown. He wanted to run his hands through her wild mane of hair. He wanted to strip off her sweat suit, touch her magnificent body with his hands and his mouth; he wanted to bury himself inside her until she cried out in sweet bliss...

"Loverboy?" she prompted.

Roman started at the name, thinking for half a second that she'd read his thoughts, realizing as quickly that she meant the killer. She let out an impatient breath. Obviously all she wanted him to do was finish his confession and leave. He'd bet he could change her mind. He suppressed a grin and scooped up his cup. "I was undercover at C & F Importers three years ago—same as your partner, what was his name...Bud Grimes. It had taken a year to gain Casale's and Fabrizio's trust, and I wasn't about to let the Seattle PD blow my cover—which you damned near did."

"Undercover?" As a cop? Unbidden her gaze raked from his mussed hair to his audacious mouth, to the way his clothes fit his incredible body. Nothing about this man said cop. Even though she didn't believe it for a minute, she asked, "Are you saying you're FBI or something?"

"Or something. My agency has a lesser known set of initials, but that's neither here nor there, except as it relates to my telling you the truth."

The truth. Did he know the meaning of the word? Maybe she should give him *her* definition and see how close he could come to it. Oh, she was sure he'd make it sound like the truth; the man could spin a fairy tale with the skill of Hans Christian Andersen.

She crossed her arms over her chest. "Why should I believe anything you say?"

"I have proof—credentials." He set aside his cup and stood slowly. Her gaze lifted with him, pulled by some invisible force she couldn't control. Damn the man looked good in Levi's. She shoved aside the images that flooded her mind. He withdrew a wallet from his back pocket and handed it to her as though he hadn't a secret in the world from her. She prayed her own secrets were fast asleep in the bedroom down the hall.

With a trembling hand, she opened the wallet and, beginning with his Washington, D.C., driver's license, examined every credit card, every credential. All claimed he was Roman Donnello. All looked genuine. Official. Her boneless grip dropped the wallet to her lap, and through a numbing fog, she gazed up at him. He really wasn't Nick Diamond. Hood or hitman. He was a federal cop whose agency, a cross between the DEA, FBI and CIA, she had heard of. Respected.

Dear God, everything she'd ever believed about this man, ever felt about him, was wrong. All lies. He'd made a fool of her. Cost her years of unnecessary anguish. Fear.

Fury, white-hot and all consuming, shot through Kerrie. Feeling returned to every inch of her. She lurched to her feet. The wallet bumped the carpet. She flung herself at Roman, slapped her fists against his chest, and screamed, "You jerk! You blew our investigation! It cost me a promotion. And set Bud back two years."

Roman grasped her wrists and held her off, infuriating her all the more. Her face felt feverish and her body chilled as if ice flowed through her veins. He said softly, "It could have cost us all our lives."

"No!" She glared at him, her scalding breath tangling with his. "Not if you had leveled with me."

"Leveled with you? The way you leveled with me?"

"I didn't know who you were. *Everything* you said to me was a lie."

He shook his head, and his eyes flickered like the amber glow of twin candles. "Not *everything,* Irish."

Heat filled her face. She didn't want to remember the truths he'd told her, didn't want to deal with them. God help her, she couldn't face them.

"Bull. This was nothing more or less than professional jealousy. The big Fed didn't want the little locals messing in his case." She meant to spit the words at him, but her anger was subsiding, the truth starting to sink in, starting to shatter the armor of anger in which she'd sheathed her heart.

She'd spent so much time hating this man she could hardly process the fact that her reasoning had been totally amiss. But it had. From day one. Roman was none of the hateful things she'd thought him to be.

Worse yet, he'd disappeared three years ago as much to save Bud and her as to keep from having his own cover blown. She'd likely have done the same in his place and could only respect his actions.

But what a mess he'd made of their lives.

Confusion dominated the emotions washing through her. What was she going to do? Tell him the truth now? Chance losing the twins? Kerrie didn't cry easily, but she felt tears now, hot against her cheeks, and was helpless to stop them.

"Don't cry, Irish." Roman cupped her face in his hands and pulled her near, gently kissing away her tears. "It's not as bad as all that."

"But it is..." The words choked her.

"No." He pulled her closer. His voice was a warm caress that whispered across her aching heart. "I'm still so damned crazy about you I can't think straight..."

Kerrie welcomed the invitation to feel, not think, and greeted his lips with her own. The kiss was tender, consoling, gently touching her mouth, then her tear-dampened cheeks, her temples, her neck. He pulled back and gazed at her with such need, her heart skipped a beat. "Just being this close is driving me wild."

Kerrie drank in his need as if she were a thirsty soul who'd wandered too long in the desert. This time the kiss was fierce, exploding with a passion she'd forgotten existed, a passion she'd missed with every ounce of her being, a passion she'd never expected to feel again.

"Mommy?"

The small voice stole the moment. Roman released Kerrie with a start, his eyes rounding in surprise, his gaze on the toddler behind them. Kerrie's chest froze, her heart seemed to stop, her lungs to lock. Which of the girls was it? Steeling herself for the worst, she pivoted.

One sight of Maureen's mop of red curls nearly brought her to the floor in relief. She hurried to the little girl and scooped her up. "Pumpkin, what are you doing out of bed?"

Was Gabby also awake? Kerrie darted a glance toward the hallway. It was empty. Slowly, she spun around to face Roman.

Roman couldn't take his eyes off the darling little girl with Kerrie's hair and her mother's eyes. He couldn't breathe. He was stunned. He hadn't thought of Irish with another man. But there had definitely been one, and judging the age of this child, not long after he'd left.

"This is Maureen," Kerrie said. "Maureen, this is Mommy's...friend, Roman."

"Hello, Maureen."

Maureen tucked her face against her mother's neck, then peeked at him a moment later, pressing the backs of her hands against her cheeks, peering through them in a shy, yet curious, way.

"She's a little beauty—" The words choked through the jealousy raging inside him. Dammit to hell, this child should have been his. But he'd never be any child's father. Where did he get off being jealous? He hadn't been a monk the past three years. Why did he think a woman with Kerrie's passionate nature should be? She owed him nothing. He hadn't made a commitment to her three years ago, and even if she were free, he wouldn't make one now.

Was she free? He felt his cheeks redden. "I guess I should apologize."

Kerrie shook her head, not understanding him.

"Maureen's father. I just assumed, presumed you were...that there wasn't a man in your life. The truth is, I didn't want—" He broke off. Didn't want what? He had no right to want anything, but he did.

"He's gone."

Gone? Did that mean he was dead...or that he'd run off? Neither was any of his business. He could see the subject made her uneasy. If she wanted to explain further, she would. "I'm sorry."

Sorry sounded so lame, and the way she'd swallowed warned him he'd best drop the subject. If the man had died, at least, he'd left a sweet legacy behind, a piece of immortality that Roman would never know. Was that why he took the most dangerous assignments, the biggest risks, looked death in the face when his peers pulled back from some sense of self-preservation he neither felt nor understood?

Maybe he could understand it...if he had someone like Kerrie to live for, someone like Maureen.

Somehow, Kerrie found her voice. "How about you...do you have a wife? Children?"

"Neither. By choice." The lie rolled sourly off his tongue, rousing the old bitterness deep inside him. He wasn't without family by any choice he'd consciously made. Fate had taken that choice from him. Silently he cursed the mumps he'd had at age fifteen. No, he'd never be able to impregnate any woman. Call it pride or sheer stubbornness, he would never marry under the circumstances.

So, in a way, the choice *was* his.

Kerrie wondered at the pained look in Roman's eyes. Something told her she knew the cause of that distress, but she couldn't bring herself to recall why or what. Not that it mattered. He'd said all she needed to hear. He didn't want a wife. He didn't want children. She hugged Maureen tighter, uncertain whether her pity was all for her child.

He reached for his jacket. "Guess I'd better get out of here, so you can get that little angel back to bed."

DIM LIGHT FILTERED into the hospital room. The killer leaned against the closed door, hugging a clipboard against the borrowed lab coat with damp hands. Soft snores echoed in the room, telling the killer the patient was fast asleep. It would be so simple to cross the few steps and silence the irritating snorts. But this patient was not the object of the killer's concern.

Two doors down the corridor from here was an armed police guard sitting outside Glynna Muldoon's room. Why? Did her daughter suspect the knife attack this afternoon had actually been meant for her mother? Was Kerrie Muldoon that clever? Or was that damned Donnello starting to put the pieces together?

The killer squinted in the near darkness, ruminating. *No. Not yet. It's too soon and I have been too clever. The plan is going as scheduled. First Donnello, then Grimes and now Muldoon. They're learning how it feels to lose someone you love. Soon, they'll learn what death feels like firsthand.*

But what to do about Glynna? Maybe I should choose another target, someone even closer to Muldoon, say one of her daughters.

Chapter Five

Trying to hide the tension gripping her, Kerrie tucked Maureen back into bed and covered Gabby who, as usual, had kicked off her covers, but was still fast asleep.

"Ni-night, Mommy," Maureen murmured.

"See you in the morning, Pumpkin." Kerrie kissed her cheek, then tiptoed to the door and quietly closed it behind her.

What a day. Her nerves were like hot wires beneath her skin, burning, jumpy. She paced the house, straightening the straightened, fluffing the fluffed and turning out lights, eventually ending up in the kitchen. The Boston fern stared forlornly at her from the sink, reminding her of Nick—no—Roman. Of the lies. His lies. Her lies.

Oh, God, all the lies.

For the second time that night tears stung her eyes. She blinked them away. Breaking down would solve nothing. What was she going to do? She plucked at the wounded plant, her mother's favorite. Suddenly the need to save it seemed all important, as if by sustaining this one small thing, she could think of a way to sustain the life she'd built for her daughters and herself.

Under the sink, Kerrie found a plastic planting pot about the same size as the broken clay one. She scooped the Boston fern and as much of the dirt as her hands could manage into it, then added more, gingerly covering the roots and finally tamping the loose soil around the fern's shoots, until it looked like one she could buy in any nursery.

But she was no gardener. Glynna was the one with the green thumb, and she'd treated this plant with a love and tenderness otherwise reserved for her granddaughters. Would the fern survive? Or had shock snatched at its life as shock had snatched at her life tonight?

Absently Kerrie turned on the faucet, splashed a little water into the plant, then turned the full force of the spray on the dirt-covered plastic bib still in the sink. Outside, the motion detecting light flared. Kerrie's attention jerked to the uncovered window over the sink. Was that a man lurching into the shadowed darkness at the corner of the house? She flipped off the inside light and peered out at the alley. Nothing moved. Except her heart thumping against her ribs.

Was it a thief? A carjacker? Perhaps, Roman hanging around to spy on her? An inexplicable uneasiness swept her. Without considering why, she collected her gun from the top shelf in the entry closet and hurried into the living room, lit now only by the soft glow of the porch light. She tugged a corner of velvet drape away from the picture window and peeked out.

Roman's car was gone. Well, what had she expected...that he'd actually spy on her? The Nick Diamond of her nightmares might have, but Roman Donnello? Not likely. He had no cause. He hadn't suspected her of keeping anything from him.

Guilt swirled through her stomach.

She craned her neck for a better look into the street, angry at the guilt. Angry at Roman. Angry that the secret she held would mean little or nothing to him. An annoyance. An inconvenience, perhaps. He was childless by choice. Single by choice. All his come-ons the past two days amounted to nothing more than his desire for another roll in the hay. Nothing that involved a lifetime commitment.

Daughters involved a lifetime commitment. Deserved a lifetime commitment.

She stayed where she was, eyes on the street, ears peeled for any sound, gun tucked in her waistband, the safety on. Was she obligated to tell Roman about his daughters if he wasn't going to give them that commitment? Seconds stretched into minutes, until she was stiff from the pose. A car came down the street. A neighbor. And Professor Plum, Sophia Sommerville's orange-and-black tabby. Was that who'd set off the light? Had the shadow she'd seen been a love-hungry cat or a sneak thief? Mirage or murderer?

Loverboy?

The thought struck her like a slap of cold wind. Loverboy? Was that why she'd gotten the gun. God, she was losing it for sure—thinking Seattle's latest psychopath had discovered where she lived and was sneaking around outside her house. Kerrie let out a taut breath, feeling as if she'd just released an invisible stranglehold on her chest, and grinned at herself. For the first time in hours the tension gripping her shifted and broke apart.

She returned the gun to its shelf, double-checked the door and window locks, reassured herself the twins were sleeping, then went to her bedroom. Talk about making mountains out of molehills. Talk about stress-induced paranoia. Oh, yes, it had been one hell of a day.

Tomorrow would be better, despite the explanations Glynna would demand of her. Kerrie wouldn't think about that now. She quickly went through her bedtime ritual and climbed between the sheets. As her head met the pillow and her eyes fluttered shut, an erotic vision of Roman, as real and seductive as an aphrodisiac, washed through Kerrie. She could almost feel his hands on her body, his mouth exploring her, his scent filling her nostrils, her limbs growing languid. An aching need coiled in her lower belly.

Hell and damnation. She punched the pillow and rolled to her side. She would not think about him, or dream about him. But she did. All night. In the morning, tired and grumpy from lack of sleep, she had made up her mind. She owed Roman Donnello exactly nothing.

She would not tell him about his daughters.

"YOU HAVE TO TELL HIM about Maureen and Gabriella," Glynna said for the tenth time on the ride home from the hospital.

Kerrie concentrated on the rain hitting the windshield, on the rush of traffic in the neighboring freeway lanes, on keeping her speed limit legal as they traversed the West Seattle viaduct. She had steeled herself for this argument, and would indulge her mom's need to express her opposing views, but her mind was made up and nothing Mom had to say would change it. "Why?"

"Why?" Glynna's voice rang with incredulity. "Because he's not the criminal you thought he was. Because he's their daddy."

Kerrie exited the viaduct and began the ascent toward California Avenue. "Only biologically."

Glynna sniffed disdainfully. "Those darling little girls of ours have the right to know their daddy."

"He's nobody's daddy." Slowing for a stoplight, Kerrie hit the brake harder than necessary, then spoke through gritted teeth. "I told you he doesn't want children."

"Oh, sure, go on. Be stubborn. But mark my word, you'll just keep on paying one price after another for loving this man."

Kerrie jerked toward her mother. Anger flared inside her. "I don't love Roman Donnello."

"Oh, dear heart." Glynna clucked sympathetically. "I saw the way you looked at that man yesterday. I was a little shaken at the sight of him myself, but I'm not blind. I know love when I see it."

The truth throbbed through Kerrie. "My feelings for Roman are not the point."

"Aren't they?" An abiding tenderness filled the softly spoken rebuke.

"No!" The wipers steady *swish-swish* was deafening in the silence that followed her denial. Kerrie took the next street corner faster than was safe on the wet pavement, causing the rear of the car to fishtail.

She could feel her mother's reproving gaze, could hear the unspoken accusation that she was protesting too much.

Glynna sighed.

Kerrie gathered her mental armor around her and pulled to a stop in front of her house.

As she disengaged her seat belt, Glynna said "You're making an awful mistake—setting yourself up for a disaster you evidently haven't considered."

"What disaster?" Kerrie snapped, her patience gone.

Glynna got out of the car and retrieved her returned Christmas shopping bags from the backseat, then hurried up the walkway after Kerrie who'd gone ahead to unlock the door. "The disaster that will occur when Gabby and Maureen are grown and discover you've kept their father from them their whole lives—all for your own selfish reasons."

The indictment stung. She didn't want to hear this, didn't want to acknowledge a kernel of truth in what her mother was saying. Her eyes felt sandpaper dry and scratchy. "I won't have them hurt by his rejection."

"They're two years old, Kerrie. They won't know about

his rejection for years to come and—if you're right and he wants nothing to do with them—well, by then we'll have had more than enough time to soften the impact." Glynna set her packages on the foyer rug, an Oriental blend of deep wines and brilliant blues. She touched Kerrie's arm. "Aren't you really afraid it's you he won't want?"

"No!" Again denial came too fast, too strong, and both women knew it. Heat sprang into Kerrie's cheeks. Was Mom right? Was her major concern at the moment not that Roman would want to be a part of his daughter's lives, but that he wouldn't want to be a part of hers? No. That couldn't be it. Whatever this feeling still smoldering inside her for Roman Donnello was—it wasn't love.

Kerrie startled to shut the door, heard her mother's gasp and glanced over her shoulder. Glynna was pointing outside, her eyes rounded in alarm. "A crow. A single crow." Her gaze shifted to Kerrie. "Sorrow."

Another superstition. Kerrie rolled her eyes.

"Kerrie Carleen, you can't ignore this sign. You must do the right thing. You must tell him today."

"Mom, I have murderers to catch today."

"Mark my words, that bird is a warning, and throwing up roadblocks won't make the problem go away. Don't put off telling him. Don't let him disappear from your life again without resolving this, or you'll never have another moment's happiness."

Kerrie sighed. "I'll think about it."

"Be sure you do." Glynna turned toward the hallway and let out another startled gasp. "Ye Gods, where's my fern?"

Perhaps, Kerrie thought, the crow was foretelling Glynna's sorrow over the plant and had nothing whatsoever to do with her. Leaving her mother tending to the fern, she hurried out to her car. The crow was gone. So much for omens.

THE HOMICIDE DIVISION of the Seattle police department bustled with the usual clatter of typewriters, telephones and people.

Tully Cage's desk faced Kerrie's. He was there, his chair tipped off its front legs, his blond crew cut smearing Brylcreem on the window they shared, a phone at his ear. His eyebrows were tugged in a frown, accentuating the scar that sliced through the left one. Like her, he wore jeans and a heavy, long-sleeved cotton shirt, his blue, hers white. His teal blue eyes lifted as she approached.

"Talk to you later." He slipped the phone onto its cradle and dropped forward in his chair, the front legs meeting the floor with a thump. "You look like hell."

"It's been that kind of morning." Kerrie plopped her shoulder bag on her desk, glanced out the window at the dismal day and sighed.

"What's going on?" He shoved aside the tablet he'd been jotting in. "Is your mom okay?"

"Mom's fine." Kerrie forced her gaze from the window. "Thanks for asking."

He nodded in acknowledgment. "Then what's got you looking like you've lost your best friend? Anything you care to share?"

Kerrie dropped into her chair. Cage stood, then settled a hip on the edge of her desk, somehow managing to look like a big brother—maybe it was the crew cut—offering his kid sister a shoulder to cry on. But she had no inclination to cry on anyone's shoulder, nor would she confide her troubles.

Cage knew she had twin daughters, but that was as far as it went. She'd told him any talk about the girls' father was off limits. He'd respected her boundaries, as she respected his. She didn't enlighten him now, but she did tell him about Roman's confession.

"Federal...huh. And you're sure he wasn't lying?"

Was she sure? She'd thought she'd been, but now that Cage brought it up, she realized she still had doubts. Had Nick lied about being Roman? Faked the proof? Stolen Roman Donnello's papers? Or did she just want him to be lying? Kerrie shook her head. "I'm not sure of much today."

"I could always check him out."

Maybe she just needed confirmation to finally accept the truth and let go of the doubts. Maybe Nick Diamond was making a fool of her. "Why don't you do that? I'd hate to think I took his word too easily, only to find out later that he really was Loverboy, yanking my chains."

Two hours later, she had her answer. Cage dropped a faxed photograph onto Kerrie's desk. "He's who he says he is all right. And furthermore, his peers think pretty highly of him, say he's a hell of a cop and a real decent guy."

Kerrie stared down at Roman's arresting image, and her throat tightened. This decent guy had turned her life upside down and inside out.

"You look like you could eat Donnello's liver for lunch. Whatever he did to you in a past life must have been brutal."

"You wouldn't believe it." And what had she done to Roman? She didn't want to think about that, about how she'd let him leave her house last night knowing full well that he thought Maureen was another man's child. Didn't want to think about that odd pain she'd seen in his eyes. Or about her mother's warning of a lifetime of sorrow if she didn't tell him he was the father of twin two-year-olds.

She scrubbed at her tired eyes and glanced toward the window again. A crow was perched on the window ledge. Kerrie reared back as if the bird could step through the glass that separated them. Her pulse skittered.

"What the—?" Cage waved his hand at the bird.

The crow ignored him. Its dark glassy eyes pinned Kerrie with a cold gaze. She couldn't look away. Her mother's warning screamed through her head.

"Get out of here, pest." Cage thumped the window with his knuckles.

The bird squawked and flew away. Kerrie shivered.

"Spooky bird. Don't often see crows this high up. Starlings, but not crows." Cage smiled wryly. "You been putting crumbs on the window ledge, Muldoon?"

Kerrie feared her face was colorless, readable. Silently, she cursed her mother's superstitions…and her own stupidity at letting a bird scare her. "I've got better things to do than worry about scavengers."

She shoved out of the chair and gathered all the info on Roman Donnello. "I think we should show this to the lieutenant and bring him up to speed."

"Be my guest." Cage went back to his own chair and planted himself with a *plop.*

"Coward." But she didn't blame him for not wanting to accompany her. This newest shift in their case wouldn't make the lieutenant happy. With the papers hugged like a bullet-proof vest to her rapidly beating heart, she struck out for his office.

She was back minutes later. A headache teased her temples. The wonder was that it hadn't developed into a full-blown thumper hours ago.

Cage looked up from the papers on his desk. "How'd he take the news?"

"One guess." Trying to make light of it, Kerrie gave her best imitation of their boss. "'I want this killer found. Instead, some damned Fed has us chasing our tails. If you run into that damned Donnello, tell him to stay out of our case. I don't care if he did know the first victim. I don't care if he was married to her. That doesn't justify his poking into this.'"

"Whew! Didn't you tell him we have another stakeout at McRory's scheduled for tonight?"

She nodded. She wasn't looking forward to another "date" with Jeremy Dane. "It didn't go far to assuage his anger."

Cage shrugged. "Look at it this way, at least you'll be able to blow off some steam at Donnello next time you see him."

Next time she saw him. The thought kicked the ache at her temples a notch higher. "Hopefully I won't have the opportunity."

SHE MIGHT HAVE KNOWN Roman would be at McRory's. At their table. Again. Seeing him was like a slam to the solar plexus. The last thing she needed tonight was to deal with him, with their personal situation. Not when she had a killer to unmask, to hopefully capture.

"Donnello is here," she whispered into the microphone hidden beneath her sweater.

Cage responded, "Are you going to relay the lieutenant's message to him?"

"I'm going to ignore him."

"What if he won't ignore you?"

Kerrie gritted her teeth. Roman *was* unpredictable. She couldn't chance his blowing this operation and scaring Loverboy off. "All right...I'll talk to him."

Roman watched Kerrie skirt the table with the Reserved sign propped in its center and start toward him. His mouth watered at the sight of her; she wore a short black skirt and a fuzzy black sweater, the color a breathtaking contrast to her wild red tresses, which rained across her shoulders with every step. Her determined expression lent an appealing glow to her striking features. She seemed unaware of the male heads turning as she passed.

He rose slowly as she neared, raking his gaze over her,

unable to hide the pleasure he felt at being the object of her attention, at being the envy of every other man in the bar. "Irish."

Kerrie's palms dampened, her insides quivered. She felt exposed. Naked. But she would not flinch. Would not let him know the power his very gaze had over her. Keeping her voice even, she asked, "Are you following me, Donnello?"

She was right on target, but Roman smirked. "The last time I checked McRory's was a public place—and I'm a public guy."

She wanted to shake the grin off his face. "We both know neither of us is here for McRory's *public* amenities. I won't brook any interference in my case tonight. Keep your distance or I'll have you arrested for obstruction of justice."

"You don't have to worry about me, Irish. I'm just going to sit here, eat, drink...and observe your technique."

Observe her technique? Suspicion flared inside Kerrie. Despite all the glowing endorsements of his peers, she didn't completely trust Roman Donnello. She glanced around and spotting her reserved table, she noted with pleasure it was too far from this one for him to hear anything that would be said.

Let him watch. It might make her nervous, but that would be all. A little extra pressure would keep her on her toes. She gave him her sweetest smile. "As long as you keep your distance—observe all you want."

Roman lifted his shot glass to her in a mock toast. Then tossed it back. She grinned smugly and left. He watched her walk away, his gaze tracing every switch of her shapely fanny. Desire pooled hot and thick in his groin, and he quickly warned himself to quit dreaming the impossible. Kerrie Muldoon deserved a man who was willing to settle down and be a husband to her. A father to Maureen. He was not that man.

Roman leaned back in his chair. Making a pretense of stretching, he inserted the nearly invisible listening device into his ear. A smile wavered at the corner of his mouth as he watched Kerrie take the chair with her back to him.

"Cage, I'm in position," she said, her voice ringing clear and true in Roman's ear. His suppressed smile blossomed. As advertised, the hi-tech bug he'd stuck to the underside of her table was state of the art.

Chapter Six

With any luck at all Loverboy would soon walk into McRory's bar. Kerrie shifted on her seat. Hadn't she been thinking this very thing just two nights ago? The image of Jeremy Dane filled her head. Had she already met the murderer she sought? Dane was definitely weird enough. Then again, so was Troy. The no-show's whiny voice replayed in her head. *Liar. Don't you know how to be faithful to one man?*

The irony of how faithful she'd been to one man, Roman, almost made her laugh. She forced her mind to the case. Had both men responded to the ads placed by Detective Leah Davis? Had both met Bud Grimes's fiancée in this very bar? Had one of them killed her?

She shook off a chill. She couldn't ask Leah—and neither of these men's names were on any of her reports. But names could be changed. Loverboy could call himself anything he wanted.

She bit down on the straw in her tonic glass, silently lamenting their lack of any real leads. And yet, she felt in her gut they were getting close. Maybe Mike Springer—the man she awaited now—was Loverboy.

Someone laughed, a voice sounding like Roman's. Kerrie's dark musings fled, and against her will, her awareness centered on him. She could feel his gaze caressing her

back, and hated the answering heat deep within her—
knowing that it endorsed her mother's accusations about
her feelings for Roman, about her reluctance to tell him
the truth.

She sighed, prompting Cage to ask what was the matter.
"Nothing," she whispered.

A man stood near the bar entrance, frowning at her,
seeming unsure what to do next. He wasn't striking like
Roman, or unassuming like Jeremy Dane. Instead he reminded her of Tom Hanks in *Sleepless in Seattle,* the kind
of man most women would trust on first sight.

He had dark, curly brown hair and eyes as warm as hot
chocolate, and features as endearing as the average boy
next door. He wore a long-sleeved, knit shirt, the sleeves
pulled down to his wrists, and rumpled corduroy slacks.
He was average height with a wiry build. Probably
stronger than he appeared.

He ambled up to the table with shy uncertainty. "Kerrie?"

His disarming, charming mien set all her cop instincts
on red alert. "Mike?"

"Yeah." He nodded, smiling his shy grin. "Wow,
you're really pret—"

He broke off, instantly embarrassed at having spoken
his thoughts aloud.

"Thanks." She blushed, too—not that she hadn't been
told before that she was pretty, but the way he'd blurted
it out said he'd had low expectations about their meeting,
and reminded her he had feelings that could be hurt. Another part of her knew this could be an act. "Please, sit
down."

"Oh, of course." He pulled out the chair and sat on its
edge as if it were either too small or he wasn't sure he
would be staying.

Cage and she had done a preliminary background check

on him and had discovered he'd given his real name when he'd answered the Introductions ad they'd placed. She couldn't say that about all the respondents. Although she already knew, she asked, "So, what do you do to keep the creditors from your door?"

His disarming grin appeared. "I'm a CP—"

The waitress interrupted, asking for his drink order.

Kerrie hated playing with people's emotions. Mike Springer might be Loverboy, or he might be as innocent as he appeared—just a nice guy trying to find a nice woman and have a nice relationship.

"What beer do you have in the bottle?" he asked the waitress.

As the waitress reeled off the choices for Mike, Kerrie considered the arguments against his innocence—such as the fact that he was twice divorced. Such as his last ex claiming he liked to beat her up, although there was no record of her having ever called the police. So, her claims could be false.

Fact was, there might be nothing wrong with Mike Springer except his inability to choose the right woman for himself.

"I guess I'll have a bottle of Red Dog," he decided.

"I'll have another of these." Kerrie raised her empty tonic glass to the waitress, an undercover rookie, who nodded and wrote on a round cocktail coaster.

But before she could leave, Mike changed his mind and selected a different beer, then grinned sheepishly at Kerrie and launched into an explanation of why he'd selected the second brew over the first. She listened with half an ear.

Regardless of personal feelings, her job wasn't to take pity on suspects. If this man was innocent the worst that would befall him was a bruised ego. She had to hang onto the bigger picture. Hang onto the reason *she* was here. Innocent women, whose names she didn't know, whose faces she had never seen, were counting on her to put a maniac away. Was Mike Springer a maniac?

If he was, it wasn't obvious. Unlike Jeremy Dane, the touchy-feely, control freak she had to share dinner with later. How was she going to stomach that?

The waitress delivered their drinks and left. Mike took a swig of beer, then launched back into his diatribe on various brews.

Kerrie nodded. She felt eyes boring into her back. Roman, again. No. She wouldn't think about him. Wouldn't play mind games with herself. The only interest Roman had in her—that mattered—was catching Loverboy.

But the subject of Roman wasn't easily dismissed. Worry about his discovering her secret had sunk tiny claws in the corners of her mind and refused to be ignored.

"Hey, Muldoon," Cage said in her ear. "Have you fallen asleep? Get this Springer guy off the blessed properties of beer and on track."

Heat spiked Kerrie's cheeks. "That's all very interesting, Mike, but I'm not a beer drinker and I'd really rather talk about you. I think you were telling me you're a CPA?"

"Yeah." He took a swallow of his beer. "I have an office in my home on Lake Washington."

"Lake Washington?" Cage squawked. "He lives with his old man in a two-bedroom rambler in Ballard. Works out of the converted garage. Why the lie?"

To impress her? Then again, why do that if he hoped to see her after tonight? "You have a house on Lake Washington?"

Mike nodded.

Kerrie's mind churned. If he expected this date to develop into a relationship, he'd know somewhere down the line, he'd have to admit this lie and explain it away. She took a long drink of tonic. Maybe he didn't plan to see her again after tonight. "Is it a new house?"

"New to me. Just moved in last week."

"Not true," Cage said.

Mike's boyish smile appeared. "Say, would you like to see it?"

"Sure." Her stomach twisted with anticipation. Maybe they were closer to catching Loverboy than even she had suspected. "When?"

"Well, finish your drink and we can go now."

Was this the ploy he'd used on Wendy Waring and Leah Davis?

"Should I call backup?" Cage was obviously thinking along the same lines as she. They could have Loverboy behind bars tonight.

"Sure," she said as much to Cage as to Mike. She didn't feel one regret that she wouldn't be keeping her dinner date with Jeremy Dane. "I'd like that, Mike."

"Irish, are you finished having drinks with this bozo?"

Kerrie jerked erect in her chair. Roman was leaning over her shoulder, his mouth so close their lips nearly brushed as she turned to look at him. What the hell was he doing? Furious, she muttered, "Go away."

"I'm not going anywhere and neither are you." He glared at Mike. "Get lost, pal."

"Mike stay where you are. Roman is leaving."

"Hey, get your hands off the lady." Mike kept his voice low, but he rose half out of his chair and scowled at Roman. "Who do you think you are?"

"Her husband."

"My—?" Kerrie sputtered, too stunned to finish. She started to shake her head, but Cage was screaming in her ear, and Mike didn't let her finish.

He reared out of his chair, still keeping his voice just above a whisper, apparently trying to squelch any attention they'd already drawn. He glared at Kerrie with pure hatred, his warm brown eyes, now as cold and hard as clumps of frozen dirt. "You...you...you..."

She could see a derogatory word hovering on his lips, but he left it unsaid. He stepped back from the table with his hands outflung as if he'd dropped a package. "Hey, you're welcome to her, buddy. Been there, done that."

He stormed out of the bar, shaking his head.

Kerrie was so angry she wanted to scream. But she was too mindful of where she was. She glared at Roman, struggling for control, her voice grating with fury. "What's the matter with you? He's the best suspect we've had so far and, right as I'm on the brink of collaring him, you butt in. I ought to have you arrested."

"Do it," Cage advised.

Roman didn't blame Kerrie for wanting his hide. He'd have skinned anyone who'd done to him what he'd just done to her. But he'd reacted without thinking—listened to his gut telling him Mike Springer was Loverboy and the next thing he knew he was standing beside Kerrie, telling the creep he was her husband. He would have laughed, but it wasn't funny.

Knowing she was well within her rights to do exactly as she threatened, he decided to try to bluff his way out of it. He strove to look innocent. "Arrested for what?"

"For obstructing an officer in the line of duty."

"Cuff him," Cage growled in her ear. "Mirandize him."

Roman planted a palm on the table, bracing his arm as he leaned close to Kerrie. "Irish, if you don't lower your voice you'll blow your cover."

Cage swore. "We've got a tail on Springer. Want me to come in and take Donnello in?"

"Forget it." Kerrie blew out a huge breath.

"Thanks I will," Roman answered, assuming she'd

been speaking to him. He slipped around the table and sank slowly into the chair Springer had vacated. "How's your mom?"

The switch of subjects threw her. She didn't want to get personal or talk about her family with Roman Donnello. "My mother is fine. She's home."

"With Maureen?"

The mention of their daughter dried her throat. "Yes."

"Alone?"

"What do you mean? Of course, alone."

"I thought you were keeping a guard on her?" Concern filled his amber eyes.

She sighed. "No one is after my mom. If it will put your mind at ease, the woman who was stabbed yesterday had her purse stolen. The murder was random, not specific. No one meant to kill my mother."

Roman wished he could believe that. But the nagging sensation he'd had at the hospital yesterday persisted like a determined gnat. Glynna Muldoon was in dire danger. He couldn't explain how he knew, but he did. "Who knows you'll be here for most of this evening?"

She tipped her head sideways. "Look, Roman, my boss said he doesn't want you messing up this case. He won't be happy about what happened here tonight. Or about the fact that I'm not hauling your nosy, interfering butt in to the station for it. So, take my advice and back off."

"Irish, the best way to keep me from messing up your case is to let me tag along with you." His voice radiated sensuality as if he'd just asked for permission to climb into her bed, instead of into her case. Unwanted heat swirled in the nether regions of her body.

"Absolutely, not." The last thing she wanted was to be in constant contact with this man who unnerved her at every turn.

He scowled. "Did you tell Springer that you were meeting someone here for dinner?"

Springer? Kerrie stiffened. He might have overheard her call Mike by his given name as he approached her table, but Roman hadn't been anywhere near when she or Mike had used his last name. Dawning rattled through her like an earthquake shaking her to the core. "You insufferable rat! You bugged this table!"

She scrambled to her feet, gathered her purse and coat and scooted across the bar to an empty spot four tables away. She raised a warning hand at him to keep his distance. "Don't even think about it."

She wasn't taking any chances on his following her and planting the bug again. But to her amazement, Roman turned on his heel and left the bar without so much as another word.

The urge to unleash her rage, to scream, to upend tables and chairs, had Kerrie gripping her muscles so tightly they ached.

"Why is it suddenly so quiet?" Cage inquired.

Kerrie sank to the chair at the new table and whispered, "Donnello left. That jerk bugged my table."

"I heard. Let it go. The most he learned were a few techniques on selecting beer."

She decided to take her partner's advice. They could pick up Springer anytime they wanted. She needed to pull herself together before… Too late. "Oh, great. Jeremy Dane just walked in."

He wore creased jeans and a dress shirt and tie beneath a tweed sports jacket. His brown hair was combed to perfection and his cool blue eyes were friendly behind his wire-rimmed glasses. He had another pink rose. Her skin crawled.

Cage said, "More bad news. Springer lost the tail we put on him."

"Great. Have someone swing by the Ballard house. If he doesn't show in half an hour, put out his license number."

"Will do."

Forcing a smile, Kerrie waved Jeremy Dane over to the table. Where *he* lived was another matter altogether. The background check on him had turned up zilch. He didn't work for Boeing as he'd told her the other night, didn't work anywhere in this state that they could ascertain. Unless it was under a different name.

"Hello, Kerrie," Jeremy said.

Kerrie stiffened. This man had a slight accent, the same as Cage. East Coast for sure. New York or New Jersey, she couldn't guess. Why had she missed it the other night? Too busy fending off his odd touching while worrying about Roman? Probably, but why hadn't Cage mentioned it?

"A perfect rose for a perfect lady." Jeremy handed her the flower, managing to caress her fingers as she accepted it.

A shiver swept her skin. His first touch and already she felt the need of a long hot shower with a gallon of disinfectant soap. Suddenly, she wasn't so sure Mike Springer was Loverboy. Maybe she'd jumped too quickly to that conclusion. She watched Jeremy take the seat across from her. Necessary or not, she dreaded the evening ahead. "I'm afraid I can't stay long."

Jeremy looked as surprised at this as she was that she'd said it. Disappointment flickered across his even features. "I thought we were going to get to know each other better tonight."

"It's my mother." Kerrie decided the truth would keep her from slipping on a lie. "She was in an accident yesterday."

"Nothing serious, I hope?" He reached for her hands.

She dropped them into her lap. Something about the glint in Jeremy's eyes prodded her suspicious nature. He seemed genuinely interested in hearing about her mother. Somehow, she felt it wasn't from politeness, but from something she couldn't pinpoint. Something sinister? Maybe she just didn't like this man. Or maybe her problems with Roman were distorting her judgment of men in general. "Mom had a bit of a shock. A woman she was standing beside was stabbed to death during a robbery."

His eyes rounded behind his glasses. "God. Did the police catch the killer?"

Did the police catch the killer? Not was she hurt? Not was she robbed? Not is she okay? Kerrie's internal antenna twitched. "No one's been charged yet."

The waitress arrived with dinner menus, took drink orders and left.

"So, your mother was a witness." Jeremy stroked the sleeve of Kerrie's black sweater as if the angora were a live cat. "Did she see the man? Can she identify him?"

Him? Kerrie hadn't mentioned the killer's sex. "No. She was looking at the ground."

"Too bad for the woman who was killed, but probably lucky for your mom that she can't identify the guy."

"Yes, lucky." Resisting the urge to jerk her arm out of his reach, Kerrie studied his face. Roman's concerns about the attack on her mother being made by Loverboy ricocheted through her brain. Was there basis for Roman's concern? She grabbed the menu and opened it. Or had Jeremy asked about her mother being able to identify the killer out of morbid curiosity? Or was he fishing to see if the police had connected anyone to the crime? Perhaps himself?

"I guess I'll have the special." She lowered the menu just enough to see Jeremy's face. "The salmon."

"Sounds good."

While Jeremy gave the waitress their orders, Cage said, "Ask him about his accent."

The waitress left. Kerrie longed for the menu to use as a barrier between herself and this creep. Again she lowered her hands to her lap, leaning back against her chair. "You aren't a native of the northwest, are you?"

The question brought a wary look into Jeremy's cool blue eyes. They shifted right, then left, then back at her. "I wasn't born here, if that's what you mean."

"Somewhere back east, I'll bet."

"Boston. But I've lived here most of my life."

"Boston?" Cage said. "No way. Wrong inflection."

"I've always wanted to visit Boston." She noted the slight slump of Jeremy's shoulders. Was he relieved? Had he counted on her not knowing the difference in east coast accents? Her suspicions of him doubled. He had to be hiding something big to risk such a blatant lie.

"Boston's okay. But I like Seattle better."

"So is Seattle where you've lived most of your life, or somewhere else?"

"Seattle."

That was all Kerrie heard. Cage let out a yelp, startling her. Then Roman's voice sounded in her ear. Apparently Cage had been about to tell her something and been interrupted before he could switch the microphone back to Listen.

She saw Jeremy's mouth moving, but her attention was on the two men she could hear in her ear as clearly as if she were in the van with them.

Roman said, "Did you put a tail on Springer?"

Cage barked, "Take a hike."

"Did you put a tail on Springer?" Roman's voice came across the line like a wild animal's growl.

"Yes, but...he lost it."

"He lost it?" Roman's disbelief was laced with ire. "If

he's Loverboy, and I think he is, at best, he's out prowling the streets. At worst, he's gone after Glynna Muldoon again.''

"Again?" Cage was incredulous. "You think *Loverboy* tried stabbing Kerrie's mom yesterday?"

"Yes."

"Why?"

"I can't explain it. Instinct. Experience."

"No offense, man, but we can't arrest him on your instincts." Cage spoke with the schooled patience of a father talking to an irate child. "If it will make you feel any better, we know where to find him."

"Yeah, if he went straight home." Roman's exasperation radiated through the earpiece. "But Springer was furious when he left here, and he knows Kerrie isn't going home anytime soon. At least dispatch a car to her house."

"Lookit, Donnello, I respect you as a cop, man. But you aren't calling the shots here and I can't give orders on your command. Capeesh?"

Ten seconds of silence followed.

"Capeesh," Roman answered begrudgingly. "I'll check on Glynna and Maureen myself."

What? Kerrie tensed. He was going to her house. Given her mother's state of mind, when she saw who was at the door, she'd likely let him in. God knew what else she was likely to do. Terror wrapped icy tendrils around her heart. Dear God, she had to phone.

"Kerrie?" Jeremy was shaking her arm. "Kerrie? What is it? You're as pale as a ghost."

"Excuse me, Jeremy." She scooted out of her chair, grabbing her purse as she stood. "I forgot I was supposed to call my mom. I'll be right back."

He half stood as she hurried from the table in search of the pay phone. Moments later, she was listening to the unanswered rings with growing aggravation. Why didn't her mother pick up? If they'd gone out somewhere Glynna would have put the machine on. But she wasn't planning on going out. Not tonight. Was Roman right about Loverboy attacking Mom at home?

Terror of another kind swept through her.

Kerrie glanced at her watch. Eight o'clock. Of course. The twins' bath time. She slumped against the wall with relief. It was short-lived. Mom ignored the telephone when she bathed the girls and would keep on ignoring it until she was done.

Roman would have arrived by then.

Panic pinged through Kerrie. She hurried back to the table and began stuffing her arms into her coat. "I'm so sorry, Jeremy. Mom's having a bad time. I promised I'd come right home."

"But..." He stood, catching hold of the pink rose. "What about—"

"I'll call you. I promise." She left him holding the rose toward her.

MINDFUL OF THE THORNY rosebushes, Loverboy knelt on the soggy garden bed beside Kerrie Muldoon's house and jimmied the window lock. There were no motion-detecting lights on this side of the house, just sweet darkness. He heard the latch give and grinned. A moment later, he lowered himself into the basement, landing, sneakers first, on what he suspected was a washing machine. The dryer hummed alongside, obviously containing a load of clothing.

He could smell laundry detergent and wet clothes.

He flicked on his flashlight, relatched the window, then took his bearings. Wet laundry was stacked on the dryer. His footprints decorated the washer, muddy testaments to his presence here. He picked a wet towel off the pile and wiped the evidence away.

A moment later he'd abandoned his sneakers to the wet towel and started across the cramped basement in his stocking feet. The stairs were old, worn and wooden. Gingerly he stepped on the first riser. Then the next. And the next.

The mother was home. She wouldn't escape her fate tonight. Light winked off the knife blade as he nudged open the door into the kitchen. The sickly sweet stench of burned peaches stung his nostrils. Damned potpourri on the stove. A radio played soft music.

Loverboy stepped into the kitchen. His eyes quickly scanned the room. No one. Voices echoed down the hall— one adult and two small children. Anticipation had his heart hammering in his chest. Kerrie Muldoon loved these people and she was going to lose them. She would feel the same loss he'd felt. But hers would be three times worse.

"Okay." Glynna's voice was closer. She had opened he bathroom door. "All done, my little princesses. Next top, story land."

Loverboy flattened himself against the corner wall and peeked around its edge into the hallway. Sweat beaded on his upper lip and scurried down the small of his back. Glynna was carrying the two pajama-clad children, one on each hip, down the hall away from him. He grinned. He'd give her a couple of minutes to put them to bed and then...he'd strike.

The doorbell rang.

KERRIE PULLED into the alley behind her house, abandoned the car outside the garage and raced up the back walk, stopping only once when she dropped her keys. She took the back stairs two at a time. She scrambled into the kitchen and rammed to a stop. She couldn't swallow at the sight. Her pulse beat so furiously she felt certain her heart would explode.

Glynna sat at the kitchen table holding Maureen. Roman sat across from her, his amber eyes hot and watery as if he had a raging fever. He was holding Gabriella.

Chapter Seven

Wet and muddy, Loverboy huddled beside Kerrie's back porch. Debilitating rage burned hot inside him, keeping the chill at bay, making his limbs feel weighted, waterlogged. *All my plans destroyed by the ring of one lousy doorbell.* He puffed out an angry breath, sending a tiny burst of foggy air away from his mouth. The last fifteen minutes had been pure hell. Everything had gone wrong.

He closed his eyes and let the memories slide through his mind like a bad B movie, each moment as vivid as if it were happening here and now.

He'd peered down the hallway toward the sounds issuing from the bathroom. The wall had felt grainy against his cheek. The switchblade heavy in his gloved hand, the peach potpourri stinging his nostrils.

The doorbell rang.

A death knell. Jarring. Loud. Terror shot through his limbs. He scurried into the kitchen and ducked back into the dark basement. He clicked the door shut. With pulse tripping and chest heaving, he listened for a clue as to who the visitor was who had so rudely ruined his plans.

Luck eluded him. Five steps below, the dryer rumbled loudly, blocking all but the squeals of the two brats. *Damned noisy machine.* Damned visitor. Damn Glynna Muldoon.

He grabbed the handrail, balancing the tremor in his legs, stumbling down the stairs. He hoisted himself onto the washer and put his shoes on. Adult voices sounded in the kitchen. His heart climbed his throat.

He levered the window open, then spread the towel over the sill and scrambled up and out. The ensuing clamor would have brought the neighborhood out to investigate— if not for the rumbling dryer. *Wonderfully noisy machine.* He hadn't planned on using this exit to leave. Should be going out the back door. He crawled out onto the rose bed, and gasped a breath of rainy night air.

He shoved off the windowsill, kicking at something bunched beneath his shoes. A second too late, he realized it was the towel. No! He spun and grabbed for it. His gloves were muddy, slick. The terry cloth slid through his grasp and landed with a plop on the washer. Swearing, he leaned into the window and made a grab for the towel. No good. It was out of his reach. He swore again. The only way to get it was to go back into the basement. What if he couldn't get back out again?

Just latch the window and go. He grabbed the latch, smearing mud on it. It refused to engage from the outside. Frustration spilled through him. The hell with it. A dirty towel, a half-open window and size eleven footprints amounted to exactly nothing as clues. Laughing inwardly, he scrambled out of the flower bed and onto the damp lawn.

Switchblade in hand, he tread stealthily toward the alley, easing alongside of the house. The motion-detecting light flashed on. Loverboy jolted. He dropped to the ground. His face pressed the wet grass. His heart pounded several minutes before he risked moving, inching on his belly like a soldier pushing toward the enemy camp.

Something hard dug into his thigh. His hand curled around a chunk of wood. In the light he could see it was an oblong, gaily painted child's building block. Perfect. He palmed it, then crouching near a rhododendron, he aimed and threw the block at the light. The glass bulb shattered, tinkling to the ground.

Once more in blessed darkness, Loverboy froze, listening to the thundering of his pulse, waiting for someone to come and investigate the noise. Seconds passed. No one came.

He started to stand. Headlights swept the alley. The sound of a car rapidly approaching struck terror through him yet again. He ducked behind the rhododendron bush. The car screeched to a stop. Its headlights swept across him, but were extinguished so quickly he doubted he'd been seen.

A second later, high heels clicked on the concrete walkway. As his eyes adjusted to the darkness, he realized the woman hurrying toward the house was Kerrie Muldoon. What the hell was she doing here? She was supposed to be occupied elsewhere. Could nothing go according to plan?

His fist curled around the switchblade, and a sudden thought brought a smile. Maybe this was better. Providence.

She didn't seem aware of the disabled motion-detecting light. Just as well. It would keep him hidden until it was too late.

Acting with speed, he reopened the switchblade and slid to his full height in one swift motion, the knife readied for the toss. Totally hidden by the dark night, the large bush, and his black clothing, he held his breath until Kerrie was within his target line. Aiming for her throat, he snapped his wrist, hurling the knife with deadly accuracy.

At the same instant, he heard a jangle. Keys hitting concrete. Kerrie swore. Crouched.

The knife zipped over her and landed in the soft grass

beyond with a dull thud. Before Loverboy could react, she disappeared into the house.

Just remembering recharged his fury. So close. So damned close. Twice tonight. He let out a low growl. Cold was finally penetrating his awareness. He ought to just burn the damned house to the ground. Serve them all right. Even the visitor, whoever the hell it was.

Suddenly he wanted to know the name of the visitor, the person who'd foiled his plan. Suddenly he wanted to know what had brought Kerrie Muldoon home in such a huff. Was it something to do with the doorbell ringer? Loverboy stared up at the lighted kitchen windows. Something perhaps to do with himself?

Fingering the retrieved switchblade, now closed in his jacket pocket, and the box of matches in his other pocket, he schooled himself against acting without planning. His father had taught him to strike when and where least expected—that that kind of random-looking kill required patience and planning. Revenge was sweetest served cold.

Right now it burned hot inside Loverboy. Because of that, he'd made mistakes tonight, one after another. Mistakes led to discovery. He must think of what to do next; then carry it out with cold deliberation.

He walked gingerly around the house and edged close to the front porch. His wet clothing made a soft swicking sound with every step. A car was parked at the curb. He intended to have a look inside that car. He should be able to do that with relative safety. The nearest streetlight was two houses over. The front part of the Muldoon house was dark. The Muldoons and their guest were in the kitchen.

"MOMMY," both girls cried at once. Kerrie was too shaken to move, too furious with her mother to speak. All the crazy ride from McRory's, she'd feared this was what she'd find when she arrived. Glynna had cautioned her to tell Roman, had made it clear where she stood on his knowing. She likely thought she was doing the best for all concerned.

But she'd done the worst.

Kerrie plopped her keys and purse on the kitchen counter. Her voice quavered with rage. "Mother, it's past the girls' bedtime."

"Of course." Glynna's chin shot up. As long as she felt she'd done the right thing, there would be no apology from her. She stood, shifting Maureen to one hip and extending her free arm for Gabby. "You two need to talk...alone."

But Roman was reluctant to give Gabriella to Glynna, wanted to take Maureen from her. "No, please, not yet."

He stroked Gabriella's raven hair as if it were the most precious thing he'd ever touched, gazed at Maureen as if she were the most precious thing he'd ever seen.

Kerrie's heart swelled inside her chest like a balloon with too much air, squashing her lungs and her ability to draw in breath. She lifted Maureen into her arms. "I'll call you in a minute, Mother."

"I'll be in my room," Glynna said, leaving them alone with their daughters.

Kerrie drew a bracing breath and leveled her gaze at Roman. Her insides were a mass of jelly. She clutched Maureen's warm little body to her, irrationally fearful that he might try to snatch her away. "I'm sure this is a shock—"

"Shock! Oh, Irish..." He shook his head. He looked as if she'd shattered every illusion he'd ever held of her, every truth, as if she'd run him through with a rusty dagger, fatally wounding him. "Why didn't you tell me?"

She arched her brows at the idiocy of his question. Wasn't it obvious to him? "I thought you were a smuggler...or worse."

"You know differently now."

"Even if I'd known sooner, I didn't know where to reach you." Anger and hurt collided inside her. Roman was every bit as much to blame as she that she hadn't told him about her pregnancy, but that didn't justify her not telling him last night. Purely and simply, her reasons for keeping her secret were selfish. But she'd be damned if she'd apologize for them. "I'm not the one who walked away...who stayed away."

Her reproach was wasted on Roman. He couldn't get past the fact that she hadn't told him after she'd found out the truth about him. And he'd been so sure he couldn't have children... "Why didn't you tell me last night?"

Kerrie bit back the desire to hurl his own words at him. He was the one who didn't want children...ever.

"Mommy, too tight." Maureen squirmed, pushing against Kerrie, protesting the tightened grip Kerrie hadn't realized she'd applied. Maureen looked ready to cry. Gabby looked just as unhappy and confused, obviously picking up the tension, the distress her parents could neither control nor hide. "The girls are getting upset. Let me put them to bed, then we can discuss this alone."

"Okay." He knew she was right. But when she reached for Gabriella it was as if she were tearing his heart from his chest. As far back as he could remember he'd wanted children of his own. As far back as he could remember, he'd known he'd never have them. But Kerrie couldn't deny Gabby was his. One look into her eyes had claimed his soul for eternity—as Maureen had the night before simply by being Kerrie's child. His daughters. He wanted to shout it to the world. And he would.

He watched Kerrie scoot them from the kitchen and ached to run after her, help her put them to bed. But he was a stranger to his own children; he wouldn't risk distressing them anymore tonight. Glynna came into the kitchen. She went straight to a cupboard, took out a bottle of Scotch, filled a gimlet glass and handed it to Roman. "I expect you could use this."

"Thanks." He hoped she knew he was thanking her for more than the whiskey.

She patted his arm, and set the bottle on the counter within his reach. "I've interfered enough for one night. I need to pay a visit to Sophia, one of my neighbors. Tell Kerrie to call when she wants me to return."

"Sure." As the front door closed, Roman tossed back the Scotch, then carried his replenished glass into the living room. Voices drifted from a room down the hall, feeding his aching joy, his desire to participate in this nighttime ritual that he'd been heretofore denied. But he was still too tense, too angry. He forced himself to sit on the sofa as he had last night.

Last night. Betrayal scored his heart, burned his stomach. He'd never forgive Kerrie for not telling him the truth when she'd had every opportunity last night.

THE SECOND SHE STEPPED outside, Glynna felt uneasy. Beyond the porch light, the drizzly night was black and uninviting. Streetlights did little to relieve the gloom. To assuage her fears. *Fears? Listen to yourself, Glynna Muldoon. You're being a silly old goose.* She turned up the collar of her coat, opened her umbrella and crossed to the steps.

The sounds of distant traffic, of water running into storm sewers, dripping off gutters and pouring from downspouts rushed into her ears. Nothing ominous. Then why did she feel jittery? She hesitated at the top stair. Maybe she should go back inside and finish the laundry, stay in the basement and read a book until Roman and Kerrie ironed out their problems.

No, Kerrie was too angry at her. She'd better give them all the space they needed right now. Her daughter would soon realize she'd done the best thing for all concerned. Roman seemed like a fine man, and unless her reliable instincts were way off base, he'd do the right thing by her daughter and her granddaughters.

If Kerrie Carleen would only let him.

She scrambled off the porch and down the walk. Rain pattered on the umbrella like an anxious voice telling her to hurry, tripling her uneasiness with every step. Sophia Sommerville's was only three doors down. Right now it seemed a mile away.

A rustling noise to her left brought Glynna up short. Her pulse kicked up a notch. She glanced sharply over her shoulder. Shrubs and bushes, whose shapes and coloring she was familiar with in the daylight, looked almost human, menacing and ominous in the dark. She picked up her pace. Her head swinging from side to side as she scurried along, scanning the shadowy landscapes on either side of her.

Sophia's porch light was off. Was she out? "Why didn't I call before I left?"

She tripped up the stairs, across the wide porch and grasped the handle of the screen door. Locked. She hit the doorbell and called, "Sophia!"

Hearing hysteria in her voice, Glynna chided herself against giving into the unnamed panic. Something struck her hard in the back. She dropped to her knees. The umbrella flew from her grasp, landing somewhere nearby. Pain centered in her knee caps. Panic revved inside her.

But a low meow doused it.

Her stomach flopped and her quickening pulse skidded as if it were a reined horse. She blew out a wobbly breath, half crying, half laughing with relief. "Professor Plum, you nearly did me in, old man."

She gathered the yellow-eyed ball of black-and-orange fur into her arms, and struggled to her feet. The usually friendly old tabby let out a yowl as if she'd hurt him. The porch light flared. In its brilliant glare, she noticed blood matting the cat's fur.

Sophia stood in the doorway. She noticed the blood, too, and let out a small yelp. "My dear, what's happened? Are you cut?"

"I don't think so." Glynna's knees stung as though the skin were scraped off, but that wouldn't explain blood on the upper part of her coat. A tremor shuddered through her. This was the second time in two days she'd had blood on her coat. "I think the Professor's cut himself somehow. We'd better take a look at it."

"Well, you're as pale as a wraith yourself." She relieved Glynna of the cat. He twisted and yowled as she tried to examine his wound. "Shush, now, Professor. I have to determine if we need to call the vet."

Glynna followed Sophia into her kitchen. It took both of them to hold the cat still enough to check the wound, a shallow slit on his side that must have been made by something with a thin sharp edge. Above the Professor's protesting yowls, she related her eerie feeling on the walk over. "I guess I spooked myself."

"Good night for it. Still, it's a shame a body can't walk in her own neighborhood at night these days without feeling afraid." Sophia released the cat. He tore off to hide and attend to his wound himself. "The Professor didn't help your nerves any."

True, Glynna mused. Plus, she'd probably been reacting to the events of the evening, to what was going on at her house, to the scare from yesterday. No one had followed her from her house. No one.

ROMAN COULD SWEAR a half hour had passed since Glynna left. His temper grew with every ticking minute. Finally he heard Kerrie coming down the hall. He stared at her as she walked into the living room. She looked edgy. Defensive. Sexy as hell in that fuzzy black sweater and short skirt, her long shapely legs inviting him to forgive her.

Dammit. How could a man want a woman in the most basic way, while wanting nothing ever to do with her again? "Why didn't you tell me last night?"

He wasn't bothering with amenities. Then neither would she. "If I'd had my way you wouldn't know now."

His raven brows flickered with disbelief. "Why?"

"I don't want you disrupting my daughters' lives."

"*Our* daughters, Irish. And I'm sorry if this will upend your life, but get this straight, I'm not walking away. I will be a part of their lives even if I have to fight you through every court in the country."

The fierceness of his statement stunned her. "You said you were childless by choice. What are you trying to prove now? That you can hurt me? Well, here's a bulletin, pal. You already have."

"Hurt you? You're the only one with feelings that count?" He scraped his fingers through his hair and blew out an angry breath. "I thought you were kidding last night when you asked if I had children. You knew damned good and well I thought I couldn't father a child."

"No, I—" But the words choked her. That flash of hurt she'd seen last night, that flicker of pain, old and seasoned, that had danced through his eyes, she had forgotten its source. Anguish dragged the bottom from her stomach, and Kerrie sank into the nearest chair.

"Yes, Irish," Roman's voice was low and cruel. "I told you. You do remember that afternoon, don't you. Yes, I can see that you do."

She closed her eyes as the memory of that hot August afternoon crept from the dark corners of her mind. They'd been in such fierce need of each other she doubted they'd have stopped if the roof were falling on them. Much less for protection. It wasn't until afterward that they'd considered possible consequences.

"At least you won't get pregnant," he'd laughed, a bittersweet, joyless laugh that had shredded her heart. He'd told her then, about the mumps, about the fertility tests that had confirmed his sterility.

Kerrie raised her eyes and looked at his accusing face. Her insides shriveled with guilt. She hadn't wanted to remember. Because she'd thought he was Nick Diamond. Because when she'd discovered she was pregnant, she'd thought he'd lied. Because he'd walked away and never returned.

But he was back now, demanding the right for a place in his daughters' lives. She could not deny him this. Could not deny her daughters this. She had to be fair, and within reason, she would be. "If I agree to let you...see Maureen and Gabby, what kind of commitment are you willing to give them? Will you move to Seattle?"

He hadn't expected her to acquiesce this easily. Nor had he considered the changes having two children who lived clear across the country from him would mean to his life. Move? Give up his job? "I guess this will be complicated."

"No, it will be simple. As simple as possible for the twins' sakes."

"You won't get an argument from me on that."

"Good. So, are you going to move to Seattle?"

"I'm sure that would suit you, Irish." He should have known she'd expect him to make all the concessions. "But it doesn't suit me. If that's a problem for you, then understand that I will do whatever it takes to have *my* daughters in my life on as permanent a basis as the law allows."

Her heart stung as if from a physical jab. She wasn't even sharing custody with him yet and already she felt the loss of her babies. The loss of Roman. The awful thing was, he'd be a part of her life forever—while not really being a part of her life at all. But her daughters would have their father.

She didn't know whether to laugh or cry.

The telephone spared her the decision. She had turned on the answering machine so Roman and she could hash this out. As far as she was concerned the hashing was over for the night. She excused herself and hurried to the telephone.

"Let it ring," Roman said, following right behind her.

She ignored him and snatched the receiver to her ear. "Muldoon, here."

"It's me," Cage announced in an oddly curt tone. "You're needed."

A chill flushed her. "Not Loverboy?"

"I don't think so."

"Where are you?"

"On my way to Bud Grimes's house."

The quaver in his voice jarred her. Her mouth dried. Cage didn't rattle easily and he was rattled. "Bud's house? Why?"

"One of his neighbors went over to complain about his dog barking. Found the door ajar and went in. Bud was lying in a pool of blood."

"Is he..."

"Don't know. Ambulance should be arriving any minute. You want me to pick you up?"

"No. It's out of your way. I'll meet you there."

She heard his radio squawk in the background. Cage told her it was the first unit to Bud's. "Hang on. Maybe I'll have something new to tell you."

He was back in a second. "Bud's dead, Muldoon."

Pain squeezed her heart. Had he killed himself? He'd been depressed since Leah's murder. But this depressed?

She lowered her voice and asked, "Was the wound self-inflicted?"

"No." Impossibly, Cage sounded more rattled than before. "His throat was slit."

Chapter Eight

"His throat was slit?" Kerrie felt as if he'd knocked the wind from her. She stifled a gasp. "Like Leah's?"

"I don't know yet," Cage said flatly, his accent pronounced.

Shivers quaked through her, starting a discordant jangling inside her head. First Leah, now Bud. Was it some grisly coincidence that they'd both been murdered in the same way? She wouldn't know until she visited the crime scene, but at the moment it called for more imagination than she could conjure. "I'm on my way."

She hung up, but her hand remained gripped on the phone. Would they find Loverboy's signature-cut on Bud's throat—like the ones they'd found on Wendy Waring and Leah Davis? Had their "Classifieds" case just taken a bizarre turn? Or had media coverage of Loverboy's hijinx spurred a copycat murderer? Someone Bud might have sent to prison in the past?

She didn't know what to think, could barely register the fact that two friends were dead, murdered in the same brutal way. "First Leah, now Bud."

She whirled around and knocked into Roman. For a few fleeting minutes, she'd forgotten her personal problems. Now they loomed as tall and large as the man himself, as dark and forbidding as his expression. She couldn't deal with their controversy anymore tonight. Thank God, she didn't have to. "That was Cage. I have to leave."

"Why did you say, first Leah, now Bud?" Roman's voice was husky, edgy. "Did someone kill Bud Grimes?"

Despite her best efforts, tears stung Kerrie's eyes. She tightened her hands into fists and tensed her whole body, refusing to give in to the grief that scraped at the corners of her mind. She needed answers right now, clues to the identity of the monster or monsters who'd killed her two friends. Crying could wait. She swallowed over the lump clogging her throat. "Yes."

"Loverboy?" When she didn't answer, Roman raised his voice. "Dammit, Irish, tell me!"

"I don't know." She realized her mistake the second the words were out of her mouth; why hadn't she denied it outright. Now, Roman would demand being let in on the investigation of Bud's death, finding links to Wendy Waring's case everywhere he looked. Damn. Knowing she was probably wasting her breath, she tried anyway, "There is no reason to believe Loverboy killed Bud."

He arched a disbelieving raven brow. "I heard you say Grimes's throat was slit."

She couldn't deny it. Nor did she have the stamina at the moment to argue with him. She just nodded and hurried from the room. A moment later she returned, carrying her coat and strapping on her gun. "Will you stay with the girls until Mom gets home? I'm needed at Bud's."

"Your mom went to Sophia's. Call and get her here. I'm going with you."

"Oh, no, you're not." She shrugged into her coat. "You're staying the hell out of this—Bud's murder has nothing to do with Loverboy."

"You don't believe that and neither do I." Roman put on his coat. "Quit being stubborn and call your mother."

Who the hell did he think he was? She gathered her car

keys. He stood like a wall between the door and her. She could go out the front door, but he'd probably follow. She couldn't leave the girls alone. Damn the man.

Muttering to herself, she sped to the telephone and punched in Sophia's number. She explained the situation to her mother, then hung up and faced Roman. Once again, he was inches from her. Her breath snagged as she lifted her head and stared into his eyes. Anger and hurt simmered in their golden depths, maybe even a touch of hatred, all provoked by, and directed at, her.

But the smidgeon of smugness tugging at his sensuous mouth sent heat spiking into her cheeks. She pulled in an angry breath, inadvertently filling her senses with the tangy scent of man and after-shave that nightly haunted her dreams.

Her temper spiraled higher. She'd love to wipe that look off his glorious face. Tell him to shove off. To stay as far away from her and her family as possible. But he wouldn't do it. Not only was he bullheaded. He was dangerous. Better watched up close than at a distance. She poked her finger against his chest, backing him away from her. "I'm letting you tag along, but I'm warning you—keep out of the way and keep your opinions to yourself."

"Yes, ma'am." He shrugged playfully, grinned crookedly, sexily.

Kerrie felt heat swirl in her belly, her body responding to the promise Roman's smiles summoned. Gritting her teeth, she spun on her heel. "I'm going to check on the girls before we leave."

The darkened bedroom was lit by the soft glow of the night-light and scented by the sweet fragrance of sleeping babies. Kerrie moved across the floor, drawing a bracing breath. Grief, love, loss, heartache, anger and fear were colliding inside her like some crazy chain-reaction pileup on a freeway. Her stomach was queasy and her hands trembled. So much for tough lady cop.

She reached for the blanket Gabriella had once again kicked off. Hot-blooded and obstinate, just like her daddy. No. She wouldn't think that way. Wouldn't think about Roman. She pulled the blanket up around the baby's shoulders, then leaned in and kissed her warm, full cheek. Thank God, she had this sanctuary to hold the evils of the world at bay.

A floorboard creaked, startling her out of her reverie. Roman. There was something indefinably intimate about his being here with her this way. Something she couldn't deal with. Watching her children sleep was her private joy, one she seldom shared even with her mother. His very invasion restirred her anxieties. Her selfishness. Her fear that he would snatch these two most precious possessions from her. She could barely breathe.

Roman moved to the other crib. Maureen, her red curls sweat-dampened against her chubby cheeks, slept with her bottom in the air, her thumb in her mouth. He said, "It's like watching an angel sleep."

The look on his face, the awe in his voice tore at Kerrie's heart, at her conscience. Was he thinking of all the nights he'd missed seeing his daughters like this? Thinking of all the nights she'd denied him this tiniest indulgence, this greatest of parental pleasures? Parental rights?

As though he'd read her mind, he said, "How could you keep this from me?"

His hard gaze pinned her. He was numb, in shock, still reeling from the realization that he'd fathered these two children. Still angry as hell at her.

"I—I…" But she had no defense. She shoved a nervous hand through her hair. If he made a genuine effort to be a part of their daughters' lives, could she really fight it? *Should* she fight it?

Without asking permission, Roman leaned over and kissed Maureen's forehead. In that instant Kerrie realized he would always take liberties. It was his nature. The more she gave him, the more he'd take…until he'd taken everything from her.

Left her nothing.

The front door opened and closed, announcing Glynna's arrival. Neither Roman nor Kerrie updated her on the outcome, or the status, of their conversation concerning the children. Kerrie told her where they'd be and how she could be reached. Then they left.

With a flashing red light issuing from the Mazda's roof, they were soon speeding south on I-5, weaving in and around traffic. The rain had tapered off to a mere sprinkle, but the freeway was slick, with standing water in places.

Roman studied Kerrie's profile, striving not to see Maureen in every line. He was still trying to make sense of this latest murder, trying to figure out how and if it fit with anything else they knew about Loverboy. "Why did you ask Cage if Grimes's wound was self-inflicted? Why would he kill himself?"

She pulled her gaze from the road and glanced at him. In the dim illumination from the headlights behind them, he could see her mouth puckered saucily. "Don't tell me you didn't know Leah and Bud were engaged?"

Roman frowned. "Engaged?"

"They were supposed to marry next month," Kerrie added. Water sprayed against the car as she drove into the far left lane and onto the ramp that connected I-5 and I-405.

Roman leaned back in his seat, his eyes focused straight ahead. He barely glanced at Southcenter Shopping Mall, barely noticed the approach of the Renton S curves. His vision was turned inward. How had his informant missed such an apparently well-known tidbit as Leah Davis being Bud Grimes's fiancée?

The connections he'd sought earlier suddenly had some disturbing links. Wendy, Leah and Grimes all had their throats slit. And only yesterday Glynna Muldoon had had a near encounter with a knife.

Kerrie exited the freeway and started into the highlands of Renton, soon pulling into an older housing development. Roman was awash in thought. That eerie sensation he could never quite shake blew through him like the cold breeze buffeting the car. From the moment Wendy Waring died at the hands of Loverboy, this case was personal. Now, he considered the idea that Loverboy had meant it to be personal. Had Wendy died because of her connection to him, Roman? Had Leah died because of her connection to Bud Grimes? Had Glynna almost died because of her connection to Irish?

Dear God...the implications were chilling. "Did Loverboy leave his signature *L* on Bud's throat?"

"We'll know soon enough." She pulled to a stop in a cul de sac. An ambulance stood like a centerpiece between numerous police vehicles before a single-story, ranch-style, brick house. A small group of onlookers, gawking and talking in whispers, hovered on the edges of the rain-soaked yard.

As Kerrie and he hustled from the car and up the front walk, Roman prayed he was wrong about Loverboy—that Bud Grimes had been killed by a revenge-seeking ex-con.

Cage's pal on the Renton PD was one D.J. Klotz, a bulldog of a man both in facial features and body build. As officer in charge of securing the scene, Klotz greeted them at the front door, reminding Kerrie that she had no jurisdiction here, that she was being admitted at his discretion—because she'd been Bud's friend and former partner. She introduced Roman.

They stepped into a tiny living room with beige carpet and brown Naugahyde furnishings. The TV blared a sports program on the latest NFL/AFL winners and losers. The abandoned remains of a Swanson Hungry Man dinner sat congealing on the coffee table, next to a can of beer, an overflowing ashtray and a remote control.

"The body's in the kitchen," Klotz said. "Cage has seen it, but I'd prefer you and Agent Donnello stayed out of there until after the lab's been and gone."

"Of course." Kerrie was relieved. She wanted to remember Bud as he'd been in life. "Where *is* Cage?"

Klotz pointed across the room. "Down the hall. I trust you won't touch anything."

Roman followed Kerrie. The house stank of stale cigarette smoke and unwashed dog and death. As they neared the end of the hall, Cage emerged from a back room. His flattop was mussed, the scar above his left eye a prominent red tonight, his teal blue eyes angry.

Cage's grim expression darkened at the sight of Roman. Roman decided not to take it personally. He hung back, leaned against the hallway wall. He knew and understood the rage that came part and parcel with a fellow officer's murder.

Tully Cage growled at Kerrie. "What's he doing here?"

"I'll explain later," she snapped, her patience as short as her partner's. "Was it...?"

Cage clamped his lips together and nodded. "Yeah, our old friend Loverboy."

Kerrie's breath left her in a noisy rush, and she slumped against the wall opposite Roman. Her question was directed at Cage. "But...why? Why Bud?" What the hell was going on? "It makes no sense. Loverboy is a psychopath who kills redheaded women he meets through the classifieds. So why Bud?"

Cage fidgeted. His unfriendly gaze shifted to Roman,

then back to Kerrie. "Was Bud in contact with you since Leah's death? You know, asking about the case, about our progress, anything like that?"

"No. Did he approach you?"

Cage shook his head.

Kerrie straightened. "You think he was investigating on his own?"

Cage let out a weary sigh and crooked his head toward the room behind him. "In his bedroom...I found some photocopies of reports directly out of our files. Reports he's not supposed to have."

Kerrie paled, her green eyes looking more emerald than ever in her drawn face. "Do you think he figured out who Loverboy is and decided to do something about it?"

Roman interrupted. "Was Grimes a stupid cop?"

Kerrie jerked toward Roman. "What? No, he was damned smart."

Roman leaned toward them. "Then ponder this—if he'd discovered who Loverboy is and decided to go after him—and it had all gone wrong somehow—would he have died in his own home? Or would we have found his body dumped somewhere—the same as Wendy's and Leah's?"

Cage and Kerrie exchanged frowns. She grew thoughtful.

"So?" Cage shrugged.

"Bud didn't go after Loverboy," Kerrie said, obviously getting the point that seemed still to elude her partner. "Loverboy came after Bud."

"Exactly." Roman nodded.

"But that's what I don't get." Cage scratched his short blond hair. "Why did Loverboy come after Bud?"

Ice lay in chunks in Roman's stomach. "I have a theory."

Kerrie rolled her eyes. He'd promised to keep his opinions to himself. She should have known he wouldn't. "I suppose this theory of yours somehow involves *you* staying in *my* case?''

''If I'm right, you and I have been involved in this case from the getgo.''

''You're delusional.'' She grasped Cage's arm. ''Let's discuss this elsewhere.'' She glared at Roman. ''Alone.''

In a complete about-face, Cage resisted. ''Muldoon, I'd like to hear what Agent Donnello has to say.''

The blaring TV suddenly went silent. The void was immediately filled with the voices of new arrivals. The house would soon be crawling with police of one breed or another. Roman tensed. What he had to say was not for strangers' ears. Hell, he wasn't a hundred percent sure he ought to trust Cage. ''Not here. Somewhere private.''

''My car?'' Kerrie asked exasperated.

Roman shook his head. He wanted somewhere with lights and heat. ''Someplace we can get some coffee.''

Kerrie's hands were on her hips and her eyes snapped with impatience. ''Downtown?''

''Too far away.''

She tapped her toe. ''My house?''

Roman shook his head. He didn't want Glynna Muldoon overhearing what he had to say and getting unduly frightened. ''Not private enough. Your mother—''

''Look.'' Cage interrupted, sounding like a referee. ''We could go to my apartment. It's closer than Muldoon's.''

''Fine.'' Kerrie sighed.

''Good.'' Roman nodded.

They broke the news to Officer Klotz that the M.O. on Bud Grimes's murder was exactly the same as the Loverboy case, currently under Seattle's jurisdiction. Klotz assured them Renton would cooperate on all levels of the investigation. Cage, Roman and Kerrie did a sweeping walk-through of the crime scene, then left.

Cage, a bachelor, lived in a new complex in Tukwila, above Southcenter Shopping Mall. His apartment was a single bedroom on the ground floor. A postcard-size kitchen adjoined a long narrow living room with a sliding glass door at its farthest end. It was sparsely furnished—just the essential sofa, recliner, TV and dining set—in shades of gray, black and red. The effect was masculine and uncluttered.

In contrast to Bud Grimes's house, it was spotless, and warm, and smelled of leather and cigars.

"I'll start the coffee." Cage shed his coat and headed toward the kitchen. "Get comfortable."

Kerrie shrugged out of her coat and tossed it on the sofa with such nonchalance, Roman wondered if she'd done it dozens of times, if she often "got comfortable" here. She tilted her head at him, sending her fiery curls cascading across her shoulders. "Is this 'private' enough for you?"

Roman swallowed hard. His body responded to this woman as it never had to another with such force of need, such desire to possess, such jealousy, such anger.

"It'll do." Somehow, he managed to keep his voice level.

"Then start talking 'cause I have this much patience left." She held her thumb and index finger an inch apart.

He bit back his own impatience and kept his gaze on her face. "Soon as Cage joins us. I only want to say this once."

"Fine." She sighed, then turned and walked to the kitchen archway and levered a shapely hip against the door frame. "Can I help, Tully?"

"Sure," Cage said. "Get out the mugs and the sugar and milk."

Kerrie ducked into the kitchen and started opening cupboards as if she were someone who knew where to find the requested items. Something unpleasant stirred inside

Roman. Why was she so familiar with Cage's kitchen? Were these two partners more than co-workers? More than friends?

Not that he cared. He pulled off his coat. She could see whomever she wanted. He had no hold on her in that area. Cage was welcome to her. She was too intractable and insensitive for his tastes.

Dropping his coat atop hers, Roman moved across the living room so he could see her better. Her long legs seemed longer than ever in that short black skirt, the fabric cupping her bottom as he longed to do. As she reached into the cupboard, her full breasts shifted beneath that soft fuzzy sweater, inviting his gaze, his touch.

He felt the tightening in his groin and hated himself for it. She'd betrayed him in the worst possible way. His body might want her, but he didn't. Period. If not for this case and for his daughters, he'd walk out of her life this minute and never look back.

Liar. Roman jerked around as if someone standing at his shoulder had spoken the word aloud, realizing belatedly that he'd only heard the word inside his head. He closed his eyes against the heartache that followed it. All right, so he might look back once. Maybe twice. But he'd get over it. Get over her.

He pulled out a chair and sat at the red lacquered dinette table. Kerrie set three mugs on a tray beside the gurgling coffeemaker, then grabbed the creamer and sugar bowl and started toward him. She walked with pride, her chin at a stubborn angle, and he knew he was in for a fight where his theory about Loverboy was concerned.

The fight for his rights with his children would be even more difficult. Especially, he feared, for Irish. She'd drawn her line in the sand, and he was going to do more than just step over it; he was going to redraw it.

Kerrie deposited spoons and a black ceramic sugar bowl

and creamer on the gray place mat in the center of the table, then sat across from Roman.

Cage joined them with the tray of steaming mugs.

Roman reached for one and curled his cold fingers around it. "I think we're agreed that Grimes's murder puts a new spin on the Loverboy investigation."

Cage scooped two spoons of sugar into his coffee. "I want to know why you think you and Muldoon have both been involved in this case since the first murder was committed."

"Me, too." Kerrie ignored her mug. "I realize you knew the first victim, but I didn't come in on this case until after Leah Davis died."

Roman took a sip of coffee, swallowing slowly, deliberately, before setting his cup down. "I don't think Wendy was selected by Loverboy at random."

Cage's eyebrows dipped. "Then how? Why?"

The pain of losing someone dear, the deeper pain of realizing you caused that loss, squeezed Roman's chest. "I believe my close relationship with Wendy was why she was murdered."

Kerrie rolled her eyes, then gazed at Cage. "Did I mention this man has an ego the size of Mount Rainier?"

Roman let the insult slide, but he had to stuff his anger. "This has nothing to do with my ego. It's the only scenario that makes sense."

"Yeah ...*non*sense."

"Look, Donnello, I'm inclined to go along with Muldoon," Cage said. "If this is another one of your gut instinct—"

"I thought you were going to hear me out."

Cage conceded the point with a nod. "Okay. Why do you think Waring was killed because of her relationship with you?"

Roman frowned. "Grimes's murder convinces me that

Loverboy is connected somehow with the smuggling bust that he and Muldoon and I were involved in three years ago. It's the only thing we all worked jointly on that would make us targets of a single murderer.''

"Targets?" The word shot from Kerrie on an exasperated breath. "You and I haven't been targets."

"Haven't we?" Roman banged his mug down. "Think about it, Irish. Wendy Waring, who's like a kid sister to me, has her throat slit." His voice ground out the points as he ticked them off his fingers. "Leah Davis, Bud Grimes's fiancée, has her throat slit. Your mother has a close encounter with a knife. Now Bud Grimes has had his throat slit."

Kerrie paled. "You're saying Loverboy set up this elaborate ruse of a Classified Killer to trap *us*? That from the start, *we* were who he was after?"

"Yes."

He could see she didn't want to believe it. He hadn't wanted to believe it himself, but it was the only explanation that made any sense of Bud's murder.

Kerrie shook her head. "It could be coincidence."

"No, it couldn't Muldoon," Cage said. "Your mom, maybe, but Bud *was* killed by the same person as Waring and Davis."

"If I'm right," Roman stated grimly. "You and I are next."

That was what she didn't want to face. He could see it in her eyes. The fear. The worry. For herself. For her mother. For the babies. For him?

"You may be on to something here, Donnello." Cage drained his cup.

Kerrie leaned her arms on either side of her mug and bent forward. "Whatever became of C & F Imports? After they closed shop in Seattle, I couldn't get a line on them."

Her voice was soft, professional, but her eyes shone with

old anger, old frustration. She couldn't let go, couldn't forgive. Wouldn't believe he'd left to protect her.

Roman leveled his own heated gaze at her. "They went underground for a month, then reemerged in New Jersey as Medici Importers. Three months later, my agency busted them. Dante Casale, the company vice president, plea-bargained himself out of serving jail time by ratting on his cousin, Tito Fabrizio, the president of the company."

"Tito Fabrizio." Cage released a low whistle. "That dude had one nasty reputation on the East Coast."

"Yeah, Tito liked violence," Roman agreed.

Kerrie shifted her gaze between the two men. "What do you mean, 'had'?"

Roman finished the last of his coffee. "Fourteen months ago, Tito escaped prison with six other inmates. Four of the six were recaptured, Tito and another man died in a fiery car crash."

Cage nodded. "Fabrizio's body was burned beyond recognition."

They were silent a moment, then Kerrie asked, "Are they certain Tito died in the crash—that he didn't use the fact the bodies were unidentifiable to escape?"

Roman grinned wryly. No matter what else she was, Kerrie Muldoon was a good and thorough cop. "I thought of that, too, Irish. Tito's dental records were used as identification."

"What about the other one…Dante?" Cage asked.

"I didn't have any reason to check on him…until now. I'll put my sources to it first thing in the morning."

"Meanwhile, Muldoon." Cage shoved his chair back and stood. "We'd better take some precautions where your family and Donnello are concerned."

"I'd better get home." Kerrie hustled up and headed for her coat, but not before Roman read the anxiety on her ashen face. She finally believed him. He felt no satisfaction, only fear for his children, their grandmother and her. He wasted no time getting to his own coat.

A high-pitched beep like a wristwatch alarm sounded.

"My beeper." Kerrie dug the object from the pocket of her coat. "It's Mom." Her voice registered the terror bobbing inside him.

Chapter Nine

Kerrie cautioned herself against the fear nipping her, but when she heard Dr. Jon Vauter's voice instead of her mother's her pulse skipped ever faster. No, she mustn't jump to conclusions. Jon often visited her mother in the evening. She cleared her throat. "Jon, Mom paged me. Is she there?"

"Now, Kerrie, your mother and the girls are fine," Jon said, apparently trying to reassure her, but frightening her instead.

Her heart hitched. "What's wrong?"

"Nothing that should upset you unduly. Glynna is more angry than anything else and the babies are still fast asleep."

"More angry than anything else?" Kerrie knew she should be relieved, but after what she'd been through this evening, what they'd decided were Loverboy's true motives, her nerves were as raw as scraped knees. "Why is Mom angry, Jon?"

"It appears someone broke into your house at some point tonight."

Her anxiety returned in a rush. "What do you mean, broke in? Where? How?"

"The basement window."

"What's going on?" Roman demanded. "Are the girls all right?"

Trepidation heated his eyes to twin globes of yellow fire. Kerrie felt Cage's curious gaze darting between them. An uncomfortable heat climbed her neck. This was not the time to inform her partner of her daughters' paternity. But she could see that was the least of Roman's concerns.

Holding her hand over the receiver, she quickly told Cage and Roman what she'd learned so far. Then she said to Jon, "I'll radio this in."

"We've already called 911. They said someone is on the way."

"Good. Don't touch anything. We'll be there as fast as possible."

Minutes later, the three of them were in the Mazda, the siren screaming, the light flashing. Hunched on the backseat, Roman felt as if he were a giant stuffed into a cardboard box, his long legs jammed against the driver's seat, knees brushing his chin, his neck bent forward.

The storm had moved on into the mountains, leaving the streets wet and the night cool and dark. He could see Kerrie's anxious expression reflected in the rearview mirror as she steered the car through the dense freeway traffic.

"Just because someone broke in doesn't mean it was Loverboy," Cage said, addressing what Roman suspected was uppermost on all their minds.

"He's right, Irish. It could have been a teen looking for something to sell for drug money."

"It could have been." Kerrie frowned, then glanced into the mirror, locking her gaze with Roman's. "Last night, shortly after you left, something or someone set off the motion sensor light at the corner of my garage."

"Something or someone? What exactly did you see?"

She glanced back at the road. "I thought I saw a man

lurch into the shadows. I suppose it could have been a teenage boy."

"But you don't think so?" Roman's voice was tense.

"I'm not sure what I saw." Kerrie recalled how she'd automatically reached for her gun. Had her instincts been right? Had the shadowy figure she'd seen been Loverboy? Last night she'd laughed off the paranoia of his locating her home address. Now Bud was dead, murdered in his own kitchen. Now her house had been broken into. She wasn't laughing anymore.

Cage shifted in his seat. "Yeah, well, speculating is a waste of time. Let's hope whoever did this left enough evidence to lead us straight to his front door."

KERRIE'S PULSE was pinging by the time they entered her back door. Two of Seattle's finest had arrived before them. Erikssen, the patrolman who'd been at the hospital the other day and his partner, the antithesis of the big Swede in every way, slight, dark haired and female. The woman acknowledged their greeting, then said, "Erikssen's in the basement."

Cage and Roman scrambled down the stairs.

Kerrie wanted to follow after them, wanted to rush to her mother, to rush to her babies. She just stood there, as if her feet were planted in cement, staring at her mother, relieved to see she was in one piece, that she was as she'd left her. Yet something was disturbingly different. Her cozy little house felt alien, awash in drama, as if she were watching a play with too many actors onstage, the action impossible to follow.

"Are you all right?" Jon Vauter asked, breaking through her immobility.

Kerrie tore her gaze from her mother. The doctor, his silver hair neatly combed, his expensive clothes immaculate, his tanned face expressing concern, sat beside her mother at the kitchen table. "I've had better nights."

"You're terribly pale, sweetheart." Glynna started to stand.

Kerrie waved her back into her chair. "Please sit down and finish giving your statement. I want to check on the girls."

"They're fine, darling. I checked not more than ten minutes ago myself."

"Just the same..." She tossed her coat on a chair and hurried to the girls' room. The moment she stepped into the softly lit haven and found her precious babies fast asleep, she drew her first deep breath in an hour. Here all was calm, here all was exactly as she'd left it hours ago. Except that Gabby had once again kicked off her covers.

"Does she always do that?" Roman murmured, startling Kerrie so badly she nearly dropped to the floor.

She spun around, took one look at the wonder emanating from his eyes and all the emotions she'd held tightfisted inside her, broke loose. Nothing at the police academy or in her experience to-date had prepared her for the violation she felt at having a stranger forcibly enter her home. Her safe place. Her family's safe place. A sob burst from her. "Someone broke in here. He could have..."

She couldn't bring herself to say what "he" might have done to her babies, wouldn't allow herself to imagine the horrors she'd seen perpetrated on children. Gabby shifted, then began sucking on her thumb. Kerrie gathered a deep breath and lowered her voice. "Was it Loverboy?"

"I don't know," he answered in an equally quiet tone. He could see the violation she felt, the anger, but most of all the fear, and even though he didn't want to share her emotions, didn't want to empathize with this woman who'd shut him out of his babies' lives, he did. So help him, God, he did. "Only Forensics can tell us that."

"This is the first time my work has…"

He nodded, understanding that she meant it was the first time her work had ever put her family in jeopardy, the first time her job had ever gotten personal, and she abhorred it.

His job had gotten personal lots of times. Usually he found the experience exhilarating. It played to his love of danger, heightened the stakes, increased the thrill, made bringing down the bad guys so much sweeter.

This time he abhorred it, too. With these innocent little girls involved, with Kerrie involved, the threat held no tantalizing edge, only genuine terror. He couldn't lose what he'd barely found. What he hadn't even had the chance to savor.

Kerrie reached for the blanket and tugged it up to Gabriella's shoulders. Her hand trembled, the only outward sign of how truly upset she was. Why did she always have to act so tough? Despite not wanting anything to do with her, he ached to comfort her. But she was holding herself so stiffly he feared she'd break if he touched her.

Kerrie could see he was as shaken as she was. Funny. She'd never thought of him as vulnerable. It just pointed out how little she really knew Roman Donnello. How little credit she'd given him for being a decent human being. But a part of her still feared him. Even feared his vulnerability. Especially his vulnerability. It made him too human.

It was easier to think of him as a monster. Had it only been yesterday that she'd worried he wouldn't want involvement in his daughters' lives? What a fool she'd been. Her biggest problem would be the unfathomable depth of his involvement with them.

She couldn't deal with this right now. Her last nerve felt ready to pop. She had to talk about something else. Anything else. She walked softly from Gabby's crib to Maureen's. "Do *you* think it was Loverboy?"

"I was afraid Loverboy would try something tonight—I don't know what I expected, but I did sense your mother was in danger. Especially after Mike Springer lost the tail Cage put on him. That's why I raced over here from McRory's earlier."

"I know why you rushed over here. I heard your exchange with Cage in the surveillance van."

"Ah." Roman nodded. He'd forgotten she was wearing a wire. So that was why she'd arrived practically on his heels.

Kerrie clenched her hands in front of her. "But could Loverboy have been here *and* at Bud Grimes's tonight?"

"If he got here before me, and left shortly after you arrived—sure. He'd have had plenty of time."

"And you're sure Loverboy is Mike Springer?"

"Don't tell me you weren't convinced before I put a stop to his plans to get you alone."

"No," she conceded. "I was sure Springer was our man, but then two minutes into Jeremy Dane's company—" She broke off, shuddering.

Despite the somber conversation, Roman smiled wryly. "Is Dane the four-eyed creep who couldn't keep his hands off you—the one you had drinks with the other night?"

She nodded. "Cage says he has a New Jersey accent, and he's lied about his employment. There's no paper on him in this state under the name Jeremy Dane. And no prints on him in the national computer."

"So, he's never served time and never been in any of the armed services." Roman's brows dipped as he grew thoughtful. "New Jersey gives him connections with Casale and Fabrizio. But he doesn't look Italian."

"Neither does Cage, but his mother's family are Northern Italian."

"As interesting as that is, I still say Springer is Loverboy. He tried getting you to leave with him almost as soon

as he sat down. And he had enough time to get here ahead
of me.''

''Then you're certain it wasn't someone who followed
us from McRory's?''

He tilted his head, considering. ''Did you notice anyone
following you?''

She frowned, trying to recall. ''No.''

''Me, either. But then I wasn't looking.''

''Neither was I,'' she admitted. Her mind had been on
preventing him from finding out about the girls.

She could see that realization dawning in his eyes. She
turned away from the accusation transforming his features,
and checked Maureen's blanket.

Choking down his resentment, Roman watched Kerrie's
tender machinations with the girls. Despite his anger and
hurt, he could see she was a good mother. That she loved
his children. He couldn't fault her that, but by all that was
holy, at this moment, he wanted to fault her for something.
He narrowed the distance between them to inches.
''You're a smart woman, Irish, a good cop and a loving
mother. So why the hell don't you have a security system
in this place? At least bars on that damned basement window?''

He had whispered the words, but he might have shouted
them for the harshness with which they struck her ears.
She didn't need to take this from him, wouldn't take it
from any other man. But she knew his concern rose from
genuine roots. She wheeled to face him, startled to find
him so close. Her chin hitched higher as she said softly,
''Because I can't afford one.''

His heated gaze warmed her face. He dipped his head
nearer. ''I'll pay for it.''

Like hell you will! But the retort melted on her tongue.
Pride wouldn't keep her safe. Wouldn't keep her babies
alive and unharmed. Her chest tightened with fright. No,

after tonight, she'd accept a security system from any source who offered it. "Thanks. I'll take you up on that."

He blinked as if she'd slapped him, obviously not expecting her to acquiesce so easily, so quickly. "I'll give you one thing, Irish, no one delivers a surprise better than you. I'll see if I can get someone on it first thing in the morning."

She nodded. "Good."

Why did he always have to stand so close? She was locked between the crib and his solid, vibrant body. He'd removed his leather jacket. Without it, he seemed stripped of a layer of armor, and yet she was the one feeling defenseless.

"Meanwhile," he drawled. "I'll spend what's left of this night on your sofa."

Her eyes widened. Her heart beat faster. The last thing she wanted was Roman Donnello within walking distance from her bed. Because despite everything, she ached to throw herself into his arms, to lose herself in his protective embrace, to let him lift her on an emotional tide of such magnitude it would wash aside all the horror, all the fear, everyone and everything, except him and the way only he could make her feel.

"Your staying on my couch—" she wiped her moist palms against her skirt "—is not a good idea."

Kerrie brushed past him and ducked into the room across the hall. Her bedroom. Roman followed, shoving the door open as she tried shutting him out. He lurched across the threshold, pushed the door closed behind him, and caught her by the elbow, pulling her hard against him.

She glared at him.

He glared back. "Dammit, Irish, we're going to have to set aside our resentments until this is over. We have two little kids who are counting on us to keep them safe."

His chest heaved as if he'd run a great distance, his

breath beating hot against her face, his warm fingers infusing his heat into her arm, holding back the chilling fog that threatened to envelop her life. Alone, she couldn't see to put one foot in front of the other. Alone, she couldn't find her way to safety. Alone, Loverboy would defeat her.

"Are you going to swallow your damned pride and work with me on this?" Roman's eyes glowed like golden beacons through the terrifying mist, offering her support and strength.

Kerrie felt her resistance weakening. Only he understood exactly how she felt. Only he had as much at stake as she did. Only he had as much to lose. She needed him.

Oh, God, but she needed him.

Every pore in her body tingled with that need. She drew a ragged breath, and never taking her eyes from his, reached her hands to his waist, and leaned into him until her chin rested on his chest.

She felt him flinch, watched his Adam's apple bob as he swallowed hard, his eyes questioning her intent. He grasped her upper arms and tried disentangling himself. "You're playing with fire. You don't want this."

She hugged him harder. "Yes, I do."

He blinked, studied her face. "I won't be gentle." His whisper was husky.

"Then don't be."

Roman moaned, "Oh, Irish."

His arms went around her, his hands skidding across her hips, her bottom, up her back until they found her face and cupped it, a second later, his lips were on hers, his tongue probing her mouth. Pent-up passion burst through her, her body responding to Roman's touch like an ignition stroked with the right key.

She clung to him, caressing his wide back with her fevered hands, gyrating her hips against his, pressing her belly against his arousal, silently begging him to address the ache of desire that only he could spark in her, that only he could assuage.

She gasped his name, encouraging him, "Please, Roman, please."

He moaned again, grasped her bottom harder. Pulling her closer, he bent sideways, and lifted the hem of her skirt. His fingers climbed her thigh, found the edge of her panties and pulled them down.

She tugged his sweater up, revealing his washboard stomach, tanned and muscled, with an arrow of black hair spearing the center and disappearing into the waistband of his jeans. She stroked his belly. It was silky and warm. Oh, so warm. She wanted that warmth inside her. She reached for his fly and began unbuttoning, her anxious fingers clumsy in the need to touch his naked flesh.

The last button gave and she shoved his jeans down his hips, then his briefs, freeing his magnificent arousal at the same moment his probing fingers slipped inside her. Her pleasured gasp collided with his, and need became demand.

Mindful of nothing and no one else, not even the houseful of investigators, they stumbled to the bed, and a moment later he was sliding between her parted thighs, filling her, huge and hard and hot, and every bit as wonderful as she remembered.

She thrust her hips toward his, matching him stroke for stroke as the firestorm inside her burned out of control, raging through her veins, searing across her nerve endings, engulfing her, lifting her toward the sky, again and again, until it roared in her ears and burst like stars inside her eyes.

Breathless, Kerrie lay sheltered beneath Roman, still clinging to him, not wanting this vital connection, this affirmation of life to end.

"Kerrie Carleen?" Glynna rapped lightly on the door. "Are you in there?"

Kerrie stiffened. Roman lurched off of her.

"I'll be out in a minute, Mom." Kerrie grabbed the panties dangling from around her left ankle and tugged them on as Roman sprang off the bed and into his own pants.

He stood, buttoning his fly and whispered, "I'm not going to pretend I understand what just happened, but it doesn't change anything...right?"

"Right." Despite knowing their lovemaking was nothing more than lust that she had initiated, Kerrie was hurt. She stood and straightened her skirt and sweater, then quickly brushed her hair and checked her appearance in the mirror over the dresser. Roman didn't love her, might wind up hating her when all was said and done. She'd better remember that. "It changes nothing."

"Yeah, that's what I thought." Roman turned away from her. For a moment there, he'd almost thought she needed him. He should have remembered who he was dealing with. Tough cookie Kerrie Muldoon didn't need anyone. Least of all the father of her children. He glanced over his shoulder. "What's changed, Irish, is you. I'm not sure it's for the better."

Kerrie felt as if he'd stuck a knife into her heart. She stiffened, lifted her chin. She'd be damned if she'd let him know it. "Don't go soft and mushy on me, Donnello. The truth is, we both had an itch. Now it's been scratched."

She yanked open her bedroom door. "Let's see if Cage has found anything important."

Roman stared after her. An itch? Scratched? He dug his fingers through his hair and followed her into the kitchen. Sex without complications. Why should her attitude surprise him? She obviously didn't need a permanent man in her life. He ought to be glad she felt that way. He wasn't offering anything permanent. He wasn't husband material, any more than she was wife material.

Besides, monogamy was not him.

Roman settled his hip against the refrigerator, watching as she conferred with her partner, his mind distracted by the images still vivid in his head, by the feel of her that lingered on his hands, the scent of her that clung to his sweater, the taste of her on his tongue.

He grabbed his coat off the kitchen chair, shrugged it on and glanced at Kerrie one more time. Sex without complications. Then why did he feel as if his appetite had just been whetted, not sated? As if his itch already needed another scratching? Why did he ache to kiss her until her lips were swollen and bruised, until she begged for the sweet release they'd just shared? Until she admitted that she needed him?

What he needed right now was some air.

"WE NEED SOME SLEEP," Kerrie told her mother, placing the last of the dirty coffee cups into the dishwasher. Daylight was an hour away, dusting the kitchen window a soft gray. Everyone had left ten minutes earlier, everyone except the patrol cars parked out front and in back, everyone except Roman, who had insisted he'd sit in his car until dawn.

Glynna lifted her right leg and scratched her heel. "Yes, the girls will be up soon."

They walked down the hall together, stopping at Kerrie's bedroom. The door stood open. One look at the rumpled bed brought all the images of the wild lovemaking that had occurred there only an hour ago rushing into Kerrie's mind. She could still feel Roman's hands on her, his heat inside her, still smell his scent on her sweater.

A blush warmed her cheeks, her blood. They'd been as rash as first-time lovers, as reckless as teenagers, as irresponsible as they'd been on the afternoon she'd conceived the twins. The thought staggered her. No, it couldn't happen twice in a lifetime. The chances were too slim. The odds phenomenal.

Kerrie bit her lip. She didn't regret any of the passionate moments she'd shared with Roman. Nor would she punish herself longing for a future with him that was never going to happen. It was time she accepted that. Sweet memories would have to suffice, would have to warm her heart on cold lonely nights.

"Did you and Roman work out your differences?" Glynna asked softly.

"No." The small word clogged Kerrie's throat.

"But you were alone a long time and when you rejoined us, I could tell something important had passed between the two of you."

Important? Kerrie wanted to laugh. "Nothing that resolved anything." Indeed it had only complicated everything.

"You should try to work out something with Roman. He's a good man."

"I'm glad you think so."

"You think so, too."

"So, what if I do?" She was too vulnerable, too touchy on this subject to discuss it. She lurched across the threshold and caught the doorknob. "I need a shower and some sleep."

Glynna took a deep breath. Her soft green eyes were heated with an intensity Kerrie hadn't seen since before her father died. "You know, Kerrie Carleen, yours isn't the only life involved here."

"I know." Kerrie sighed and shifted from one foot to the other. She had heard this argument too many times in the past thirty-six hours. "My daughters—"

"Of course, Maureen and Gabby are to be considered."

Her mother cut her off. "But, for once, I was talking about myself."

Surprise darted through Kerrie. "Oh?"

Glynna nodded. "I guess you just thought I'd be here forever to help you raise the girls. Guess I thought that, too. But the past few days have made me realize I also have a life. One I've put on hold for over three years now. Not that I haven't done it willingly, gladly. Nevertheless…"

Kerrie felt stunned, numbed. Was her mother saying she was leaving them? Until this very moment, until it was pointed out to her, she hadn't realized how much she took for granted her mother's position in their little family unit. How Glynna's support allowed her to have her career and motherhood at the same time.

She blushed with shame and contrition. "Is that why you keep turning down Dr. Jon's marriage proposals?"

Glynna frowned. "I suppose it has kept me from seriously considering them."

Guilt wound through Kerrie. "Do you want to marry Jon?"

Glynna lifted her right leg and scratched her heel again. "He asked me again tonight…before we discovered the break-in."

"And…?"

"And…this time I'm seriously considering saying yes."

Kerrie nodded. How odd life was. Her mother was on the brink of a new happiness, while she was on the edge of an old sorrow. She had some hard decisions to make. Given the choice she'd pick happiness every time—but happiness wasn't being offered to her. Still, she could choose it for Glynna.

She stepped back into the hall, draped an arm around her mother and kissed her cheek. "Whatever you decide, you have my blessing, Mom."

"Thank you, darling." Glynna smiled and hugged her. "You know, my heel has been itching all night. That means I'm going on an unexpected trip soon."

Kerrie grinned. "Maybe a honeymoon?"

Chapter Ten

Kerrie's nerves were as taut as the braid holding her unruly hair off her face. Despite the loss of sleep, despite the mess her life was in, a part of her felt more alive than she had in years. She strode into work with purpose, determined they would beat Loverboy at his own game...now that they knew what the game was.

Cage was at his desk, conferring with Roman, who stood with his back to the window. One glance at the father of her children and her heart hitched. She didn't want to notice the autumn sunlight on his blue-black hair, the warmth it gave his tanned, olive skin, the depth of onyx it added to his raven brows and lashes, the catlike gleam it lent his golden eyes.

Instead she concentrated on the tiny lines at the corners of those compelling eyes. They were prominent this morning as were the whiskers on his square jaw. Had he gone home at all? Slept at all? The image of him in bed flashed into her head, set her pulse thrumming.

Forcing the unwanted vision aside, she greeted the men, crossed to her uncluttered desk and deposited her first latte of the day and her shoulder bag. "Hey, Donnello, I saw your car being towed away from my house this morning. Engine trouble?"

"Nope." His husky response sent shivers across her

skin, pulling her gaze to his. His expression was somber. "Someone slashed my tires."

Kerrie frowned. "Last night?"

Tully Cage nodded. "Yep, a regular crime wave going on in that peaceful little neighborhood of yours."

For the first time she noticed her partner looked every bit as tired as Roman, but there was a glint in his eyes, the kind of spark she'd seen before, whenever an investigation was progressing to his liking. What was going on? "What have you two been doing since you left my house?"

"Among other things, checking on Dante Casale," Cage answered.

As though she'd just emerged from a thick fog and could suddenly see colors sharper, could detect innuendo and mood, she realized both men vibrated with an underlying edginess. Her breath snagged. They had discovered something. "What did you find out?"

Roman leaned against the window, his long legs crossed at the ankles, his jeans distractingly tight, hugging him in places that stirred provocative images in her head. She concentrated on not noticing. "Tell me."

Roman arched a dark brow. "Dante's missing."

"Missing?" She shrugged out of her distressed-leather bomber jacket. "As in...disappeared?"

"Yes." He rolled his neck and a lock of hair swung onto his forehead, making him impossibly more handsome.

Cage rocked back in his chair. "The Casale family claims he ran off with his secretary."

"The thing is—" Roman jammed his hand into his hair, shoving the wayward lock back. "No one has seen or heard from him for at least four months. He's just vanished."

"A regular milk carton candidate." Cage grinned.

He'd been missing since Wendy Waring was killed.

Kerrie eyed them speculatively. "What do you think happened to him?"

"Nothing. I think he went into hiding." Roman braced his arms on the windowsill. "I think he's in Seattle running this operation."

Kerrie suppressed a shudder and dropped her jacket over the back of her chair.

Cage reached for his coffee mug.

Kerrie sat down. "Why would Dante care enough to launch such an elaborate ruse...just to get us?"

Roman's gaze swept her, appraisingly, as though he were remembering last night, as though he wanted her as he'd wanted her last night. Heat filled her face, flickered like tiny electric surges in the most private areas of her body and heart, everywhere except her mind. He didn't want her. He only wanted a sex partner.

He said, "I suspect Dante regretted testifying against his cousin Tito—especially since Tito's arrest led straight to Potter's Field."

"An eye for an eye. Blood for blood." Cage put his cup down with a thump. "In families like Casale's it's considered an obligation to extract vengeance on the person or people foolish enough to bring shame or death to kin. Your investigation not only led to death, but it came between Casale and Fabrizio, blood cousins. A double whammy."

She removed the lid from her latte. The high spirits she'd arrived with minutes before deflated.

"Detective Cage is right." Roman leaned his palms onto her desk and bent toward her. She caught a light whiff of the aftershave that still lingered in her memory from the night before. No, she would not be sidetracked with thoughts of making love to this man.

She pulled the latte close and inhaled. Casale was too old to be Loverboy, and he'd never bloody his own hands, so who was executing the murders? She took a sip of espresso. Would Casale enlist the help of strangers? Hired guns? Could a hired gun pull off the kind of passionate kills that Loverboy had? She was more inclined to go with Cage's notion that Casale would keep it in the family. "Did Fabrizio have any sons?"

"Naw." Cage shrugged dismissively. "Just daughters."

"Oh, I see," Kerrie snapped, instantly angered. She had to deal with gender prejudice in one way or another nearly every working day of her life. She wouldn't take it from her partner. She started up out of her chair. "You think women are incapable of this crime. This is the nineties, Cage. Purdy is full of women who committed murder for revenge."

"Whew, somebody's running on a short fuse today." Cage looked amused. "If you recall, Muldoon, we put some of those women into the state facility ourselves."

Chagrined, Kerrie blinked, and sat back down. "I'm tired, riding on my last nerve. I probably overreacted."

Cage chuckled derisively. "Probably?"

"She's right." Roman interrupted. He hitched his hip onto the edge of her desk, his back to her. "We shouldn't underestimate a daughter's love for her father."

Kerrie stiffened. She couldn't see his face, but his message came across loud and clear. He meant to gain his daughters' love, with or without her cooperation.

She clamped her mouth shut, reining in her anger, trying to swallow the knot in her throat. She didn't need these constant reminders that she'd kept Roman's children from him, kept him from forming any kind of bond with them. She sipped the espresso.

Cage shoved his coffee mug to one side. "So, we'll check on the daughters, and any sons-in-law while we're at it."

"Only one of Tito's daughters is married," Roman said.

"To a minister. The oldest daughter is a librarian, the youngest, a widow, is a kindergarten teacher."

A minister's wife, a librarian and a kindergarten teacher. All gentle souls by nature. Kerrie shook her head. In light of this information, her argument about nineties women lost its punch. Nineties women they might all be, but revenge-seeking, switchblade-wielding mamas? The stretch was too much for her to accept. She sipped her latte, thoughtfully. "What about Casale? Any children?"

"None we're aware of." Roman shifted his body until he was facing her. "But he liked the ladies...so it's possible he's fathered children who've never lived with him."

There was a subtle hint of fierce emotion in his eyes. She braced herself, knowing what she was about to ask would hit to the heart of his anger. But the question couldn't be avoided. "Would he have acknowledged them...kept in close contact?"

"If the mother allowed it."

She narrowed her eyes at him, straining to keep her flush of anger from reaching her face.

Cage seemed to pick up on the tension between them. He frowned. "I thought your agency was checking on illegitimate children."

"They are." Roman let out a heavy breath.

"So tell Muldoon about the nephew," Cage urged him.

"What nephew?" Kerrie grabbed at the switch of subject as if it were a lifeline.

Roman stroked his whiskered chin. "I recalled Casale bragging about a nephew, his sister's son, who by all accounts could very well be Loverboy. He's the right age. And apparently has enough looks and charm to gain a woman's interest and trust."

"And you've tracked the nephew here?" She felt a sudden swell of hope.

"Not exactly," Cage interjected.

She glanced at him, then back at Roman. "What then?"

"Reportedly he's on vacation at a beach house Dante owns on the Atlantic seashore."

"Reportedly?" The swell of hope flattened. "Is he, or isn't he?"

"I've got somebody watching the place now. They'll contact me as soon as they verify whether or not he's there. Maybe as early as this afternoon."

"Good." She took another swallow of espresso, wondering if the caffeine would ever kick in, would revive her rapidly waning energy. "Anything new on my break-in?"

Cage shuffled through the papers spread out on his desk, then handed her a sheet. "That's the lab report. This one has the techs puzzled."

"Why?" Kerrie asked.

"You'll note the footprints were made by size eleven Nikes, but the usual height and weight equation doesn't play in this instance."

"Why not?" She glanced up from the report.

Roman said, "The imprints indicate the perp was abnormally lightweight to wear such a big shoe."

Kerrie sighed. "So what are you saying—the perp was tall and reed-thin, small-boned with oversize feet, a woman wearing men's shoes, what?"

Cage shrugged. "Don't know."

She had an awful thought. "A teenager, after all?"

"Not in this case, Irish. Those footprints belong to Loverboy."

She frowned at Roman. "How can you be certain?"

"Because—" Cage leaned toward her, his arms outstretched in front of him, a smug smile in his teal eyes. "Just before you walked in, the lab called with an update. The same knife was used on Bud as on the other victims, likely an eight inch switchblade of some kind."

"How does that connect Bud's death to my break-in?"

Cage narrowed his eyes, inadvertently accentuating his scar. "The lab techs found some oddities in Bud's wound, deposits they suggest must have been on the knife."

"What?" Her stomach churned anxiously.

Roman bent toward her. "Some teeny specks of mud and a few strange fibers—rubber fibers, the kind of rubber used in tires."

Her eyes rounded. "As in your slashed tires?"

"Bingo!" Cage's grin spread across his face.

Kerrie's mouth dried. Proof. Solid and undeniable. They were another step, maybe more, closer to catching Loverboy. He'd gotten careless. Anxious. She flattened the empty latte container between her hands as she hoped she'd soon be smashing Loverboy's plans.

She tossed the cup into the waste basket. But why had he gotten careless? Was he getting bolder? More desperate? Growing tired of his game? A shiver slithered along her spine.

Cage stood and came to sit on the edge of her desk opposite Roman. "I haven't run this past Agent Donnello, yet, but I think he'll agree with me that you and your family should move out of your place and into a safe house."

The suggestion stunned Kerrie. She'd never considered it. Not even last night. She wasn't about to let someone drive her out of her own home. No way. Thank goodness that wouldn't be necessary.

"Thanks anyway, but a state-of-the-art alarm system is being installed in my home at this very minute." She avoided Roman's gaze, but she could feel him looking at her, likely wondering whether she would credit him for the alarm system. "The workers were starting on it when I headed in here. They're even putting some steel bars on the basement window. The Seattle PD couldn't supply me with a more secure site."

"But we could give you some place that Loverboy doesn't know about," Cage argued.

"And what am I supposed to do, just sit at this safe, secret house and twiddle my thumbs hoping you and Donnello bring Loverboy in before he finds us?"

"Nobody's suggesting you take a leave of absence. You'd still be on the case."

"You forget we don't know who Loverboy is. He could follow me from here to wherever I went. No, I'm not moving out of my house."

"Besides, she's got to consider her kids," Roman added.

Cage made a face at him. "What?"

"Kids don't like their routines disrupted," Roman explained.

"Well, excuse me, 'Daddy.'" Cage's retort had the effect of a bomb blast, startling Roman and Kerrie, then rendering them silent. Too silent.

Kerrie's cheeks burned. Crimson climbed Roman's neck. Tully Cage's gaze shifted between them, a thoughtful frown that was a testament to the wheels churning in his clever mind. He already knew Roman and she had a past, he was smart enough to put two and two together and come up with twins.

"Donnello's the father of your little girls?" Cage let out a low whistle. "Holy moly."

He stiffened, instantly contrite, apologetic. "Sorry, partner. I crossed the line. No questions, none of my business. But you've got to admit it's a mind blower."

"I'd appreciate it, Tully, if you didn't spread this around." Kerrie felt as if she'd just stepped off a stomach-jarring carnival ride.

Roman scowled. "As far as I'm concerned, Irish, he can tell the world. I'm not ashamed that what we once shared produced those two beautiful girls."

"Yeah, well, you don't have to work here," she growled. *And you're not a female in a predominately male office. And you don't understand or care how I feel about any of this.*

"Aren't you afraid you'll collapse under the weight of all that pride, Irish?"

Before she could respond, Cage interceded, "Kiddies, kiddies, could we get back to trying to identify Lover-boy?"

Roman nodded. It took Kerrie several deep breaths until her anger was banked, then she nodded, too.

"All right then." Cage returned to his chair, found a pen and opened a legal pad to a clean page. "Let's share thoughts about the suspects."

Roman grabbed a chair and positioned himself between their desks. "Which suspects?"

Kerrie understood exactly what and who her partner was referring to. "The men who've participated in this classi-fied ad ruse so far. At least one of them had to have been enlisted by Casale."

"Maybe more," Cage suggested. "Don't forget the un-known factor—Troy with the whiny voice."

"Who?" Roman asked.

She explained about the caller who'd stood her up the first night Roman had found her in McRory's and sat at her table without being invited. "Apparently he arrived, saw me with you and took off."

"We've never seen him," Cage added. "Don't have a last name and he's made all his calls from a pay phone."

"The same pay phone each time?" Roman asked.

Cage shook his head. "All different locations."

An anxious knot formed in Roman's stomach. Under-cover investigation, using oneself as bait to catch a mur-derer, was fraught with inherent dangers. But this was different. How many unsavory worms had running this classified ad stirred? Worms who had nothing to do with their case? Was Irish in jeopardy from other, unsuspected sources?

He curbed the urge even to mention it, knowing she'd likely dig her heels in deeper out of sheer orneriness. Maybe he was getting upset about nothing. Maybe his distress stemmed from their new knowledge about this case. He rubbed his bristled jaw with the palm of his hand. Her new role in his life.

Or was it related to what they'd shared last night? No. No way. That had been sex. Just sex. She'd made that clear enough. Too bad he couldn't brush it off as lightly. But how did he really feel about her? Hell he didn't want to examine *that*. "Mike Springer gets my vote. What have you got on him?"

Cage tapped the tablet with the pen. "Nothing that fits the profile we've worked up with Dante Casale at the head of this."

"Why not?" Roman frowned.

"Because Springer *does* check out," Kerrie said. "He's a CPA who has lived in this state since he was a teenager. And he lives with his father."

Roman arched a dark brow. "His birth father?"

Kerrie and Cage exchanged glances, instantly recognizing what Roman was getting at. She shrugged. He shook his head. "Have to admit, I don't know. Yet." He wrote himself a note.

Kerrie tilted her head sideways and studied Roman. "Why do you favor Springer?"

"Because the creep tried getting you to leave McRory's with him almost from the moment he arrived."

His answer surprised Kerrie. She could have sworn he sounded…jealous? No. She was hearing intonations where none existed. If she didn't curb all hope of Roman ever loving her, she'd have no one to blame but herself when she got hurt again. She lifted her chin. "That's hardly grounds for arresting the man. Surely you have a better reason than that."

Better reason? Roman narrowed his eyes. *Because Springer had a boyish charm that appealed to you, Irish. Because my gut instinct told me so. Because...I don't know, just because.* "Because...he had time to get to your house ahead of me last night."

This reason sounded ridiculous even to Roman. He glanced at Cage, avoiding the certain mockery he knew would be in Kerrie's emerald eyes.

Cage stopped tapping the pen. "Why are you so certain he broke into Muldoon's house before you got there?"

"Well, I, ah." He started to tell them about his instincts, then reconsidered. "I guess I don't know why, I just do."

"That famous instinct again?" Cage chuckled derisively.

"This is so lame," Kerrie said, before Roman could reply. "His instincts, indeed." She glared at Roman. "What makes you think your instincts are any better or any more seasoned than ours? I wasn't aware you had psychic powers."

"I don't," Roman defended, but he had to admit she was right. He hadn't given Cage and her much credit. Had thought he alone could figure out who Loverboy was. He grinned wryly. "Touché, Irish."

Kerrie's scowl deepened. "Are you working with us or against us on this?"

He sobered. "With you, of course."

"Then let's deal with facts and not instincts." She nodded at Cage to continue. He looked concerned. He'd talked the lieutenant into letting Roman participate in this investigation. Their boss had agreed only if Cage accepted full responsibility for all screwups. Roman's ego might cause a major one.

Cage said, "My money's on Dane. He's told us one lie after another—starting with where he lives."

Roman wanted to ask why a tail hadn't been put on Dane any of the times he'd shown up at McRory's, but knew it would sound like criticism and, at the moment, he'd bruised enough sensitivities.

The mention of Jeremy Dane brought the hair prickling on the back of Kerrie's neck. "He's obsessively neat and we can't discount his East Coast accent."

"Given that criteria," Cage said, in his most pronounced New Jersey voice. "Then even *I'm* suspect." Smirking at her, he extended his arms, wrists together, as though she might want to cuff him.

"Careful, she might take you up on it." Roman teased, his smile warming her insides.

Kerrie smiled, too, glad that her partner had found a way to lighten the tension Roman and she generated. "I'd say arresting you would fall into the 'guilty by being the least suspicious' mind-set. I'd rather stick with the lying Mr. Dane."

"You're a hard woman, Muldoon." Cage chuckled. "But we don't know anything about the man."

"How about fingerprints?" Roman asked.

Cage shook his head. "Not in the national computer."

"But," Kerrie added, "on the plus side, he is the age indicated in the ad."

Roman's golden eyes gleamed with purpose. "There must be some way to get a lead on him."

Cage scratched something on the tablet and stood. "I'm going to log-in some computer time and see if I can't do just that."

Kerrie reached for her purse and shoved out of her chair. "Meanwhile, I'm going to take a drive to Ballard and have a little chat with Mike Springer."

Roman leaped to his feet. "I'll go with Irish."

She donned her jacket. "I don't need a bodyguard, Donnello."

"Well, I do. You're not the only gift on Casale's wish list, you know." Roman retrieved his own coat. It was time she learned she hadn't cornered the market on stubbornness. He followed her out of the office and fell into step beside her. "I still say something about Springer is cockeyed—maybe even dangerous."

Kerrie rolled her eyes and shoved open the door to the stairwell, starting down ahead of him. "If you're trying to scare me—save your breath. I'm the one who's armed and dangerous."

Roman hastened down the stairs right on her heels. Damned woman was too obdurate to admit she had a vulnerable bone in her sexy little body. If she wouldn't watch out for herself, he would. He wasn't about to let a man like Springer anywhere near the mother of his children. The wayward thought surprised him. He didn't want to think about Irish as the mother of his children. That implied something tender and precious, two words that did not apply to his feelings for Kerrie Muldoon.

KERRIE PULLED THE MAZDA to a stop in front of a shabby, two-story house in one of the older neighborhoods in Ballard, a bustling community in northwest Seattle. The house, likely built in the forties, had gray shingled siding and white-trimmed windows, all in dire need of paint. A detached garage, that had been converted into an office, sat at street level.

Roman and she got out of the car and approached the makeshift office. A sign hung above the door: Michael C. Springer, CPA. But butcher paper with red poster paint lettering covered the windows, announcing that the accountant had moved to better digs.

Kerrie was writing down the new address and telephone number when the front door of the house opened.

"Hey, you there, whatcha want?" A man in his late sixties stood in the doorway.

Roman and she skirted the garage and climbed the concrete stairs to the porch.

The man had a stooped body and thinning gray hair combed over from a side part. Eyes the color of tarnished pennies peered suspiciously at them from behind thick glasses. He wore an old cardigan with leather patches on the elbows and rumpled slacks. "If you're looking for Mike, he's at his new place."

Kerrie crossed the porch, reaching into her purse for her ID. "Are you his father?"

"Who's asking?"

"I'm with the Seattle PD." Kerrie showed him her ID. "Agent Donnello and I just wanted to ask him a couple of questions."

The man's eyes rounded behind the glasses. "Mike in trouble with the IRS?"

"What?" Kerrie frowned, wondering how the IRS had suddenly become involved in her murder case.

The man pointed to Roman. "You said that fellow was an agent."

Kerrie glanced at Roman, taking in his mussed black hair, his whiskered face, his black leather jacket and tight jeans, his scuffed cowboy boots. An IRS agent? Not unless the agency had changed its dress code to biker casual. She bit back a grin. "I said, I'm with the Seattle PD."

"Yeah, I know what you *said*."

The man apparently didn't believe her, even though she'd shown him her ID. Her humor departed. Why was Donnello always a complication? A thorn in her side? If only she didn't need him on this case... The thought stopped her silent tirade. She did need Roman, in fact, though she'd never tell him, having him near lessened her fear of Loverboy.

"She called me agent out of respect," Roman said, stepping up beside Kerrie. "I'm a former FBI."

Kerrie couldn't hide her surprise at the lie.

The man noticed and nodded warily at Roman. "If you say so."

Kerrie pressed on. "Could we get back to Mike, Mr....?"

"Springer, Joe Springer."

Roman butted in. "Are you Mike's natural father?"

Joe swallowed as if an egg were stuck in his throat. "What's it to you?"

"Maybe nothing," Roman said pointedly. "Which is it?"

"Mike's my stepson." Joe's hand started to tremble. "I met his ma when I was working back east. Mike was ten when we married."

Roman smirked and winked at Kerrie, excitement dancing in his eyes. She wanted to remind him this bit of information might be nothing. It was only a crumb. They needed the whole cookie. But her own pulse had kicked up a beat and she couldn't keep the hope from her eyes, couldn't keep from returning his grin.

Joe's face turned an unhealthy red. Maybe he had high blood pressure. She strove to calm him. "Mr. Springer, we just want to ask Mike some questions in connection with a case we're working on. Nothing for you to worry about."

This seemed only to frighten him more. He shook his head and clutched the doorjamb with one hand. "Oh, Lordy, Lordy. I warned Mike there was something fishy about that man. No one pays a CPA that much dough for crunching a few numbers. Had to be mob money."

Chapter Eleven

"Mob money?" Roman repeated.

Joe Springer clamped his liver-spotted left hand over his mouth. Obviously he had said more than he'd meant to. "Are you gonna arrest my boy?"

Kerrie didn't like the color of his complexion. She shook her head. "No, Mr. Springer." At least not today.

"She only wants to talk to him." Roman gripped her arm. "Come on, Irish. The afternoon isn't getting any younger."

Joe stepped back into his house and slammed the door.

Roman started to hustle her down the porch stairs.

Halfway down, Kerrie twisted free of his grip. "Why are you in such an almighty hurry?"

Roman stared dumbfounded at her. "Are you kidding? Joe there just confirmed his *stepson's* association to Casale—and you can't figure out why I'm anxious to question the jerk?"

She laughed and continued down the stairs. "That's the swiftest conclusion-jumping I've witnessed in ages."

"I'm not jumping to any—" He broke off. "Oh, all right, I may have made a couple of fast connections, but don't tell me you didn't."

"Well," she conceded, opening her car door. "Okay,

maybe one or two connections clicked, but this is all speculation. We haven't got anything concrete.''

"Yet." Roman got in on the passenger side.

As she drove away from the curb, he gazed at her intense expression. "How do you want to play this?"

"Play what?"

"Questioning Springer."

"*Play* it?" She peered over at him quizzically, but as their gazes met the fervor he exuded stole her very breath. She was suddenly too aware of the short span of space between them, too aware of the magnetic pull between them.

She forced herself to concentrate on her driving. "Mike Springer may have been bribed by Casale to play a deadly game with us, but all my chips are turned in. All I want is to fold the board and put the game away."

"Precisely. But I think we should have a plan before we get there."

"Why am I sure you already have a plan?" Why was she sure she wasn't going to like his plan?

"Guess you're starting to understand me."

"That's a scary thought." She sighed. "I'm listening."

"It's simple. Just let me do the talking."

Kerrie chuckled. "Have you forgotten that you're not on this investigation in any official capacity? That you're only involved by the special circumstances? By the good graces of my boss?"

"I haven't forgotten. But what Springer can tell us may lock up this case."

"That's right. So, *my* plan is that *I'll* question him."

"And what am I supposed to do?"

Nothing. But she knew that was something Roman Donnello could never manage. "Keep your eyes and ears open and take down his answers for me."

Roman arched an eyebrow and the corners of his mouth

tipped slightly upward. He scooted down in the seat,
leaned back on the headrest and closed his eyes. "Sure,
Irish. Whatever you say."

Kerrie shook her head. The man was impossible.

Almost as impossible as the traffic on I-5. Rush hour
was in full swing and immediately after merging onto the
freeway, they became one of the multitude traveling at a
stop-and-go pace.

Kerrie tried to keep her mind off the man beside her.
There was something so infinitely sexy about the way his
ebony lashes brushed his olive skin, something compelling
about his expression, something she didn't want to notice,
something that wouldn't be ignored. If traffic were moving
at normal or even half its normal speed, she would have
been occupied with driving.

But she was preoccupied...with Roman. Traitorous images filled her head, stirring remembered sensations, arous-
ing new longings. The drive was sheer torture. Try as she
might to direct her thoughts to the case they remained
stubbornly on the man beside her—until Kerrie exited the
freeway forty-five minutes later.

"We're nearly there," she said, just as she located the
street they sought. It was an older Mercer Island neighborhood, and although none of the houses were new, all
had trim lawns and fresh paint. Many had views of Lake
Washington. Many did not. Mike Springer's fell into the
latter category.

The house sprawled on a corner lot. It was a brick-
fronted rambler with another converted garage, this one
attached to the house at one end. Roman unlatched his seat
belt. "It's nothing to jump hoops over, but definitely a
rung or two up the old ladder from his stepfather's place."

"According to his financial records there is no way he
can afford this house." Kerrie parked and got out of the
car. She took stock of the neighboring houses, instinctively

checking the peripherals for anything or anyone suspicious. "Do you think the man Joe Springer spoke of—the one who gave Mike all that money for crunching a few numbers—is Loverboy?"

"That's what we're here to find out."

They strode to the converted garage, that had apparently been used as a family room or den and was now metamorphosing into an office. The door was glass paneled with Springer's name and occupation in tiny gold leaf letters printed at eye level. Closed miniblinds covered all the windows. The door was locked and a Sorry sign pressed against one pane.

Roman rapped on the glass panel.

A red sports car pulled behind the Mazda and a shapely young brunette emerged carrying a fast-food bag. She was two inches taller than Kerrie's own five-seven. A brown sweater covered her narrow hips and tan stretch pants her slender legs. She hurried toward them with the grace and surefootedness of a trained runner.

Her dark brown hair was cut short around her face. She wore too much makeup for afternoon, causing her sable brown eyes to stand out disproportionately to the rest of her features, which were bold in their own right. Something about her was familiar to Kerrie. The woman asked, "May I help you?"

"We need to speak to Mike Springer." Kerrie stepped toward her. "Is he around?"

"Oh, well, we're not open for business yet," the woman explained. "I'm Cindy Faber, his assistant. If you want to leave your name and number?"

"We need to see him now," Roman said.

"Okay." Cindy eyed him warily. "May I ask why?"

Kerrie showed her ID. "Police business."

Cindy blanched.

"Is Mr. Springer here?" Kerrie tried again.

Cindy blinked, color returning to her cheeks, but confusion and alarm were evident in her jerky movements. "Oh, you mean because the blinds are closed? We're just setting up the office. Mike's here. That's his BMW over there." She pointed across the street. "Come in."

She reached for the doorknob. Amazement registered in her brown eyes when she found it locked. "That's weird. I just left a short while ago." She shook the fast-food sack at them and giggled self-consciously. "We're working through lunch."

Cindy knocked on the door and called Mike's name. When he didn't answer after three tries, she said, "He must have gone back into the house for some reason and can't hear. I've got a key." She dug into her purse.

Kerrie's mind raced. Maybe Mike Springer's dad had called and warned him. Maybe he'd seen them drive up, recognized them from the other night at McRory's and knew they were on to him. He might have ducked out the back way. That would explain his car still being here.

As though his mind had traveled the same path, Roman said, "I'll check the back of the house."

Kerrie nodded and withdrew her gun from her purse. Cindy unlocked the door, then turned, saw the .45 Magnum and let out a startled yelp.

Kerrie shushed her. "You stay out here until I tell you otherwise. Understand?"

Cindy swallowed and nodded. She edged away from the house.

Kerrie shoved the door open. She swept inside, holding her gun readied. Overhead lights blared. Her eyes widened. The office looked like a cyclone had blown through it. Upended boxes, emptied folders and papers of every imaginable shape, size and color littered the desk, the two barrel chairs, and the carpeted floor.

She stepped into the room. Paper crunched. Crackled.

Louder and louder with every step until her heart slammed her ribs. She crossed to the hallway. Then darted into the kitchen. Her pulse roared in her ears. If someone else were moving inside the house, she couldn't hear them.

She spotted Roman at the back door. Relief slowed her pulse. She hurried and let him in. Together, they searched the three-bedroom rambler. Boxes were everywhere. "Most of these are still packed," Roman said.

Kerrie nudged open the master bedroom closet. "Look at this. One pair of slacks and one shirt."

Roman moved up beside her, then glanced down at her. "Seems like ol' Mike hasn't decided whether or not he's staying."

"At the moment, he's definitely gone."

Roman nodded. "Joe probably called him the second we left."

"Before we were in the car," Kerrie agreed, putting her gun away. "No telling where he's gotten to by now."

"His car's still here." Roman holstered his own weapon. "If he left on foot, he'll turn up sooner or later."

A shriek brought them hurrying back to the office. Cindy Faber stood in the center of the mess, looking scared and shocked. "Who...who did this?"

"We don't know," Kerrie answered.

"Where's Mr. Springer?"

"Don't know that, either."

"He isn't here?"

"No, ma'am." Kerrie moved toward her. "Would you have any idea where he might have gone?"

"Without his car?" She looked exasperated, near hysteria. "Nowhere."

Roman asked, "Would you know if anything is missing?"

Cindy Faber gaped at him in disbelief. "You can't be serious?"

Half an hour later, Kerrie was still chuckling about that on the way back to Seattle. Roman grinned sheepishly. "I guess I should have left the questioning to you as per our plan."

"It was a good tension breaker. Probably spared the woman a fit of hysteria." She smiled at him. His golden eyes softened as if offering her a silent thank-you. The moment was tender and warm. Kerrie's throat tightened. Warm and tender seemed to get quickly out of hand whenever Roman and she were alone. Like now.

She shifted the conversation back to Mike Springer, got Roman speculating on where the man was, why he'd run. As soon as they reached her office, they sent someone to watch his house, then retrieved their messages. Cage hadn't turned up anything new, and none of Roman's informants had reported in. But Glynna had called; the security system was up and running.

Cage came in long enough to grab his coat. "I don't know about you two, but I'm going for a steak, a bath and bed, in that order."

"Sounds good to me," Roman agreed. "Can you drop me at my hotel, Tully?"

"Sure."

"See you tomorrow, then." Kerrie was equally anxious to get home to her daughters, a warm bath, and a hot meal. She wasn't certain how well she'd sleep. *If* she'd sleep.

She'd been home two hours when Roman arrived on her doorstep, showered, shaved and wearing a white shirt and fresh jeans. He was accompanied by two, uniformed security guards. The men stayed on the porch as he introduced them to Glynna and her. "I wanted you to meet and personally get a look at Charlie Wong and Arnie Schmidt."

Kerrie and Glynna acknowledged the introduction. Wong was the older of the two, a tall, solidly built Asian/

American with a shaved head and intelligent black eyes. Schmidt was younger, shorter, but just as solidly built. His hair was cut close to his head, a silver stud nestled his left ear, and his gray eyes had a feral gleam.

Roman said, "They'll be watching the house every night—one in front, the other out back. If for any reason either of them can't make it one night, I will personally check out their replacement and we'll go through this again."

In Kerrie's judgment, Roman was going a little overboard in the security area, but she had to admit, her prospect of a good night's sleep had improved one hundred percent with the addition of the guards.

"It's a sensible plan, Mr. Donnello," Glynna said.

"Call me Roman."

She nodded. "Thank you, Roman."

Then she said to Arnie and Charlie, "I'll sleep better knowing you two are within shouting distance."

"Me, too." Kerrie admitted. "Thank you, Roman."

He shrugged, seemingly embarrassed by their gratitude, making Kerrie fervently aware that *her* safety hadn't been his main concern. He said, "We're going to walk the perimeter before they go on duty."

Kerrie closed the door and reset the security code.

Ten minutes later, Roman was knocking on her door again. This time he was holding a department store shopping bag. She let him in. Up close, he smelled wonderful, looked better.

"I wondered if I might stick around awhile tonight—so the girls could get to know me a little?" His voice was thick with emotion.

"Sure." How could she deny him this? He'd bought her a security system, hired protection for her family. What surprised her was that he hadn't insisted on staying on her couch tonight. Maybe he was as afraid of being in this house all night with her as she was to have him here. He might not love her, but he knew as well as she the chemistry they shared. That was the trouble. Like a rare flower, their passion bloomed vibrant and fast, would not be denied, but sadly, once it blossomed, could not flourish.

"I brought them each something."

"Oh?" On the other hand, how safe would Roman be out there with Loverboy on the prowl? What security measures had he taken for himself?

"I hope this is appropriate?" He held the department store bag open so she could view its contents, two fuzzy bunnies. "I didn't know what they had. What they like."

She felt as if a fist were lodged in her throat. "They're perfect. The girls will love them." The old fear of losing her children to him—as she'd lost her heart to him—rushed her. She struggled to control the slight trembling in her hand as she moved to the wall unit and reactivated the security code. "This is quite a system you purchased."

"State-of-the-art."

"Indeed. I think I've nearly mastered setting the code without triggering the alarm."

"Just don't forget the code."

"I couldn't do that. It's Gabby and Maureen's birth date."

He nodded, and that emotion she couldn't quite define was back in his eyes, clawing at her heart.

Squeals of childish delight erupted from somewhere in the house. Roman eyed her curiously.

"They're just finishing dinner," Kerrie explained, leading the way. "Mom's in her room, talking to a friend on the phone."

"Moman," Gabby said, the second they entered the kitchen.

"Moman," Maureen repeated, dropping her spoon and staring at him from behind her hands.

But Gabby grinned at Roman as if they were old friends and offered him a spoonful of her spaghetti. He laughed and accepted, making a big deal over how "yummy" it was. Gabby giggled and offered him more. Not to be left out, Maureen entered the game. Soon he had them both laughing.

Kerrie's heart felt like one of the antique teacups in her mother's hutch, feathered with cracks, so fragile merely touching it could cause it to shatter into a thousand pieces. She began putting away food, rinsing dirty dishes and putting them into the dishwasher, busying herself so she didn't have to watch or listen, didn't have to admit that for the first time, *she* felt like the outsider.

Once bibs were removed and smudged faces and sticky little fingers washed, Roman produced his gifts.

"Bunny, bunny." The twins chimed in unison. Gabriella toddled to Roman and reached for the yellow bunny, said "Peas and tank you," much to Roman's delight.

Maureen hung back, her green eyes steadied on the pink rabbit. It was obvious she wanted it, but she was too shy to walk over and take it. Finally she reached out and pointed. "Peas."

Roman brought her the fuzzy pink toy. She smiled shyly at him and said, "Tank you."

To Kerrie's surprise, her shy daughter allowed Roman to tousle her hair, then she hugged the bunny, and kissed it and showed it to Gabby, spouting something unintelligible.

Roman frowned at Kerrie. "What did she say?"

Before Kerrie could answer, Gabby responded to Maureen in the same unintelligible language. Kerrie laughed. "Twinese. Only they understand it."

In words both adults understood, the girls insisted Roman read their bedtime story, and both refused to settle down without a kiss good-night from him.

Before he left, he assured Kerrie his hotel had plenty of security, and that he wouldn't take any unnecessary risks. She closed the front door behind him, then reset the alarm. Her heart was heavy, her body weary. She got ready for bed, then reassured herself all the little red lights were glowing on the security pads. Her last stop was the girls' room. Both were asleep.

Maureen's pink bunny had fallen away from her as the child's grip loosened in sleep, but Gabby held tight to hers as if she somehow sensed it was from her father, a blood link she was too young to understand but instinctively recognized.

Kerrie's head ached with indecision. Her life was already changing and not for the better. Roman's being here, tucking the girls into bed, had left her mind full of him, her heart full of longing for him. This was not going to work.

She started for her own room, meeting Glynna in the hall. "The next time Roman shows up and wants to spend time with the girls, I can't stay. You and he—"

Kerrie broke off. She'd momentarily forgotten her mother was on the verge of leaving this house for good. The next time Roman showed up, her mother might not be here. She couldn't just walk out and leave him alone with the girls. He didn't know their routine. It would upset them terribly. "Sorry, Mom. I wasn't thinking."

"That's okay, sweetie. You've had a long, stressful day." Glynna leaned down and scratched her heel. "Just so you'll know, I'm moving closer to accepting Jon's proposal."

"I'm glad for you." Tomorrow she would have to start deciding what she was going to do without her mother.

KERRIE DROPPED OFF to sleep as soon as her head hit the pillow. Hours later, she woke with a start. She sat bolt upright. Her heart thudded. What had awakened her? One of the babies? The house was completely silent. She threw off her covers. Raced to the girls' room.

The quiet was broken only by the soft sounds of even breathing. Both babies were still fast asleep. As usual Gabby had kicked off her covers. Kerrie held onto the crib rail, willing herself to calm down. She reached to pull Gabby's blanket up. Her hand stilled. Where was the yellow bunny? She checked every corner of the bed, under the crib, under the little girl. It was gone.

How could that be? Her pulse lurched. Fear tingled her scalp. Had her mother come and taken it for some reason? She hustled into Glynna's room. Gentle snores greeted her. She rushed over and spoke in a loud whisper. "Mom! Mom, wake up!"

Glynna started awake, much as Kerrie had done minutes earlier. Alarm registered in her eyes. "What is it, Kerrie Carleen? Has the alarm gone off?"

"Did you take Gabby's bunny?"

"What?" Glynna was shaking her head, squinting at her as if she'd lost her mind. "Now why would I do that? Surely you didn't wake me to ask about a bunny. What's wrong?"

"I don't know." Kerrie's heart was leaping like a herd of jackrabbits. "Get up and go into the girls' room, will you?"

Glynna was out of bed and struggling into her robe before Kerrie reached the door.

Kerrie sped down the hall. She got her gun, loaded it and stepped into the foyer. Her gaze zeroed in on the new alarm system. None of the red lights glowed. The alarm was turned off. Her heart nearly stopped. Had the system failed? A worse thought sent a chilling flush through her.

Was Loverboy in the house? Had he gotten past the guards somehow? Disarmed the security system?

She punched in the code and the system responded at the touch of her fingertips, all the lights reactivating. Moving as fast as she dared, she turned on every light in the house. Two seconds later, Charlie Wong was on the front porch, banging on the door. "Ms. Muldoon, what's wrong?"

She threw the door open. "I don't know. The alarm was turned off. And something's missing from the baby's room." She told him about the bunny, about her fear of who had visited them. "I'm afraid it's Loverboy. That he's still in here somewhere."

"Then gather your family in one room while I search the rest of the house."

Five minutes later, he joined them in the girls' room. The babies were still sleeping, so he motioned both women into the hall. "If there was an intruder, he's not in here now."

To reassure herself, Kerrie insisted Charlie wait until she'd tossed a sweat suit on over her sleep shirt and then join her for another check of the house. The second search took twice as long as the first with the same results. Kerrie was confused, but definitely relieved.

Until they returned to the kitchen. Glynna was peering out at the backyard, a troubled expression furrowing her brow. "Is something wrong, Mom?"

Glynna shrugged. "Where's the other guard? It's three o'clock in the morning. Why hasn't he noticed all the lights on and come to investigate?"

Charlie made a face. "Maybe he saw something or someone and is in pursuit. I'll check."

"I'm coming with you," Kerrie said. "Mom stay inside and activate the code as soon as we close the door."

Glynna complied.

Kerrie flipped on all the backyard lights and followed Charlie Wong outside. They moved down the back steps, cautiously, alertly. The patrol car was still parked next to her garage. They could see a man seated behind the steering wheel. His head was tilted toward the side window. Had he fallen asleep?

Charlie yanked the door open. "Arnie, what the hell are you—"

He broke off as the interior light flared. Arnie wasn't asleep. His throat had been slit. Something yellow was perched between his belly and the steering wheel. Gabby's missing bunny.

Chapter Twelve

"He was in the girls' room." Kerrie studied Roman's face as revulsion and anger pulsed through her. Somehow she'd coped with getting the necessary calls made to set in motion the crime scene techs, managed to keep the girls calm, despite the agitation of strangers prowling all through the house, managed to hold herself together as Glynna fell apart, managed to remain calm as she'd arranged for Charlie Wong to escort her mother and the twins to Sophia Sommerville's where he now watched over them.

But seeing the horror and shock and fear she felt reflected in Roman's expression was more than she could bear. Her restraint slipped. Tears stung her eyes. "He touched Gabby, maybe Maureen."

Roman swore. He looked as if he wanted to hit something. Instead he gathered her into his arms with tenderness and strength of purpose as if she were a delicate rose petal he wanted to preserve for eternity. She clung to him with all her might, accepting the comfort, but refusing to cry. Police personnel were in nearly every room in her house, out in her yard. She couldn't, wouldn't break down in front of her co-workers.

Instead she pressed her face against Roman's white shirt, fighting the tears, inhaling his familiar scent, finding it reassuring, a trace of normalcy in a world of craziness.

"You don't have to be tough all the time, you know? No one expects it." He stroked her back, speaking softly. "Let it out."

Kerrie shook her head, silently willing him to try to understand.

Roman walked her into the bathroom and closed the door. "We're alone now. No one else will see."

It struck her that he knew her better than she'd realized. Her throat tightened. Her lower lip trembled. At this moment it no longer mattered that he didn't love her. This was about their children, and only Roman knew exactly how she felt.

He folded her against him again. "I won't tell anyone, if you don't, Irish."

As though he'd opened a spigot, release came, tears spilled uncontrollably from her, and she burrowed against him as snugly as any lover. But for the first time since they'd met, desire hadn't preceded this hug, this intimacy. Kerrie cried for the violation she felt, cried for her murdered friends, cried for all of Loverboy's victims and their families and their friends, until the tears were gone, until only rage and determination remained.

She shook herself mentally, stepped away from Roman and reached for a tissue from the box on the counter.

He leaned against the wall, seemingly unaware of his damp shirtfront, and watched her reflection in the mirror. "I checked on the girls and your mother just a minute ago."

Kerrie gave him a grateful nod. "I called Jon right after I called you. Is he here yet?"

"Yes. He was arguing with Glynna over whether or not she needed a mild sedative. She told him to quit fussing— that she wasn't some hothouse flower who wilted at the first sign of frost." Roman grinned wryly. "Guess that's where you get your st-strength."

Kerrie could have sworn he'd been going to say "stub-bornness." She smiled, and glanced at herself in the mirror. She looked a mess, no makeup, her nose all red, her hair a wild, tangled mop. She daubed some powder on her nose and ran the brush through her hair, capturing it at her nape with a scrunchie. That was better. Not great, but not "Lady Distress," either. "Arnie Schmidt's murder is the third to touch Mom's life in the past two days—I can't understand how she's holding up as well as she is."

Roman arched a brow at her. "I have an idea fortitude runs in the Muldoon family."

Someone rapped at the bathroom door. "Muldoon, you in there?"

It was Cage. When had he gotten here? She yanked open the door. Cage raised his scarred brow at seeing both of them. There was a well-rested freshness about him this morning. Obviously he'd gotten a full night's sleep. He nodded at them both. "This is a hell of a thing. You're all right, though?"

"Peachy," Kerrie answered. Roman and she joined him in the hall. "I tried inviting you to this little come-as-you-are-party at 3 a.m., but got no answer."

Cage grimaced guiltily. "After yesterday's all-nighter, I turned off the bell on my phone, but I had my beeper on. I guess I just didn't hear it."

"At least one of us got some sleep," Kerrie said. Somehow being awake to see the dawn two mornings in a row ought to be romantic. Revitalizing. Not grisly. "Do they know how he got in here yet?"

"Apparently he planted a bug in the foyer, a listening device. The security people say whoever deactivated the alarm did so with the code. Did you tell anyone what the code was?"

Kerrie didn't have to answer him, the color draining from her face did that. Dear, God, she'd stood right in the foyer and told Roman the code was the girls' birth date. And Loverboy had been listening. A sickening chill dragged the bottom from her stomach and she had to throw her hand over her mouth to keep from gagging. The monster knew when her babies were born! She shuddered. *She'd* brought this new horror on her family. It didn't matter that she'd done it innocently.

She led the two men into the living room and sank to the sofa. Roman sat beside her. Cage took the chair across from them.

Kerrie drew a calming breath. "I can't figure out why he didn't kill us in our sleep."

"He's playing with us." Roman spoke softly, but his words were as disturbing as stones dropped in a glassy pool. "Telling us he can get us no matter what precautions we take."

She clenched her hands together in her lap, trying to hide their trembling. "What are we going to do?"

"Maybe now you'll consider a safe house?" Cage said.

Kerrie glanced at Roman and their gazes locked. Fear stood bold in the depths of his golden eyes. This man feared few things, much as she feared few things. Loverboy was one of those few things. Kerrie shook her head. "That's no answer, Tully."

Roman concurred. "I know what has Irish concerned. Arnie Schmidt specialized in guarding people. He was one of the best in the country. Somehow Loverboy ambushed him."

"Are you saying Seattle PD can't do better?" Cage asked offended.

Roman leveled a cool stare at him. "Can you give me a one hundred percent guarantee my children will be safe, Detective Cage?"

Cage blinked first. "Well, I—"

"Look, whatever we decide—" Kerrie interrupted "—I

want my babies and my mother to survive this with as
little trauma as we can manage.''

They all fell silent. This was the second morning in a
row Roman hadn't shaved. He rubbed his whiskered jaw,
considering their options. What they needed was a place
with high security. What they needed was someone who
could be trusted, someone who understood firsthand the
danger Loverboy presented. Someone who wouldn't underestimate the killer's intelligence and cunning.

He thought he knew the ideal place. The ideal person.
He looked at Kerrie. "I have to leave for a while. Don't
make any decisions until I get back. I won't be long.''

Kerrie's heart lurched. She didn't want him to leave.
But she didn't know how to ask him to stay. As he stood
and moved away from her, she clenched her hands tighter.
Why was it less personal to need him sexually than it was
to need him emotionally?

ROMAN WAS RUNNING on pure emotion. He didn't want to
use Kerrie's telephone until he was sure there weren't any
more listening devices. Wouldn't risk Loverboy getting
hold of her telephone records for incoming and outgoing
calls.

He took a taxi to his hotel. In his room, he called a local
number and spoke with an old friend, collecting on a long
overdue favor, then packed his clothes. When his newly
ordered car arrived, he checked out of the hotel.

Next, he visited the department store he'd patronized the
day before. His third stop was a pay phone. He stood on
the street corner, his leather coat collar turned up. The day
was overcast and crisp with a breeze as bitter as his rage
for Loverboy.

He dialed the familiar number in Middleburg, Virginia,
and spoke quickly to the man who was as much father as
friend to him, explained the situation and gave him an

updated report on the investigation. Satisfied with the outcome of the call, he next phoned a travel agent, then lastly, Sophia Sommerville and made sure the girls were safe.

It was nearly eleven when he returned to Kerrie's house. He'd been gone over two hours, longer than he'd expected. Cops still swarmed the grounds and inside. Curious neighbors stood near the yellow crime scene tape, apparently oblivious to the chilly wind. He wouldn't doubt they staved the cold off by entertaining one another with tales of the gruesome murder.

Roman found Kerrie in the girls' room. She stood at the dresser, one drawer open, her hand inside, tenderly stroking an item of toddler clothing. The act was personal, private, her emotion filling the room. She'd changed into jeans and a long-sleeved, faded denim shirt. Her hair floated around her face, a fiery cascade of wavy curls that accentuated, instead of softened the strain around her mouth and eyes.

The sight of her this way, all vulnerable and needy and scared, caused his heart to skip, and he had to remind himself that although Loverboy's attack last night had brought them together as parents, it didn't change anything between them as man and woman.

His body still ached to ease itself within her. Maybe it always would. He cast the thought aside. He was strong enough to overcome the feeling. The want. The need.

He was.

"Hi." Her spirits lifted at the sight of him, but her body responded to him on a more erotic level, as if it were a separate entity. She curbed her awareness of it, of him. She shut the drawer and turned full toward him. "Cage and I haven't been able to agree on what will keep the girls and Mom safe. Tell me you've come up with an idea."

He grinned at her. "I have, actually."

"Great." Relief swept her. "Tell me."

"Not here."

Kerrie started to protest, then realized he was concerned that Loverboy might have planted other bugs. The search for them was ongoing.

"The only people who will know about this plan are you, me, your mom and Charlie Wong."

Kerrie's eyebrows lifted in surprise. "I can't tell Cage?"

Roman shook his head. "No."

The cop in her objected to his exclusion of her partner, to the implication that Cage couldn't be trusted, but the mother in her dominated today. She knew the fewer people in on their plan, the safer her family would be. She wasn't about to gamble with that. "Okay, when do we start?"

"Immediately—as soon as you get the kids and Glynna packed."

Glynna and the kids. Not her. Roman wasn't trying to take her off this case. He understood she wouldn't go. That she *had* to be in on catching Loverboy. The wall around her heart shifted. He might not love her, but he respected her. Every day, in every way, he was proving himself a man she could be proud to call the father of her children.

Her children. Reality squeezed her chest. She was going to have to be separated from them until Loverboy was caught. It was the only safe and sane solution. But the thought of not seeing her babies every day... No, she wouldn't think about that. Whatever Roman's plans were, the separation would be hard on the girls, too, harder still if she allowed them to view her fear or her sadness or her anger. "Are there laundry facilities where they'll be?"

"Yes."

She moved with purpose to the closet and hauled out a huge duffel bag. "A week's worth of clothing should be plenty, then."

As soon as she had the bags packed, they loaded them beside his in the trunk of his rental car and drove to Sophia Sommerville's.

Charlie Wong let them in and reported that all was secure, then told them the others were in the den. Roman asked Charlie to join them there. Sophia and Glynna were seated on the sofa watching the girls play on the floor at their feet.

Gabriella let out a squeal of delight the second she saw, "Moman" and "Mommy."

Surprising everyone, she raced right to Roman and let him scoop her into his arms. Maureen made a beeline to Kerrie, grasping her pant leg in one hand and her pink bunny, that she'd been halfheartedly sharing with her sister all day, in the other. She peered shyly at Roman through Kerrie's legs.

Roman, grinning from ear to ear, hugged Gabby and kissed her cheek. She laughed, then squirmed. "Down."

Roman squatted, lowering her chubby legs to the floor, but before he released her, he produced the new yellow bunny from inside his jacket. "Look what I found."

"Gabby, bunny." Her eyes, so like his, rounded in surprised delight. She snatched the toy from him and toddled to Maureen.

Maureen released her grip on Kerrie and touched her sister's toy with her free hand. "Gabby bunny."

"My bunny," she added, hugging her own toy. Both girls plopped down on their bottoms and began chattering in their own special language.

Glynna was the first to break the moment. "I hope you've come to tell us we can finally go home."

Kerrie glanced at her mother in amazement. Glynna looked perfectly composed. A few hours ago, she'd been atremble with fright, awash in tears. Now, there was a determined glint in her soft green eyes, an acceptance in the tilt of her head, defiance in the jut of her chin. Roman was right about the Muldoon women having fortitude. She hoped her mother had enough to accept the news that home was not where she'd be going.

Kerrie asked, "Is Dr. Jon still here?"

"No, I sent him to his office." Glynna scratched absently at her heel. "He had 'sick' people to see."

Kerrie suppressed a smile, then glanced guiltily at their hostess. "Er, Sophia, Roman and I need to speak to Charlie and Mom. For your own safety it's better if you don't hear any of what is said."

"I see." Sophia levered herself up off the sofa. Her fierce brown eyes full of understanding. "You know, I need to get Professor Plum some cat food."

Charlie walked her to the door, waited for her to don her mauve coat, then saw her safely to her car. The second he returned, Roman and he rechecked all the locks, then rejoined the women again in the den.

Kerrie took the spot Sophia had vacated and Roman and Charlie sat opposite the women in recliner chairs.

"Perhaps now someone will tell me why we had to chase Sophia out of her own house." Scarlet dots stood out on Glynna's cheeks. "Why didn't we just go home and talk?"

Kerrie told her about the listening device found in the foyer and their concern that there might be others. Glynna flinched. Kerrie grabbed her hand. "It's all right, Mom. Roman has a plan."

Roman leaned forward, his arms resting on his legs, his gaze leveled on Glynna. He wore a solemn expression, but a muscle twitched at his temple as he explained to her the arrangements he'd made. "You'll be flying to Middleburg, Virginia, this afternoon."

"Virginia?" She glanced at Kerrie, who could only nod. She, too, was hearing this for the first time.

"Yes. You'll stay at the mansion of my friend Philip Waring," Roman said. "His house is the most secure place I can think of, and Loverboy won't know where you've gone. Where to look for you. Only the four of us and Philip know about this."

"Okay." Glynna frowned thoughtfully. "Waring? Why does that name sound familiar?"

Roman closed his eyes. Kerrie cleared her throat. "His daughter Wendy was Loverboy's first victim."

"I see." Glynna studied Roman a moment. "Then Mr. Waring knows the dangers of taking us in?"

Roman nodded his head gravely. "Only too well."

She sat straighter. "What about his wife? Other family members—won't they be endangered by our presence?"

"Philip is a widower. Wendy was his only daughter. He's a good man and he'll watch over you as if you were his own family."

"Well, then." Glynna started to stand. "If we're flying out this afternoon, we'd better go home and pack."

Kerrie waylaid her. "I've already packed. We're leaving from here, Mom."

Glynna settled back onto the sofa and looked down at herself in dismay. She had on the sweat suit she usually wore over her tennis outfit. "I'm not traveling dressed like this."

"No one expects you to. I packed your navy pantsuit and your makeup."

"Where are they?"

"In my car," Roman said. "You'll be able to change at our next stop."

"Which is?"

"It's a surprise."

"This day has been full of those." Glynna smiled wryly. "I've heard Middleburg is a charming area, close to the nation's capitol and yet rural with spectacular horse farms and wineries.''

Roman nodded. "Philip makes his living with his stud farm.''

"Interesting.'' Glynna reached to scratch her heel and stopped in midmotion. She stared at Kerrie with a dawning look in her soft green eyes. "Oh, my. I *am* taking an unexpected trip, but it's definitely not going to be a honeymoon.''

"Mom, I'm so sorry.'' Kerrie felt directly responsible for this. It was her work that had visited this evil upon them. Now her mother's plans with Dr. Jon would have to be put on hold indefinitely, as she'd been putting them on hold for three years already.

"Don't be silly. It's not your fault some madman is loose in this city. We'll do what needs doing to stay safe.'' She stood and everyone else did the same. She began putting Maureen's coat on her, while Kerrie did the same to Gabby. "Well, Kerrie Carleen, I take it we are leaving now on this adventure?''

"I won't be going with you, Mom.''

"Why not?'' she challenged. The first sign of trepidation flicked through her eyes.

Roman stepped up to Glynna and helped her with her coat. "We don't want Loverboy to know the girls and you are gone until it's too late. With the precautions I've set up, we should be able to guarantee that. Charlie will be accompanying the twins and you.''

"And what are Kerrie and you going to do?''

"I'm moving in with her.'' Roman glanced at Kerrie, then back at her mother. His voice rang with heartfelt fierceness. "I promise you, Glynna, I'll keep her safe.''

Glynna took his hand in both of hers, and gazed up at him. Her own eyes glowing with the strength of her determination. "And I promise I'll keep our little girls safe.''

As though someone were walking on her grave, Kerrie felt a sudden bone-chilling fear. Would either of them be able to keep their promise?

Chapter Thirteen

It seemed to Kerrie that Roman's previous car, the one needing four new tires, had been a typical rental compact. Its replacement, this elegant Lincoln Continental, was anything but snug. The backseat more than accommodated her mother and herself with the twins between them. She could actually stretch her legs. But the part she liked best was the opaquely tinted windows; if Loverboy was following them, he couldn't see them.

Roman, at the wheel, and Charlie Wong, monopolizing the front passenger seat, were chatting in voices too low to be heard above the twins' jabbering. Kerrie sat directly behind Roman, who still hadn't told them where they were going, where it was that Glynna could change into proper traveling clothes. Neither had any of them asked. At this point they trusted his judgment. Had to trust his judgment. Their lives depended on it.

She glanced at his intense expression reflected in the rearview mirror. For a split second his golden gaze locked with hers. Her pulse skittered. She blinked and looked out the window at her side, trying to concentrate on downtown Seattle's looming vista, instead of on the sexy, passionate, generous man whose very glance could command her heart. Her body.

Her hand brushed against the buttery smooth leather of

the seat, pulling her back to her perusal of the car. For the first time, she realized how richly potent the pearl gray leather smelled. How new it smelled. A frown tugged her eyebrows. What rental company leased brand-new Lincoln Continentals?

In the front seat, Roman and Charlie fell silent. Gabriella tugged on Kerrie's sleeve. "Mommy," she said. "I wanna sit wiff Moman."

Maureen said, "We go bye bye wiff Moman."

Gabby stretched her hands toward him, indicating she wanted him to lift her into the front seat, and whined, "Moman."

"You can't sit with Roman right now, sweetie." She hugged the child to her side and kissed the top of her head. Each little girl was strapped into a seat belt; their safety car seats had been abandoned for this ride. "Roman's driving."

In the mirror, Kerrie saw the grin in his eyes, the pure delight such a small moment gave him.

Maureen nodded at Gabby. "We go bye bye wiff Moman and Mommy and Gammy." She snuggled against Glynna's arm.

"And Tarlie," Gabby added, pointing to Charlie.

Kerrie's heart swelled with love, and she realized, like Roman, she also cherished these small moments. Sadness and anger stripped all warmth from the thought. She would soon be putting her babies on a plane that would take them a couple of thousand miles from her. For how long? How long would it be before they caught Loverboy? How long before her children and she were reunited?

They weren't even on the plane and her heart felt bereft. Her arms empty. She stroked Gabby's silken hair with one hand, stretching to caress Maureen's cheek with the other. Maureen giggled and twisted out of her reach, burrowing her face against Glynna's side. Glynna chuckled and grinned at Kerrie. Kerrie laughed, too, but tears stung her eyes.

She glanced quickly toward the window and blinked them away. She'd promised herself she wouldn't break down in front of the girls or her mom. That she'd send them off with as brave a face as she could put on the situation. By all she held dear, she intended to keep that promise.

"We'll be there in just a minute," Roman announced, exiting the freeway at Seneca and advancing onto Sixth Avenue in downtown Seattle.

As usual, traffic was thick, crowding all three lanes of the one way street. It was nearly lunchtime on a day that had already been too long for most of the Lincoln's occupants. Foot traffic bustled along the sidewalks, colorful umbrellas and raincoats brightening the otherwise drizzly day.

Six blocks later, Roman pulled to a stop in front of an old three-storied parking garage with construction barriers blocking its entrance. Two men darted from the shadows just inside the arched opening. Both wore beige raincoats and felt hats. Both appeared to be federal agents of some kind; Roman's associates, Kerrie guessed.

The shorter of the two nodded at Roman, then helped his partner roll open the metal gate. Roman drove through the gap, and the gate was rolled back into place.

Kerrie's eyes widened at the abandoned look of the garage's interior. "Are you sure this building is safe?"

"As a fortress," Roman assured her. He lowered his window and spoke to the short man. "Are we set?"

"Second floor, Donnello. Just been waitin' on you."

"Thanks, Harp. I owe you one."

"Damned straight." The short man nodded and stepped back. As Roman drove ahead, Kerrie saw the man speaking into a two-way radio.

The ramp to the next floor was dark, creepy, but they emerged onto a fully lighted second floor. Like the show-room of a new car dealership, five other Lincoln Conti-nentals were parked at angles to one another. All had blacked-out windows. All were forest green—exactly like the one they were riding in. Several men, each tall and well built, much like Roman and Charlie, milled about smoking and talking.

"What in the world?" Glynna asked.

"For security," Charlie said.

Kerrie grinned at the cleverness of Roman's plan. "Hide in plain sight, Mom."

Roman stopped the car and shifted around to look at Glynna. "If our nemesis thought to follow us, this is our best bet to lose him when we leave here."

"I see." Glynna smiled. "He can't go after all six cars at once."

Roman smiled and nodded. "Exactly."

Kerrie could see her mother visibly relax for the first time since they'd left Sophia's house. Roman activated the trunk release and yanked open his door. "We're also switching cars."

Kerrie disengaged her seat belt, then Gabby's and soon they were all out of the car. The garage smelled of mold and dirt and spilled crankcase oil. She hoisted Gabby into her arms. "Hang onto Maureen, Mom, or she'll get filthy."

"Let me," Roman said, taking Maureen from Glynna. The shy little girl, who'd been clinging to her grandmother and staring at all the strangers, went gladly into Roman's arms. He noticed, and Kerrie could see the look of sheer pleasure in his eyes as he hugged his daughter close.

"Glynna." His voice was thick with emotion. "You can get whatever clothes you'd like from your suitcase. Charlie, see if one of these other Palookas will help you transfer the luggage to another car. I'm kind of busy right now.''

"Sure thing, boss.'' Charlie strolled over to the group of men.

Glynna got busy digging the clothing she wanted from her luggage. Three minutes later, she stood in front of Roman, hugging navy cloth to her chest and frowning. "Where am I supposed to change?''

He shifted Maureen closer and pointed to a far corner. "Bathroom's over there.''

Kerrie glanced to where he indicated, spotting a grease-blackened door. She hated that her mother was forced to use such distasteful facilities. Hated the man who was the cause of it.

Roman had the decency to look sheepish. "It's not the Ritz, but I had it swept and disinfected before we arrived. I'm afraid all it's got is cold water.''

Glynna gathered her clothes to her chest and lifted her head proudly. "A bit of cold water won't kill me.''

The fact that Loverboy might, sent impotent rage swirling inside Kerrie. But she was proud of her mother for taking it all in stride.

As Glynna walked toward the bathroom, Kerrie said, "This isn't easy for her.''

He glanced down at her, his expression serious. "This isn't easy on any of us, Irish.''

She sighed and juggled Gabby in her arms. "Tell me something. Where, or should I say how, did you find this many cars the same make, model and color?''

He offered her his heart-stopping grin. "Friend of mine owns a Lincoln dealership in Factoria. I explained the situation and he loaned me these for the afternoon.''

"Generous friend.''

Charlie Wong rejoined them with another man in tow. "Roman saved the life of the car dealer's wife a few years back. Get him to tell you the story sometime. It's quite interesting.''

She gazed speculatively at Roman. He shook his head. "Why don't you stick to your job, Wong. Get the luggage transferred.''

"Whatever you say, boss." Charlie ran his hand across his shaved head as he turned to his companion. He and the second man moved to the trunk and began the transfer.

A moment later, as Charlie started past, a suitcase in one hand and a shopping bag in the other, Roman stopped him. "Wait. I'll take that sack.''

It was, Kerrie noted, from the same department store where he'd purchased the girls' bunnies. She made a face. "You're going to spoil them.''

"This isn't toys. It's a little added insurance for their escape. Let's get in the new car.''

Once all four of them were settled on the backseat, he opened the bag and produced two new, toddler-size winter ski-type jackets, one an array of blues and greens, the other a solid soft yellow. The coats were completely different than the denim ones the girls were wearing. The new coats were even different from each other in both style and design.

He steadied his gaze on Kerrie. "In case, he's been watching the house and knows how you dress the girls.''

She nodded and tried swallowing past the lump in her throat. Gabriella was delighted with her new "lellow" jacket which accented the golden depths of her beautiful eyes. Maureen wasn't as certain, but once she had the green and blue jacket on, she decided that she looked every bit as good in her new coat as her sister did in hers.

They both thanked Roman as he zipped the jackets closed and told them they were going bye bye again. Glynna appeared, wearing a navy pantsuit with large gold buttons, her makeup on, and her hair twisted into a french roll.

Roman got out of the car and met her at the trunk. She packed her sweat suit and the girls' denim jackets into her bag. "Well, it looks like I'm ready."

"Almost." Roman reached into his wallet and produced a handful of bills.

Glynna shook her head. "I don't need your money. I've got my checkbook and my credit cards."

"You won't be traveling under your real name. I don't want you cashing any checks or using any credit cards until…"

She paled. "Oh, I hadn't thought."

Roman put the money in her hand and curled her fingers over it. "It's two hundred in small bills. When that runs out, Philip will give you more."

"I'll pay you back every penny of this."

"I wouldn't expect any less of you."

She put the cash into her purse. Then Roman and she climbed into the back seat of the car with Kerrie and the twins. He lifted Maureen onto his lap. Next to him, Kerrie held Gabby on hers. Charlie sat in front with their driver. He spoke into a two-way radio. "It's showtime folks."

Car engines started and moments later all six Lincolns were pulling out onto Sixth Avenue. One after the other, like floats in a parade, they moved down the street. At the first stoplight, the lead car turned left, the second car turned right and the other four went straight ahead.

At the next streetlight the procedure was repeated until the cars were all going in different directions. All would travel circuitous routes, through the occasional alley, pulling over to the odd curb. The agents in each car had instructions to watch for tails, obtain any suspicious-looking vehicle's make and license number, and execute any appropriate action.

Holding his own child was something Roman had thought he'd never do. He hadn't allowed himself to even imagine what it would be like to wrap his arms around a tiny person who existed because of him. Hadn't expected that children could touch his very soul, infuse every fiber of his being, rouse such fierce protective instincts.

But this squirming little girl, who weighed next to nothing, who chattered with such delight at everything in her world, whose tiny hand felt like a velvet seashell in his, left him awestruck. Blessedly the gaping emptiness, which had resided in his heart since he was a teenage boy, shrank with every second he held his daughter, with every mile closer to the airport.

How was it possible? He pondered the enormity of it, the simplicity of it, then decided, why question what likely had no explanation? Why not simply savor the indescribable bliss?

Roman gathered a huge breath and hugged Maureen, reached out to grasp Gabby's hand, too. He closed his eyes and let joy wash through him. The car swerved unexpectedly. He stiffened. His eyes sprang open. But there was nothing to get excited about. No reason to panic. Just a car in the next lane veering too close to theirs. Still, if this ride were only a celebration of fatherhood, Roman knew his muscles wouldn't be edged with tension. His body on full alert.

He counseled himself to calm down. But in his gut he feared he'd missed some detail, hadn't covered every base, that Loverboy would discover their plans. Would come after his little girls. God help him, he wanted to board that plane with them and see them safely into Philip's care.

Impossible. Kerrie and he had to get back to her house. Soon. Had to act as if Glynna and the girls were still in town and would be returning shortly. As if, despite the murder in their backyard, everything else was normal. Normal. He touched his chin to the top of Maureen's head. Would any of their worlds be normal again? His wouldn't. It would be both better and worse. Without Loverboy, he might never have known about his children.

A deep sadness filled him. Without Loverboy, Wendy would be alive to hold his children, to one day hold her own children. Some pains, he realized, never left a person's heart. Accepting Wendy's death had been awful enough, dealing with her loss on a daily basis… His throat muscles tightened.

It must be killing Philip. Before coming to Seattle, Roman thought he'd understood his friend's grief. Shared it. He hadn't, not really. He'd felt as if he'd lost a sister. That wasn't the same as losing a child.

He shifted Maureen on his lap. Oh, how he understood now. Oh, how he empathized now. Oh, how empty his arms would soon feel—and he wasn't losing his daughters, only putting them on a plane. It would be the hardest thing he'd ever done.

As SeaTac International Airport came into view, he glanced at Kerrie. The sorrow in her emerald eyes told him she was dealing with the same demons.

The driver pulled to a stop on the departure level. Everyone vacated the car. The men unloaded the luggage from the trunk, including Roman's. Then the driver left in the Lincoln. Roman, Kerrie, and their entourage entered the terminal.

Roman said, "Charlie, you know what to do and where we'll be?"

The big man nodded his shaved head. "I'll join you shortly."

Charlie gathered the luggage and hustled to a check-in counter. Hefting his own bag, Roman led the women and girls to a private room the size of a small bedroom. It had no windows, smelled faintly of cleansing solution and was sparsely furnished with two rows of armless, metal framed chairs with black Naugahyde cushions. Two oblong, folding tables stood against a back wall.

The girls immediately toddled over to the first row of chairs and began playing with their bunnies, jabbering to each other with serious faces. Silently the three adults sat and watched with rapt attention as though the child's play were as fascinating as a Broadway production.

The door to the room swung open, startling Kerrie from her thoughts. It was Charlie, she noted with relief. The adults all stood. Charlie closed the door behind him and strode straight for her mother, offering her an airline ticket. "The plane is leaving on schedule. They're boarding now."

Roman hoisted Maureen into her grandmother's arms. "Glynna, I want you and this other redheaded beauty to go directly to Concourse B, Gate 16, and board the plane. Charlie and Gabby will follow in a few minutes. Philip will contact me when you've arrived safely."

Glynna frowned, then glanced anxiously from Roman to Kerrie. "You're not coming to see us off?"

"We can't." Roman looked as if he'd lost his best friend.

Kerrie swallowed around the lump in her throat. But she knew Roman was right. "We'd be too easy to spot if we all went together, Mom."

Glynna nodded, and Kerrie saw strength and determination in her mother's eyes. She'd proved a real trouper when all the chips were down. Kerrie was extremely proud of her. She gave her a huge hug. "I love you, Mom. Be careful."

"I will, and don't you worry about the girls. I won't let any harm come to them."

"I know." Kerrie told Maureen to mind Grammy, then hugged and kissed her. "I love you, angel."

Roman tousled Maureen's hair and kissed her cheek. Glynna shifted the child onto her hip, and they left.

The second the door closed on her sister, Gabby frowned and tears welled in her golden eyes. "Gabby, go. Gabby, go."

Kerrie scooped Gabriella into her arms. "You are going, sweetie. With Charlie."

Gabby shook her head. "No, not go wiff, Tarlie. Go wiff, you. Go wiff, Moman."

Gabby began crying in earnest, and Kerrie felt as if her heart were being wrenched from her chest. She strove to comfort the little girl. Time was running out. Charlie and she had to board that plane.

Roman came up beside them. "Gabby, Charlie has some candy for you and he's taking you to see Maureen and Grammy."

"Now?" She sniffed and gazed at the candy bar in Charlie's outstretched hand. She reached for it. Kerrie transferred her into the security guard's arms. Gabby took the candy bar and bit into it. Like a thin coating of gloss, chocolate smeared her heart-shaped lips.

Grinning sadly, Roman kissed her cheek. But Kerrie stepped back, fearing they'd never reach the plane if Gabby sensed her mother's distress and threw another fit. "Mind Grammy and Charlie. I love you, Gabby."

"Love you, Mommy."

"Love you, Moman."

"Hurry," Roman instructed Charlie in a hoarse voice, opening the door and sending them on their way.

Fighting tears, Kerrie spun away from Roman and struggled to compose herself. She was grateful he didn't try to fill the thick tension in the room with conversation. That he didn't try to console her, or reassure her. Right now, any of those gestures would have reduced her to a quivering mass of motherhood.

They waited another minute, then hurried to the baggage claim level, stepped outside and hailed a taxi. Roman instructed the driver to take them to Southcenter Shopping Mall. There, he ordered another taxi. On the ride back to her house, neither spoke. *We're like two lost souls,* Kerrie thought, *who can't reach out to anyone else, not even to each other, in our sadness and anger. How infinitely sad.*

Since the back alley way was still officially a crime scene, Roman directed the taxi driver to her front door. One car remained parked at her curb. It belonged to patrolman Erikssen. He stepped out of the house and onto the porch as they climbed the stairs.

His gaze flicked over Roman's bag, and one eyebrow arched slightly, but he kept whatever he was thinking about it to himself. He faced Kerrie. "Thought I'd wait around until you returned, Detective."

Roman frowned at him. "Why?"

Erikssen looked offended.

Kerrie sighed. "Don't mind Agent Donnello. His protective instincts are on overload."

"I'm just being cautious, Irish."

"It's okay, man." Erikssen nodded understanding. "I would be, too. But you can both relax. Whole house was electronically swept. You're bug-free."

He ran his hand through his thick white-blond hair, and added, "Thought you'd like to know no one else had been in here while you were gone. And that only one bug was found. The one in the foyer."

"That's a relief." Kerrie stepped over her threshold. "Thanks, Erikssen."

He pressed his lips together, reached the top step, then glanced back. "Oh, by the way, Detective Cage has been trying to locate you since noon. Left his office number."

"I'll call him right away." She stepped into the house

and as soon as Roman joined her, shut the door. "I've come up with a new code."

Roman watched her set the alarm and committed the new numbers to memory.

Kerrie spun toward him. As usual he stood too close. He needed a shave, needed sleep. But it was the other more basic need standing hot in his smoldering eyes that sent her heart skittering, her imagination careening out of control. She stepped past him and ran into his suitcase.

Great. She'd just locked herself in with Roman Donnello. The man and his need were here to stay. Heat stole into her cheeks. In truth, she was more worried about her own need, her need for him. "You can have Mom's room. The sheets need changing."

She led the way, stopping only long enough to gather clean linen from a closet and hand it to him. "I'll find out what Cage wants while you settle in."

"Sure." He looked appealingly ill at ease, the pink floral sheets in one hand, his bag in the other. "I'd like to shower and shave."

"Of course." The last thing she wanted was to imagine Roman shaving in her bathroom, naked in her shower. The images filled her head anyway. Reminding herself that she had a call to make, she left him, placed fresh towels in the bathroom and rushed to the kitchen phone.

Moments later, Cage barked, "Hello."

He sounded annoyed, anxious.

She braced herself for a different kind of mental onslaught. "It's me, Tully. Has something come up?"

"Muldoon." His voice lost none of its tension. "It's about time. Yes, actually. We located Jeremy Dane."

"That's great." Eager to hear, she pulled out a chair and dropped into it. "So, tell me."

"His real name is Jerry Danko. He lives in Puyallup, behind the mortuary he owns and operates."

Kerrie grimaced. "He's a mortician?"

"Yep."

"You still think he's Loverboy?"

"No. He was panicked that we'd tell his wife about his picking up women through the classifieds. Apparently her family financed his business, but they never liked him and would jump on any excuse to convince their daughter to divorce him."

She sighed. "Maybe Roman's right. Maybe Mike Springer is our boy. Anything new on the security guard's murder?"

"Nothing we didn't expect."

"It was Loverboy, then?"

"Natch. I tried reaching you all afternoon to tell you this." Impatience echoed down the line as if it were a vibration.

"Had some errands to run." Her gaze flicked to the wall clock. Too soon to hear from Philip Waring. Too soon for the plane to have reached Virginia. "I wanted to get Mom and the girls out of the house while…until everyone was gone."

"Don't blame you." There was a heavy pause. "Everyone's okay, then?"

"Absolutely." She hated lying to her partner. Hated lying period. Loverboy had reduced her to this. Somehow she kept her angry frustration out of her voice. "We're going to settle in for a quiet night. Hit the sack early. It's been a long day."

"I hear you. Maybe we'll have something new in the morning. Get your R & R."

"Will do," she said, hanging up. But Kerrie would neither rest nor relax until they heard from Philip Waring. The house was too empty, too quiet without her mother. Without her children. She realized this was what it would feel like when Glynna married Dr. Jon Vauter and the girls spent weekends or longer with Roman.

Roman. The steady beat of the shower echoed through the house and threatened to waylay her with erotic thoughts. She lurched out of the chair. She needed to keep busy, to pass time. Food. She was starving. The only thing she'd eaten all day was a slice of toast.

She went to the refrigerator, and to her surprise, found it in dire need of restocking. She couldn't recall when she'd seen it this empty. It was usually too full. She leaned against the open door, the cool air brushing her face like a cold swipe of reality. Her mother did the grocery shopping. Just one more chore Kerrie didn't have to see to, one more task Glynna performed that allowed her to have her career.

Major changes awaited her in the very near future.

"Whatcha doing, Irish?"

Kerrie tensed. She closed the door and smiled halfheartedly at Roman. "Looking for something we can eat, but I fear the pantry's bare."

He wore a chest-hugging, bronze T-shirt, that deepened the golden highlights in his eyes, black jeans that cleaved his male assets in all the right places. His raven hair was damp, slicked off his forehead. His aftershave lightly teased her senses.

He shrugged. "Is Salty's still open?"

"Yes." The restaurant was just down the hill and, in her opinion, served the best fish and chips in all of King County. And, it offered a reprieve from this forced and dangerous isolation with Roman. "I'll get my purse."

FORTY-FIVE MINUTES later, with their bellies filled, they left the restaurant. Roman steered up the hill toward California Avenue. Kerrie settled against her seat. "I forgot to tell you—Cage found Jeremy Dane.'' She recounted her partner's information.

Roman said, ''Looks innocent enough, but I'm not ruling anyone out until we have the creep.''

They were silent the rest of the way. A light rain tapped against the roof of the car, reminding Kerrie of the minutes ticking slowly by, of the long wait still ahead. She dreaded returning to the empty house. Dreaded being alone with Roman. Alone with her need for him.

As they came level with Sophia Sommerville's house, a furry orange-and-black object darted into the Mazda's headlights. She screamed, ''Professor Plum!''

Roman hit the brake. The tires bit the pavement with a squeal. Kerrie's heart was in her throat. She flew out of the car and dropped to her knees, searching for the cat, praying she wouldn't find him beneath the tires. ''Professor Plum! Where are you?''

Roman knelt beside her. Rain fell into her eyes as she gazed up at him. The car's interior light touched his concerned face. ''Is he there?''

''I don't see him. What do you suppose spooked him like that?''

''I—'' A deafening boom cut off his words. Windows shattered and burst from frames.

Swearing, Roman threw himself on top of her, flattening her to the wet pavement. The wind whooshed from her. Shouts and screams mingled with falling glass. Roman said, ''What the hell?''

Kerrie heard an unusual roaring. Roman eased his weight off her and pulled her up. ''Are you all right?''

She was shaking like a leaf, but as far as she could tell, she was all in one piece. She nodded, pulling air back into her lungs. ''What was that?''

''Explosion…'' Roman helped her to her feet. Her knees felt weak. Roman's eyes rounded as he spied something over her shoulder. Kerrie spun around to see what he was looking at.

Black smoke and huge flames poured from what remained of her house.

Chapter Fourteen

"My house." Kerrie's voice rasped the words. The house she'd purchased through blood, sweat and tears, that held her every material possession, the only home her daughters had ever known, was rapidly being eaten by the hungry flames. She ducked past Roman and started for it at a dead run.

"No!" Roman caught her by the upper arms and jerked her to a stop. He spun her around to face him. Both of them were oblivious to the steadily falling rain. Like a huge campfire, the high, hot flames gave off a brilliant illumination in the dark night. Roman could see Kerrie's face clearly, and he didn't like the shock glazing her eyes. He leaned toward her. "There's nothing in that house worth your life. Nothing that can't be replaced."

"What?" She didn't seem to understand.

"The girls and Glynna are safely gone from here." He spoke firmly, softly, sanely. "Anything left in the house can be replaced."

The fact that her children and her mother were not inside the burning inferno somehow penetrated her shock-riddled mind. She drew a noisy, shuddery breath. "They are safe, aren't they?"

"Yes, Irish. They are." He prayed to God he was telling her the truth. He pulled her against him and held her trem-

bling body close. The stench of smoke in the air stung his
nostrils.

"Oh, my God!" A woman, Sophia Sommerville, he realized, identifying the wild-eyed woman in the purple
sweat suit, bustled up to him. "Oh, my God! Are either
of you hurt?"

"No," Roman said. "Has anyone called 911?"

The bleating of a fire truck in the distance answered his
question. He hoped an ambulance was accompanying it.
Other neighbors were outside now. Several looked in need
of medical attention—if for no other reason than shock.
Like Irish.

"Why don't you take Kerrie to my house," Sophia suggested. "I'll move her car to the curb."

Roman nodded. He turned Kerrie slightly and began
leading her. She resisted. "No. I want to stay here."

"You're in shock, sweetheart." He leaned down so she
could see his eyes. "You're getting soaked. Let's go in
and dry off. Let the firefighters do their job."

She stood stock-still for a few more seconds, then Roman felt her going limp. He quickly scooped her up into
his arms. Kerrie came easily, like a child. He carried her
through the growing number of stunned gawkers, and
headed to the purple house, where the door stood wide-
open.

Inside, he laid Kerrie on the living-room couch and
wrapped her in a lavender comforter, tucking it around her
tightly, warmly.

"Do you have any towels?" he asked Sophia as she
came in the door.

"Sure." She handed him Kerrie's car keys and hurried
down the hallway, returning a moment later with a handful
of bath towels. "My goodness, I've never had such an
awful fright. Rattled every window in the place. Why if I

hadn't been sitting down already it would have knocked me off my feet."

Roman took Kerrie a towel and blotted her face and hair. She gazed at him. "What do you suppose caused it?"

"I don't know." He hadn't considered the cause. He'd just been reacting. Not thinking.

"Gas leak, maybe?" Sophia suggested, towel-drying her own face and hair.

Roman shrugged. Kerrie frowned.

"Well, whatever it was—" Sophia stood beside an armchair. "Thank the Lord neither of you were inside."

"Yes." Another minute, Roman thought, and they would have been.

Professor Plum poked his orange-and-black head out from under the sofa and rubbed against Roman's leg. Roman bent to pet the cat's damp fur. "Actually this guy is the hero of the day."

Instead of being pale like Kerrie's, Sophia's face was overly pink. "A hero? How's that?"

Roman told her about the cat darting out in front of the car.

"Why ever did he do that? He usually steers clear of the street." She drew a sudden, sharp breath. Her hand flew to her chest and her eyes rounded with new horror. "Glynna and the girls!"

"They were not in the house, Ms. Sommerville."

Sophia sputtered, "Are you certain, I thought—"

"I'm positive." Roman cut her off.

Relief loosened her taut expression. "Where are they?"

"Somewhere safe from this."

"I see." She seemed to realize he wouldn't say more and dropped the subject. She looked ill at ease for one second, then brightened. "I think I'd like some hot chocolate. Anyone else?"

"Please," Roman told her. "For both of us."

He squatted beside Kerrie and took her hand in his. She gave him a wan smile, but the color was returning to her cheeks. The hiss of air brakes announced the arrival of the fire trucks. Kerrie heard it, too. She flinched, then gazed at him with intensity. "Can they save it?"

He considered lying to her. Knew she'd resent him for it and decided honesty was best. "I'm not an expert on fires, Irish, but it seemed to me that it was burning too hot. I'm sorry."

Kerrie nodded and swallowed hard. "Was Sophia right about a gas leak?"

He read the unasked question in her eyes. *Or has Loverboy added arson to his list of crimes?* Roman recalled the ear-splitting boom. Demolitions? Or an open gas jet? He knew they couldn't rule out Loverboy until an investigation said otherwise. But speculation wouldn't ease Kerrie's mind. And right now, that was all he wanted to do. "Why don't we wait and see what the experts have to say?"

Sophia entered the room with the cocoa. They all drank in silence. Gradually Kerrie's natural color returned.

"You know," Sophia said. "I saw a stranger, a man, lurking around the neighborhood the past couple of days. I told that nice Detective Cage about him earlier today."

"Oh?" Roman's attention was immediately piqued.

Kerrie set her cup on the coffee table. "What did this stranger look like?"

"Well…" Sophia set her cup down. "He reminded me of that actor Tom Something—the one who won all those Oscars—the one who was in the movie about Seattle. Has curly hair. Not real handsome like this one." She gazed at Roman and blushed. "More wholesomelike. Kind of guy you could trust on sight."

"Mike Springer," Roman said with assurance.

"No, that's not the actor's name." Sophia shook her

head, her face still scrunched as she tried recalling who the stranger reminded her of.

Kerrie sat straighter. "I wonder if he's turned up at his house yet?"

"We're not going to worry about that tonight." Roman put his cup down, set the towels to one side and stood. He offered Kerrie his hand. "Right now, I'm recommending a hot bath and a warm bed for you."

"You're both welcome to stay here," Sophia offered, lurching from her chair.

"Thanks. But I don't think that's a good idea." Roman wasn't about to put this kind woman in jeopardy. Plus, he wanted Irish out of this neighborhood.

"Well...if you're sure." Sophia gathered the towels, but she didn't pursue the issue.

They both thanked her and left.

The night smelled of wet smoke and ash. The rain had stopped and the air was eerily calm. Kerrie caught Roman's arm. "I want to see my house."

They approached slowly. The brilliance of the flames had been snuffed, but there was no mistaking the extent of the damage even in the dark. The house was gutted. Arcs of water still streamed from hoses, hissing and sizzling on hot coals that refused to die.

They spoke to the first firefighter they saw, a tall middle-aged man with a smoke-streaked face. "Nothing we can do now, Detective Muldoon," he told her. "Except contain the burn. I'm real sorry, ma'am."

Roman thought she took the news well. Too well. Her face was a mask. Whatever she was feeling, she was hiding it. This had to be agonizing for her, but no one would guess it. Roman wished to hell she'd let down and mourn this loss. Scream. Cry. Something. Anything but this blasted calm acceptance.

She said, "When will you know what caused the fire?"

The firefighter shook his head. "Not until the ashes cool. Couple days at least."

Kerrie sighed loudly.

Roman wondered if he should call Glynna. Maybe talking to her mother would help. Trouble was, telling Glynna would only result in her immediate return to be with Kerrie. That was out of the question. She and the girls were safe as long as they stayed in hiding. He had only to look at what remained of their house to know that.

"Come on, Irish. Let's get out of here."

To assure no one followed them, Roman drove in a roundabout way to a downtown hotel. He booked them into adjoining rooms, and immediately ran Kerrie a hot bubble bath, insisting she get into it.

She was too wiped-out to argue.

As soon as he was sure she was out of earshot, he placed a call to Philip Waring.

Philip answered on the third ring. "Roman, good. I was just about to call you. Let me put your mind at ease. All arrived in fine fettle and are now settling into their rooms for the night."

For the first time in what seemed like days to him, Roman smiled. He felt as if a stone had been lifted off his heart. His daughters and Glynna had arrived safe and sound. He thanked God. "I'll breathe easier knowing they're with you, Philip."

"I'll protect them with my life."

"I know that."

"Your daughters are a delight." Philip chuckled as if recalling something sweet. It was a nice sound to Roman's ears. His friend had found little to laugh about since Wendy's murder.

"And their lovely grandmother is a pleasant surprise."

"Glynna Muldoon is a pretty special lady."

"Not unlike her daughter?"

Roman wasn't about to participate in Philip's fishing expedition. Instead he gave him the number of the hotel and told him Kerrie would call her mother in the morning.

"Glynna told me about the guard that was killed at her house. Is that why you've decided not to stay there?"

Roman tensed. "One of the reasons. Actually I'd prefer you didn't mention the hotel to Glynna, unless it's unavoidable."

"Curiouser and curiouser. I'll not mention it." The lighthearted tone in Philip's voice was gone. "Are you getting any closer to finding Loverboy?"

Not for one minute did he consider telling Philip about Kerrie's house nor that, at the moment, Loverboy seemed to have the upper hand. Bad news could wait. Right now it was enough that they were all safe. "We've got some solid leads."

"Glad to hear it. Now get some rest and don't worry about your girls. Oh, and Roman, as far as Loverboy is concerned, break a leg."

"Your theatrical roots are showing." Roman teased. Philip had been an off-Broadway actor in his youth, and still embraced some of the superstitions he'd acquired during that time.

Roman hung up, then tapped on the bathroom door. "Irish, the girls and your mom arrived without a hitch. I told Philip you'd call Glynna in the morning."

"You didn't mention the house, did you?"

"No."

"Good." Kerrie sank further into the tub. She felt numb now that her anger had subsided. She didn't know what she'd tell her mother when the time came. For now, however, she didn't want Glynna worried about anything but her own safety and the safety of the girls.

Roman's voice filtered through the door again. "I'm going out for a few minutes. Be right back."

Kerrie lathered her skin and scrubbed every inch for the fourth time, then laid back and drenched her hair. None of her efforts erased the stench of smoke from her nostrils. She supposed the smell would linger in her memory for a long time.

She watched a drip of moisture meander from the showerhead to the faucet taps as though it were the most fascinating thing she'd ever seen. It seemed a minute passed, but when the water felt suddenly tepid, she realized she must have been staring at the wall for at least half an hour.

Her fingertips and toes were pruny and white, her hair slick with suds. She emptied the tub, then pulled the shower curtain into place and stood beneath the hot beating water until she could no longer feel any soap in her hair.

She stepped out of the shower, wrapped herself in a towel and twisted another turban-style around her wet hair. What was she going to wear to bed? The thought of sleeping naked held little appeal, the thought of putting on the clothes she'd worn since morning even less. Especially since they were the only clothes she now owned.

She fought down the wave of outraged grief this thought resurrected. Loverboy may have destroyed her house, but he would not destroy her. She'd buy new clothes tomorrow. Meanwhile she supposed she could wear the robe the hotel provided. She'd wash her undies in the sink. Hopefully they'd dry by morning.

When she approached the bathroom counter, she saw the clothes she'd left there were gone. In their place were three brand new pairs of panties, her size, and a sleep T-shirt with a Seattle SuperSonics decal. Next to them was a new hairbrush and her favorite perfume.

She put her hand over her mouth to catch the gasp that slipped from her throat, and blinked hard against the tears that instantly sprang into her eyes. How could she have remained so tough through the past twenty-four hours only to be brought to her knees by one thoughtful gesture?

"Save me from this man and his effect on me," she murmured. She uncapped the bottle of perfume and drew in a deep breath. The sweet scent did what nothing else had been able: chased the stench of smoke from her nose. She closed her eyes and daubed perfume on her pulse points. "The woman who wins your heart, Roman Donnello, will be one lucky lady."

FORTITUDE, Roman thought, as Kerrie came into the room. Loverboy had taken her home from her, but he hadn't taken her spirit. It hovered around her like an invisible mantle, an aura. Roman admired her for it. And yet, he realized, it was the very quality that made her too strong for her own good on occasion, a quality that made her build walls he couldn't penetrate, a quality that both attracted and repelled him.

Although, at this moment, it seemed impossible that anything about her could repel him. Her fiery hair, still damp from her bath, curled gently around her face, whispered over her shoulders, and sweetened the air with its heady fragrance. The neck of the sleep shirt filled the V of the tightly belted terry-cloth robe that ended just above her knees—a look both innocent and seductive. Her shapely feet were bare, her toenails painted an enticing shade of coral pink.

He felt an immediate and fierce stab of desire. How could a woman, no, he corrected, why did *this* woman affect him so? Why had he always been more attracted to her than any other? Why had he never been able to get her out of his blood? Off his mind?

"Thank you. For...the clothes." The words seemed to choke her.

He nodded, feeling suddenly self-conscious in his own

knee-length robe. "I sent our clothes out to be cleaned and pressed. We'll have them back by morning."

An awkward silence hung between them. Finally Roman moved toward his own room. "It's late. You really should get some sleep, Irish."

"'Night," she said, sounding more like one of her two-year-old girls than their mother.

The need in her eyes tugged at his soul. He ached to hold her, to comfort her and join with her. What he didn't want was meaningless sex. Not tonight. Not with Irish. He wanted to make *love* to her, with her. It took every ounce of willpower he possessed to step into his own room and begin to close the door.

"No." Her stricken look stopped him.

"You want me to keep the door open?"

"I—I don't want you to go."

He wasn't sure he could share the same space with her and not touch her. Not love her. Somehow he would have to manage it. He stepped back into the room.

Kerrie bid him to move closer. Every wall she'd ever built between them had shattered into oblivion with the destruction of her house. Right now, she needed him with the same hungry need she'd seen in his eyes earlier tonight. She wanted him to hold her, to kiss her until every inch of her tingled with feeling, with life. If he couldn't give her his heart, she would take whatever he could give.

As though she'd said this aloud, Roman strode straight for her and pulled her into his arms. She clung to him, her hands flattened against his back. The thrum of his accelerating heartbeat pulsed beneath her palms, sending its life force through her like some bizarre surge of electricity. It seemed to say she was not alone. Would never be alone as long as he was with her. That together they could vanquish all their foes.

She wanted to believe that. Needed to believe it. If only for the moment. "Make love to me, Roman."

He pulled back from their embrace, gazing down at her with a querulous expression. Desire radiated in his golden eyes, but reluctance mingled with it. Why did he study her face so intently? What was he looking for? His hands moved into her hair, his fingers dipping gently against her scalp. She sighed, "I need you so."

Her words dissolved his indecision. His mouth descended on hers, not fiercely as always before, but gently, reverently, as though she were something delicate...or something so delicious he wished to savor every taste, every touch.

Her blood began to stir and heat, and an odd tingling sensation moved through her veins, her nerves, as though her circulation were being reawakened, as though her body was emerging from the desensitized lethargy that had held her in its grips for hours now. It felt painful at first, a sweet sharp ache from her head to her toes, a wet hot throbbing from her mouth to her womb.

He stepped back, his gaze steadied on her, his eyes like liquid gold as he slipped his robe off his shoulders, letting it slide from his arms onto the floor. He stood there, permitting her to drink in his glorious nakedness. She caressed him with her gaze, then closed the gap between them and laid her hand on the soft ebony hair across his chest, and gradually trailing a fingertip down his belly and into the denser, springy hair at the core of him.

Roman moaned, "Irish, you drive me wild."

"Show me." She couldn't resist touching him, holding him, his desire hot and hard and throbbing in her hand.

He moaned again, the sound low, feral, pleasing, pleased.

"Not so quick. Not this time." He stepped back, and reached for the belt on her robe, deftly loosening it. He grasped the lapels and eased it off her shoulders. When it lay pooled at her feet, he smiled and moved to her again, kissed her again, and soon his hands were skimming her back, her waist, her bottom. He pulled her against his erection, pressing his hips to hers, his desire to hers, igniting tiny explosions of pleasure and need in the very essence of her.

His hands slipped under the T-shirt and he lifted it up and over her head, tossing it aside as his gaze feasted on her breasts. "You are the most beautiful woman, Irish. I could never tire of seeing you like this."

The compliment sent a heating blush into her face and hardened her nipples as though he'd teased them taut with his tongue. He did touch them now, delicately as if they were breakable crystal, and the sting of desire she'd felt earlier heightened to such intensity she didn't think she could contain it a moment longer. "Please, Roman, now."

"Patience, my love." He ducked to taste her breasts, his demanding mouth capturing one, then the other. Impossibly Kerrie's need leaped higher, and a honeyed groan slipped from her throat. Roman ran a hand lovingly over her flat tummy, then dipped his fingertips inside the elastic waistband of her panties and fondled the thick curls nestled there. Soon his finger was inside her, stroking her.

Kerrie could barely breathe. Her own hands were busy, exploring, caressing, bringing her joy in the very feel of him.

Roman stripped her panties off, lifted her onto the center of the king-size bed, and stretched out beside her. In the middle of his palm he held a condom. Where he'd produced it from she couldn't say. She arched an eyebrow at him and grinned wryly, spoke breathlessly, "Prepared this time?"

"I thought..." His gaze was glazed with desire, his

voice husky with passion as breathless as her own. "...since I can't trust myself around you, Irish..."

His confession went straight to her heart. She reached up and kissed him, her tongue twining with his, plunging and thrusting, a mini rehearsal for the full-blown gala ahead. As she slipped the protection onto him, she parted her legs. Roman found the heart-shaped birthmark on the inside of her upper thigh and gently traced it with his fingertip, then kissed it, then tasted her, teased her, and finally, raised his body over hers and pushed into her with one hard, luscious lunge that sent her over the edge of ecstasy.

She wanted this to continue forever, feared they would both give into the rush of need that usually made up their lovemaking, but he was in no hurry. Every thrust was slow and loving and pleasure-giving. The affection in his eyes as he gazed down at her seared her very soul, healed her emotional wounds, filled her empty, lonely heart, lifted her to heights of passion she had never before reached.

Inside her, ardor swelled, and she cried out for release, cried out his name, a sweet song of the love she felt for him. She reached the pinnacle seconds before him, and when he joined her there, she stayed at the peak, shudders quaking through her in never ending shock waves of rapture.

The downward spiral was slower than the ascent, sweeter, more languid. For a long time after, Roman stayed joined with her, raining tiny kisses across her face, at her temples. Eventually he rolled to his side and held her close, until she fell asleep in his arms.

Roman's reluctance to leave her, further convinced him that what he shared with Kerrie had deeper meaning than either of them had admitted. He wanted to talk to her about it, make her acknowledge what he had just faced: that their sexual encounters were more than an itch being scratched.

But life and reality had played enough tug-of-war with her emotions in the past twenty-four hours.

Having her children wrenched from her, her house destroyed, along with every material thing she owned except her car, was more than most people could stand without collapsing totally. Kerrie was stronger than most, but everyone had their limits.

He gazed down at her sweet expression and knew that he had put it there, that he had provided her some inner peace. The knowledge warmed him, gave him the courage to confront his feelings for her. He loved this stubborn, contrary woman.

But did she love him? He gazed at her contented expression. It gave him hope. "First thing tomorrow, Irish, we're going to talk about us."

Chapter Fifteen

"Hey, sleepyhead. Wake up."

Roman forced his gritty eyes open. Kerrie stood over him, looking freshly showered. His first thought was, *Too bad she'd dressed.* He kept the thought to himself, struggled to his elbows and grinned at her. "Good morning, Irish."

"'Morning, yourself."

He arched a brow at her. He'd had more cordial greetings from archenemies. What was going on? He took another look at her, noticing this time that her glorious mane lay tight against her head in that fancy braid she favored, as controlled as her demeanor. He considered grabbing her wrist, hauling her back into bed and giving her attitude a carnal adjustment.

"Our Continental breakfast was just delivered." Kerrie swept out of his reach, strode to the table and helped herself. Her energy was palpable. "While you're showering and eating, I'll call Mom."

She carried a sweet roll and coffee into the next room and kicked the door shut with her foot before he could protest. Or insist on the talk he wanted to have with her. Roman grunted in frustration, threw off the covers and sat up. Their lovemaking had restored her all right—back into Ms. Efficient Cop with all her impenetrable walls repaired.

His cleaned clothes lay on the unused bed across from his. He shook his head. Breakfast on the table, his clothes readied, she was acting more like his mother this morning than his lover. He definitely didn't need a mother. He definitely would set her straight on that fact.

He headed into the bathroom, returned a minute later and downed a cup of steaming coffee. Feeling better, he ate two pastries with the second cup of coffee, then showered, shaved and dressed. As he poured a third cup of coffee, he realized he felt somewhat restored this morning, too. Best night's sleep he'd had in a long while.

Kerrie interrupted the thought. "Are you ready?"

"Just about." As before, his blood quickened at the sight of her, but this time he noticed there was a freshness about her that he hadn't seen in days. She was remarkable. Her kids taken away, her house in ashes, and she kept focused on their goal of bringing in Loverboy. Admirable. But there was another, equally important issue she seemed eager as hell to avoid. "Irish, we should talk about last night."

"Not now. I have to get to the station." She had her purse and was dragging on her coat.

"Fine." Roman set his cup down and grinned to himself. *Run away, my love. But you can't run forever. We will have this talk at the first opportunity. Today.* He put his coat on and hauled his cell phone out of his pocket. It had gotten crushed when he'd knocked Kerrie to the ground last night. He held it out to her. "I need to stop and pick up a new cellular phone on the way. This one's on the blink and I'm expecting some agents to call in."

"No problem." Kerrie glanced at her wristwatch. "Cage won't beat us in by much."

"DETECTIVE CAGE isn't here," the fifth-floor receptionist told Kerrie, pointing to the sign-in/sign-out board. "But he is on line one. I was just writing down his message for you.''

"I'll take the call at my desk." Kerrie hurried to her phone with Roman close behind. She motioned him into Cage's chair. "Use his phone."

She dropped into her chair and snatched up her receiver. "Donnello is with me, listening in. Where are you, Tully?"

"I've taken the stakeout at Springer's house." The phone connection sounded odd, as though he were actually calling from some greater distance than Mercer Island.

"And?" Kerrie asked, hoping he had something to report that would advance the case.

"He hasn't shown yet."

She sighed with disappointment. Where was the wily CPA? "How about his BMW?"

"Still sitting at the curb," Cage said. "Locked up tight."

Roman asked, "Anybody been there at all?"

"Not this morning."

Roman frowned at Kerrie. "Not even his assistant, Cindy Faber?"

"What's she look like?"

Kerrie described her.

"Nope, haven't seen anyone like that," Cage answered. "But why would she come back if she knows he's not here? More likely she'd telephone or leave a message on his answering machine."

"Or," Roman added, meeting Kerrie's gaze, "she could have left him a note before she locked up yesterday."

Both those suggestions were logical, Kerrie realized. But so was something else. "Or maybe Mike called her."

Roman's look was questioning. "Why don't we check on that?"

Kerrie nodded.

"Hey, Muldoon." Cage broke in. "I'm sorry about your house."

Kerrie felt as if he'd choked her. "Thanks."

Roman hung up, giving her a modicum of privacy.

"Last night's news report said no one was injured," Cage continued, his accent prominent. "None of you were, were you?"

"Not physically." She shoved the demons back into the corners of her mind. She would not deal with them right now. Not until they had Loverboy sitting in a cell, awaiting prosecution.

"Was it arson?"

She knew Cage was really asking whether or not Loverboy had set the fire. "Won't have any answers for a few days."

There was a weighted pause, then Cage said, "If you need anything…"

"Thanks, partner, I'll keep that in mind." She hung up.

Only someone who knew her as well as Roman would realize that she was rocked by having to talk about the fire. A sadness she couldn't quite hide flickered in her eyes, but she quickly squared her shoulders and stuck out her chin as though daring Fate to punch it.

Roman leaped to his feet. "Looks like we've got a house call to make."

"Two, actually." Kerrie gathered her purse again and strode toward him. "I want to talk to Cindy Faber *and* Joe Springer again."

He handed her the Mazda keys.

The address Cindy Faber had given them was for an apartment house in Ballard, about twenty blocks from Joe Springer's place. The complex was old, but someone had tried maintaining it and now it had the look of an aged actress who'd had one too many face-lifts—the outer skin smoothed too tightly over the sixties modern-chic bone.

"Naturally, since there's no elevator, she'd be on the top floor," Kerrie complained.

"Don't tell me you aren't in good enough shape to climb four flights, Irish." Roman leaned seductively close to her. "I know better."

Kerrie blushed, picked up her step and stayed slightly ahead of him until she reached the fourth floor. Last night had been wonderful. Roman had delivered her from the horrors threatening to engulf her. He'd made her feel alive, given her comfort and compassion, restored her sense of self as nothing and no one else could.

But he hadn't declared any undying love. She wouldn't fool herself into thinking his tenderness was anything more than technique. He could no more help that he was a lusty, sensuous man, than she could help being a natural redhead. She just wished she wasn't so susceptible to him.

The sharp tang of fresh paint floated on the air, getting stronger as they approached number 4G. The door to 4F hung open, the obvious source of the pungent fumes. Drop cloths covered the carpet and hung across the threshold, and the slap of a paint roller hitting a wall echoed from within.

4G was the last apartment on this floor. When their knocking went unanswered after three minutes, Roman glanced down at Kerrie. "We should have called first."

"Guess I was in too big of a hurry."

What she'd been was antsy. Roman understood. Cops were trained for action and during high stress cases like this one, with the stakes as personal as they were, the tension was relentless, the need to *do* something unbearable. Plus, she hadn't wanted to talk about last night—and she knew that's exactly what they'd be doing if she didn't focus on the case.

Kerrie stepped away from the door. "Maybe we'll have better luck with Joe Springer."

As they started back down the hall, a middle-aged woman stepped into the open doorway of 4F. She was nearly as tall as Roman, skinny and long legged, with a bandanna covering every speck of her hair. Thick blond eyebrows dominated the features in her long face. She wore paint-splattered jeans, sweatshirt and sneakers. "By any chance you folks wouldn't be looking for an apartment to lease?"

"Not today." Roman smiled. "We were hoping to catch Cindy...Ms. Faber in."

"Catch her in?" The woman's blond eyebrows lifted. "Hers is the other of these two apartments that are up for rent."

"Ms. Faber has moved?" Kerrie exchanged a glance with Roman. "When?"

"Earlier this week."

Roman stepped closer to the woman. "You wouldn't happen to have her new address by any chance?"

The woman's affable manner grew suddenly leery. "Who are you two?"

Kerrie dug into her shoulder bag and showed her ID.

"Oh, my." Interest beamed in the woman's eyes, the kind of gleam that marked her as a lover of gossip. "What's she done?"

"Nothing that we know of, ma'am," Kerrie said formally. "We just wanted to talk to her."

"Oh, I wish I could help you out. Surely would love to. But she didn't leave a forwarding with me. No reason to. She paid her rent on time every month and kept pretty much to herself. Only had a couple visitors I ever saw. An older woman, her mother maybe, and lately a nice-looking young guy who...don't laugh now...but he reminded me of Forrest Gump."

Kerrie handed the woman her card. "You've been more

of a help than you realize. If you hear from Cindy Faber again, would you get her new address and call me?''

"You betcha." The woman studied the card, stuck it in the pocket of her jeans, then dug into another pocket and brought out a card of her own. Gazing at both of them, she offered it to Kerrie. "And if either of you hear about anyone who wants a one-bedroom fully furnished—I can be reached at that number."

Once in the car, Roman said, "Why did Cindy Faber give us this address when she'd already moved?"

"If we could find her, we could ask her." Kerrie started the engine.

Roman buckled his seat belt. "Do you suppose she moved in with Springer?"

Kerrie pulled away from the curb. "It is quite a coincidence that they both moved in the same week."

"Yeah, and apparently her apartment was furnished, so she wouldn't have much to move except her clothes."

They looked at each other. Kerrie said, "Some of the unpacked boxes in Springer's house could be hers."

"Too bad we don't have grounds for a search warrant."

"We need something more concrete than the man not being at home when we want to talk to him. In reality, we don't have one solid lead that connects him to Loverboy or even to any of the other suspects."

"If only one of my agents would call with a new lead." He cursed the silent cell phone residing in the inside pocket of his leather jacket. Tracing and retracing the same paths for any missed clue was part and parcel of daily police work, especially on a case as perplexing as this one, but Roman found himself agitated with the routine today. "All we've unearthed are more suspicions."

"Maybe she's shown up at the Mercer Island house by now." Hopeful that this might be the case, Kerrie checked at headquarters. To her disappointment, Cage hadn't re-

ported in since she'd spoken to him earlier. She got the
number for the cell phone he was using and had Roman
try him.

"No answer," Roman said, putting his phone back in
his pocket. "Either he's turned the phone off or he's away
from it."

"We'll try again when we finish here." She pulled to
the curb beside Joe Springer's house.

Joe Springer was not happy to see them. As before, he
wore an old cardigan with leather patches on the elbows
and rumpled slacks. His thinning gray hair was combed
over from a side part and he kept them standing on the
porch.

Behind his thick-lensed glasses, he peered at them anxiously. Roman wondered if he was hiding something. Say
Mike? Or Cindy? He'd have loved to ask, but this was
Kerrie's show. He stepped back to the porch railing and
leaned against an upright post.

"Mr. Springer, we are still seeking your son for questioning. Have you seen him or heard from him since yesterday?"

Joe Springer's tarnished-penny eyes widened with
alarm. "Why are you badgering me?"

"I'm not badgering you, sir." The tolerant voice Kerrie
was using on the man amused Roman. She was very good
at this. Calm him down, then throw out a question that
would hopefully catch him off guard. He listened as she
went through the routine and saw it was having the desired
effect. Joe Springer nodded and he seemed to relax
slightly.

Then Kerrie asked, "Do you know a Cindy Faber?"

Roman tensed, but this expected bomb landed with all
the explosive force of a feather.

"Cindy?" Joe Springer shook his head, his expression

one of classic confusion. "No. Never heard of her. Who is she?"

"Mike's new assistant," Kerrie explained.

Roman's cell phone rang, startling him. Kerrie glanced over her shoulder as he pulled it from his pocket. "Donnello, here."

"It's Green." Chuck Green was one of the agents he had watching the beach house in Wildwood, New Jersey.

He covered the receiver. "I have to take this. I'll be right back."

Leaving Kerrie to continue her questioning of Joe, Roman scrambled down the steps to the curb. His pulse was zinging. "What have you got, Green?"

"The pigeon arrived at the coop in the wee hours this morning."

"Description?" Roman held his breath.

Green said, "Tall, slender, average looking, with short hair."

Sounds like Jeremy Dane, Roman thought, feeling justified that he hadn't ruled out the mortician from Puyallup. "Brown hair?"

"Not this guy. He's got blond hair, crew cut.

Shock traveled Roman's veins. What the hell? Tully Cage? "Do you have a name yet?"

"No, but I'm working on it."

Roman shook himself, trying to make sense of this new information. When they'd spoken to Cage earlier had he actually been calling from Mike Springer's Mercer Island house, or from New Jersey? A chill swept his gut. "Keep at it, Green, and let me know if anything else develops."

Roman would do some checking on his own. At this end.

"Wait, you haven't heard it all," Green said loudly, catching him just as he was about to disconnect. "The pigeon's not alone. Another guy showed up a while ago."

Roman's mouth went dry. "Does this other guy look like Tom Hanks?"

"Hey, how'd you know that?"

"Contact the locals, Green, and tell them I'll call within the hour. Have them haul both men in for questioning in the Loverboy murders."

Roman hung up and sprinted back up the stairs, his step as frantic as his thoughts. If Cage was behind this, how would Irish take it? Hell, they finally had a break in the case and it might break her heart. Cage…and Springer. His head was spinning. He hated dirty cops, hated to think of Cage as one, but it would explain why no tails were put on Jeremy Dane after Kerrie's "date" with him; Cage would have already known Dane wasn't the perp.

As Roman approached, Joe eyed him belligerently, pleadingly. "I swear I haven't seen Mike in days. I can't reach him at his new phone number or nothing."

Roman nodded. "I believe you, Mr. Springer. Thanks for your cooperation."

Joe's look shifted to suspicion. "Why you believing me all of a sudden? That phone call have something to do with my boy?"

"No, it didn't." Roman lied. He spoke to Kerrie. "We have to go. Now."

She nodded, and spoke to Joe, "We'll be in touch, Mr. Springer. Don't leave town."

Kerrie didn't ask Roman anything until they were inside the Mazda. "What's happened? You look like you've lost your best friend."

"Not me. Maybe you." Roman cursed himself at the alarm that immediately sprang up in her emerald eyes. "No, no, it's not the girls or your mom. It's Cage. At least, it may very well be." He explained on the way downtown.

As soon as they arrived at the station, they tried contacting Cage again without result. Kerrie didn't want to believe Roman's fellow agent was right about Tully, but she determined to keep an open mind, in case she had to face that very fact. If she'd learned anything in the past twenty-four hours, it was that she could count on nothing remaining the same.

She brought the lieutenant up to speed. He told her Cage was not assigned to watch Springer's house today. Someone else was doing that. They'd just reported no activity there all day. Kerrie's stomach sank, her worst fears confirmed. Tully Cage, the man she'd trusted daily with her life, was not the straight arrow she'd believed him to be.

Over the next hour, they applied for a search warrant for Mike Springer's house and sent a unit to look for the missing Cage.

The lieutenant and the New Jersey police granted Kerrie special permission to accompany Roman and sit in on the questioning of Mike Springer and the other man, whom they had not yet identified. No one had told them the other man might be her partner. They wouldn't brand Cage a rogue cop until they were certain. Roman and she left for the airport.

As soon as they were settled in the middle of the 737, Kerrie felt uncomfortable. The seats were too close together, forcing her into an intimacy with Roman that she'd tried avoiding all morning. Every time he glanced down at her with those warm golden eyes, she felt her insides stir with heat. Every time he shifted in his seat, his aftershave teased her senses.

This was going to be one long flight, with nothing to talk about. She pulled a paperback out of her purse and opened it to the folded page she'd left off reading.

Roman studied the novel Kerrie was reading. A romance by a popular female author. He ached to bring up the subject of their own romance, but this was not the place for such an intimate discussion. Given both their tempers, he doubted it would be a quiet exchange.

But the longer the conversation was delayed, the more doubt crept into his mind. She harbored feelings for him. He was sure of that, but how strong were those feelings, how deep?

The long flight seemed interminable, the food dry, the movie dull, and comfort nonexistent. He was glad to see the night skyline of Newark and feel the 737 touch down on New Jersey tarmac. As they deplaned, Roman spotted Chuck Green waiting in the crowd. What the hell was going on? The closer he strode toward Green, a medium-size black man, whose handsome face was usually a coffee color, the more anxious he became. Something was wrong. Damned wrong. Tonight, Green's skin tone matched his name.

But that wasn't the only thing giving Roman a queasy stomach. He hadn't made any plans for Green to meet them at the airport. He was going to rent a car and drive to Wildwood.

With barely concealed impatience, he introduced Kerrie, then snapped, "What are you doing here, Green? What's wrong?"

Green tipped his head in acknowledgment, then he steadied his dark brown eyes on Roman. "The locals arrived to bring our pigeons in for questioning, but when they went into the house they found one dead and the other gone."

Chapter Sixteen

"Dead?" Roman said louder than he meant, startling several passersby, who jerked his way and stared. He lowered his voice. "What do you mean? What happened?"

"He was murdered," Green explained.

Murdered? The way Roman had it figured, Cage and Springer were in the Loverboy scheme with Dante Casale. Had there been some sort of falling out among them?

"Who was murdered?" Kerrie's face was ashen.

Roman didn't know which would be harder for her to accept, Cage being murdered or being a killer. He wanted to take her hand, put his arm around her, but with all those walls of hers in place, it would be useless. He held his arms stiff at his sides. "Was it Cage?"

"Cage?" Green shook his head. "No, it was the pigeon you called a Tom Hanks look-a-like." He consulted a tablet he'd taken from his pocket. "His real name was Springer. Michael Casale Springer."

Roman gaped at him in surprise. Cage, not Springer, was Loverboy? He'd have laid odds that the opposite was true. But his feelings hardly mattered right now. He glanced at Irish, concern sliding through his belly. Her eyes were awash with pain, but he could see she was dealing with it and wouldn't appreciate his acting on his need to comfort her. Why did he both admire and resent her strength?

She let out a breath and gazed up at him with her head tilted to one side. "So, your hunch about Springer was right. There *was* a connection with Dante Casale. He was his nephew."

"I told you to trust my instincts, Irish." He winked at her, glad to see the color returning to her cheeks. But Springer's death soured any satisfaction he might have felt in being right. If they'd proven his connection to Casale sooner, he'd still be alive. Now he couldn't be questioned, couldn't testify against Loverboy.

"Apparently," Green went on. "He was Casale's sister's son."

"I guessed that." Roman imparted what they knew of Mike Springer's life, starting with his move to Washington State as a teenager and ending with his career as a Seattle CPA. He pursed his lips.

What did Cage being Loverboy do to his theory about Dante Casale's involvement? Shot some pretty substantial holes in it, he surmised. Had he been wrong about Loverboy's motives? No, otherwise Casale's nephew wouldn't have been involved. But if Casale was behind this operation, why had he allowed his nephew to be murdered? A shiver spiked his spine. Maybe Casale didn't know about the murder yet. "How was Springer killed?"

Green glanced uncomfortably at Kerrie, as if what he had to say might offend her. "His throat was slit."

He asked Green, "Did the killer leave a tiny *L* at the cut?"

"Man, I swear you're psychic or something." Green shook his head at Roman, a look of awe on his face. "How'd you know that?"

"It's Loverboy's trademark," Kerrie informed him in a

voice as cold as the ice forming around Roman's convictions.

Green frowned at her and Roman enlightened him. "Detective Muldoon is the officer in charge of the Loverboy case."

Green's eyebrows arched slightly and he gave her a shrewd, appraising once-over. His brown eyes warmed with respect. "I hope you catch this vulture real fast, ma'am. He's a nasty one."

She leveled a stony gaze on him, her lush lips tight. "You don't know the half of it."

"Just to make this official, Chuck, would you look at this photo." Roman pulled a photograph of Tully Cage from his jacket pocket and extended it to Green. "Do you recognize this guy?"

Green peered at the picture, then nodded. "No question, that's the rooster who flew the coop all right. I'd recognize him anywhere."

Kerrie stiffened as if he'd smacked her, and Roman realized some small part of her had been holding out hope that Green would tell them Cage wasn't the murderer, that he would say it was some other blond man with a crew cut. He grasped her arm, gently, firmly, letting her know he was there if she needed his strength. She'd had worse blows than this one in the past few days, but there was no telling what might be the last straw.

To his relief, she didn't shake off his grip. He said, "What I don't understand, Chuck, is how he got past you."

"I don't understand it, either." Green shook his head. "I swear, Donnello, I never took my eyes off that house. But the bird was gone before the cops arrived."

"I hope they put an APB on him." Kerrie's voice was hard-edged.

"They've worked up a sketch of him from my description, but this is better.'' He tugged a pen from the inner pocket of his suit, flipped Tully's picture over and asked, ''What did you say this turkey's name is?''

''Tully Cage,'' Kerrie said flatly. ''He's my...a Seattle cop.''

Green's head jerked toward Kerrie, his eyes rounded. ''Crap.''

''Yeah,'' Roman said. ''Lookit, there's no telling where this guy is or what his next move will be, but he should be considered armed and dangerous.''

''I'll get right on the horn to the locals. But we *do* have an idea where he is.''

''What!'' The word jumped from Kerrie. She leaned toward Green as if she'd shake the information out of him if he didn't hurry up and spill it.

''He left this for you two.'' Green withdrew a piece of paper from his overcoat pocket and held it out between them. Roman thought Kerrie would snatch it out of Green's hand, but she just stared at the paper and made no move to take it.

Green said, ''It's a copy. The original is being run through a local police lab.''

Roman unfolded the paper and held it so both Kerrie and he could read the typewritten missive.

If you're wondering where I am, you could check the C & F warehouse. But just a word of caution. Remember what happened at your house Muldoon? It's going to happen again—because I'm one step ahead of you.

                                                                L

Kerrie shifted her gaze between Roman and Green. ''Where is the C & F warehouse?''

''Jersey City,'' Roman told her. ''Twenty, thirty

minutes drive from here. But I'm wondering who left this note, Casale, Springer, or Cage.''

Kerrie seemed to ponder the problem. "Well, Casale would deem it appropriate to kill us at his defunct factory—since he holds us responsible for his losing the business.''

"Are you ducks sure Cage isn't related to Casale?" Green asked.

Kerrie and Roman exchanged an I-hadn't-thought-of-that glance. Her expression was bitter. "Don't ask me. I thought I knew the man inside out.''

"Seattle is double-checking his personnel papers," Roman told Green. "Digging further into his background. If the connection is there, they'll find it.'' But he was already warming to the idea, could feel the holes in his theory shrinking.

Kerrie asked Green, "Has the warehouse been checked out?''

"The Jersey City squad is watching it, but they decided to wait for the two of you before going in.''

As though his faculties were abruptly more alert, the noises in the airport intruded, reminding Roman where they were. He glanced surreptitiously up and down the concourse. It seemed as crowded as it had when they'd arrived, maybe more, but no one appeared to be paying them any attention. He didn't see a soul who looked even remotely like Cage or Casale.

In fact, he had an odd sense they were not in any danger. Here. Too much security in the airport. But what if they ventured out into the streets of New Jersey? How vulnerable then? He shifted back to Green. "What do they need us for?''

Green shrugged. "The detective in charge said you might have an angle on how this guy operates. I think he wanted your take on this note. What it means—that stuff about Muldoon's house.''

"You can tell the detective that this psycho blew up my house last night. That's what it means. It means the guy's dangerously crazy.'' Kerrie spoke with all the anger she'd been stuffing down. "And he has nothing to lose.''

Roman added, "He wants to kill Detective Muldoon and me and he's not going to stop until he does. Or until he's caught. I'd suggest they call in the bomb squad to comb that warehouse.''

"This means you're not coming back with me to Jersey City?''

"No, we're not.'' Roman's gaze collided with Kerrie's and he could see she concurred with this decision. He stepped protectively closer to her. "That's exactly what Loverboy wants. That's why it's exactly what we're not going to do.''

He wasn't about to walk into a trap. Not with Kerrie. He gazed down at her and his pulse tripped. There were two little girls counting on him to keep their mommy safe. Two little girls *he* intended to see grow up.

"Seems like you wasted a trip,'' Green said, seeming unsure what course he should take now that his plans had gone awry the second time in one day. "Are you heading back to Seattle, then?''

"Soon as we can exchange our tickets.'' Roman gave him a lopsided smile. "Be careful, Chuck. Call me when you know something more.''

Green agreed. "The minute there's something new to report.''

As soon as he was out of earshot, Kerrie snapped, "Green's right. This was a wasted trip. He's got us running all over the country, playing 'catch me if you can.' Cage. God, I can't believe it. How could I have been so wrong about him?''

The question was rhetorical, but Roman couldn't bear the pain emanating from her eyes. "Look—I've got an idea. If you don't want to fly straight back to Seattle, we could take a side trip to Virginia."

He was rewarded with a wobbly smile. "Can we? Is it safe?"

It was all he could do not to sweep her into his arms and kiss that glorious mouth of hers. "Absolutely. Our nemesis doesn't know where we are."

They exchanged their tickets for a flight to Dulles International that would depart in two hours. Kerrie suggested he call the Waring farm so they'd be expected, then excused herself for a trip to the ladies room. When she returned, she asked if he'd made the call. Roman assured her he had, but it was a lie. Without exception, Philip Waring retired every night by ten. It was after eleven. All a call at this hour would have done was disrupt security and alarm Philip, who would in turn alarm Glynna.

Their visit would take place tomorrow. He'd deal with where they were spending the night when they arrived in Virginia. God knew how Kerrie would react if he told her now.

AS THE PLANE SET DOWN at Dulles, Roman said, "Middleburg is about thirty-five minutes away."

Kerrie's heart seemed too full. She would soon be seeing her children. Granted they would be asleep, but at least she could kiss their chubby cheeks and caress their beautiful heads. Roman hired a taxi and they settled back on the lumpy seat as soon as he'd stated their destination. Kerrie could see little besides neon signs and streetlights. The ride ended not thirty-five, but ten minutes later.

Puzzled, she glanced outside. The taxi was parked beside a two-story, town house. Definitely not in the driveway of a lavish horse farm. "Where are we?"

"Centreville, Virginia, ma'am," the cabdriver told her.

As soon at the taxi left, she asked Roman, "Why are we in Centreville instead of Middleburg?"

"This is my place."

"Your...?" After years of wondering about him. Where he was, where he lived, now, without warning, she was standing outside his house—about to go inside. In rapid succession, anxiety, trepidation, curiosity and anticipation whipped through her. But why were they here? "You wanted to get your own car?"

"Not exactly." He dipped his head toward hers, the porch light spilling over him, making his eyes seem more golden than usual. His expression grew sheepish as he admitted his lie and told her why he hadn't called Philip.

She glared at him. "You couldn't simply have told me this? Donnello, I don't like being treated like a porcelain doll. Or being lied to."

"I don't like being lied to, either, Irish, and I think we should discuss that. Preferably inside." He deactivated his alarm, unlocked the door and shoved it open. "Are you coming in?"

She hesitated, not because she feared the conversation he'd proposed, but because she feared Loverboy. Would he do to this residence what he'd done to hers? "Are you sure it's safe?"

Roman's raven brows twitched. But he seemed to understand what held her back. He grinned wryly. "If Casale wanted to kill me here, he would have done it long ago. No, as far as he knows, as far as Cage knows, we're either in New Jersey or Seattle, but I'll check for bombs if it will make you feel better."

"It will." She stood her ground, fighting worry for Roman and feeling foolish and vulnerable. She stepped into the house and shut the door. Finding herself in a compact entry with black and gold tile, she moved ahead, striding onto the gold carpet of a spacious combination kitchen/ living room.

A reflection of the man who lived here, it was furnished in blacks and golds, soft leathers and hard edges, very masculine, very sensuous, very inviting. Very much a bachelor pad. She felt a nudge of jealousy.

She could hear him upstairs rummaging through closets and cupboards. She drew in an unsteady breath and realized the room held his scent, mingled with a light touch of lemon oil. Obviously someone kept the place dust free.

Was that someone young and pretty? Someone he was involved with? The nudge of jealousy became a stab. How could she know him so well and yet know so few details of his life? Did it mean a person's past was only important in as much as it shaped the person they were today?

On the mantel a brass-framed photograph caught her eye, and she strode across the room and picked it up. It was of Roman and two other people, a man whose dark hair was graying at the temples and an auburn-haired woman in her early twenties whom Kerrie recognized as Wendy Waring.

Her heart felt suddenly heavy, suddenly sad. She set the photo down and feathered a finger over the top edge of the frame.

"THERE ARE NO INCENDIARY devices anywhere," Roman said as he came back into the room. She stood with her back to him, but from the slump of her shoulders he knew something was amiss. "Hey, what's wrong?"

"How am I going to tell Mom about the house?" Her voice wobbled.

His heart ached for her. His body longed for her. But she'd kept him at arm's length all day. He doubted she'd appreciate his affection when she was feeling so vulnerable. Hell, he had to do something. Say something. A dozen reassurances sprang to mind, but she wouldn't believe them. He could imagine how she was feeling, but he couldn't empathize. All he could do was remind her that she hadn't lost what mattered most. "You'll find the words."

"Will I?" She faced him. Unshed tears stood in her emerald eyes. "You were wrong, you know, about everything in my house being replaceable. How do I replace all the photos of the girls when they were babies? The photos of my dad? How will Mom replace every item she garnered in her life with him? How do we replace all our memories?"

"You haven't lost your memories, Irish." He gave in to his urges, closed the gap between them and pulled her into his arms. Her body trembled within his embrace. "Just the mementos of your memories."

She lifted her head. He gazed into her luminous emerald eyes and was instantly lost. It was so natural to kiss her, he couldn't help himself. Kerrie responded, kissing him back with ardor, with abandon, and like a wildfire, desire exploded between them.

Kerrie moaned, then struggled free and out of his arms. "No, I can't do this right now."

"Why, Irish?" He loomed over her, challenging her. So help him, she'd lied about this for the last time. "Because when we're together it isn't just mindless sex? Because that's the biggest lie of all?"

She blushed to her roots. "What do you want from me?"

"The truth." But could they get to the truth about their feelings for each other without some basic forgiveness? He dragged his fingers through his hair and inhaled deeply, blowing the breath through his nostrils. "Maybe we'd better settle something else first."

"What?"

He paced to the opposite end of the hearth and turned slowly toward her. "What's the real reason you didn't tell me about the kids after you knew I wasn't Nick Diamond?"

Kerrie blanched. She couldn't stand the hurt in his eyes. Maybe for the girls' sakes, it was time to start healing. Maybe clearing the air was a good step. She ran her tongue over her lips, which still tingled from his kiss. "I—I didn't want you to ever know about them. I—I was afraid you'd turn my life upside down, that you'd walk in and demand your rights, that you'd—" she swallowed hard over the crux of the matter "—you'd take them away from me."

She was still terrified of that. And she realized with a start, more terrified still that he wouldn't forgive her.

Oddly, he was smiling at her. A sweet, sad smile that held no resentment, only compassion. There didn't seem to be enough air in the room. His gaze unnerved her. She ducked her head and stared at her clenched hands.

"I would never take the girls away from you, Irish. I only want to be a part of their lives. I want to be their dad."

The simple declaration ripped at her heart. Silence followed. To Kerrie it seemed the force of that silence might very well push her further away from him. She'd never felt so helpless. She twisted her hands.

Roman said, "I forgive you."

Her head jerked up, and her gaze collided with his.

He narrowed his eyes. "Can you forgive me?"

She caught the sob that climbed her throat. "F-for what?"

"For not being there for you when you needed me. For what you must have suffered—the hardships of going through an unexpected pregnancy. The strain on your career. The difficulties you've faced being a single mother, a cop, raising two kids on your own."

Her mouth dropped open and she quickly clamped it shut. "Are you for real? You've actually thought about all of that?"

"Thought about it long and hard. I can't make it up to you and I don't know if you can forgive me."

She shook her head at him. Was he daft? "How could you have been there for me through any of that when I never told you I was pregnant in the first place?"

"Then maybe it's Fate we should blame." He waved his hands, his expression intense. "But we should forgive ourselves and each other. We need to. It's the only way we can move on, get past this."

She knew he was right. So damned good-looking, so damned sexy, and so damned smart. She smiled at him. "I forgive you, Donnello."

"Truce, then."

"Yes." Her smile broadened. "Our daughters are lucky to have you for their daddy."

She had selected her praise carefully. She had chosen right. It was the first time since he'd discovered he was the twins' father that she'd seen him smile at her without a trace of hurt. It warmed her heart, stole some of her fear about his relationship with the girls.

He moved closer, so close she was nearly pressed to the fireplace. His feral energy was as potent as an aphrodisiac. Kerrie struggled against the desire flaring within her.

He lowered his face toward hers. "What we shared last night was more than sex."

When he was this near she couldn't think. Somehow she managed to admit, "No, it was sweet and tender and giving."

He leaned closer, his lips hovering over hers. "It made me feel whole."

"Me, too," she murmured.

"I need to know how you feel about me."

She slammed her eyes shut. Could she tell him what was in her heart? Could she risk his rejection? Wasn't it better to reject first? No. She'd done that, and what had it gotten her? Hell, it wasn't as if she hadn't risked anything before now. This very relationship had been a risk from the moment she'd met this man.

She gazed up at him, intending to be one hundred percent honest. One look at his smoldering gaze and her resolve faltered. "I—I have strong feelings for you."

"Strong feelings? I was hoping for a better definition. Like 'I love you Roman'...because with every ounce of my being, I love you, Kerrie Muldoon."

He nuzzled his jaw against her temple, but didn't touch her otherwise—as though he were afraid that she didn't return his feelings. Tears burned her eyes, her throat.

He whispered, "Do you think that strong feeling you have for me could be love, Irish?"

She reached up to stroke his face, to touch his thick rich hair. "I know it is, Donnello."

He let out a low moan, then a laugh, then he gathered her against his body and kissed her until they were both breathless. He lifted his head, cupping her face in both his hands. "Marry me, Irish?"

Chapter Seventeen

It took Kerrie a long moment to realize that the alien feeling swirling through her was happiness. Sheer utter joy. "Yes, I'll marry you, Roman Donnello. Just don't say later that you didn't know what you were getting into."

"I promise." Laughing, he took her hand, led her to the sofa and pulled her down beside him. "Oh, God, this is incredible. First I'm a father, and now I'm going to be a husband."

Kerrie laughed. "Most men do it the other way around."

"Well, I'll get the rest in the right order." He leaned back, lost in plans. "I'll list the town house with a Realtor right away. We'll get a house somewhere near here, big enough for all of us, with a huge fenced backyard where the girls can play and you can grow herbs and vegetables, if you like. A big kitchen."

Kerrie was momentarily taken aback. "You want me to quit my job and move to Virginia?"

"Of course." He looked as if he couldn't believe she would consider anything else. "Your house is gone. What's to keep you there?"

Her ire flared. "After all that understanding talk about all I've suffered to hang onto my career, you expect me to give it up and become a full-time wife and mother?"

"The girls need you at home and I've got plenty of money. Why should you work?"

A red haze fogged Kerrie's eyes. The gall of the man. She leaped to her feet and poked her finger in the air near his chest. "I'm proud of what a good cop I am. I thought you were proud of that, too."

"I am proud of you." Roman scowled, his face as dark as a thundercloud, his demeanor unmistakably macho. "What do you want me to do—give up *my* job?"

"Why not?"

"For one thing, I probably make more money than you."

"Oh, it's back to money again?"

"You aren't being practical about this, Irish. Up till now, your mom's looked after the kids. But is she going to live with us after we marry? I doubt it. What if she gets married? Do you want some stranger watching the girls?"

"Why can't their daddy watch them?"

"Stubborn..." He rolled his eyes at her. "Woman, you've got your priorities all messed up."

"No, that's not it at all. You just expect me to make all the compromises—because I'm the woman."

"I'm making compromises. I'm selling my town house."

She bit her lower lip. "I thought you loved me..."

"I do..." His scowl wavered into abject confusion. "I thought love was supposed to solve these kinds of problems."

"So did I. Looks like we were both wrong."

ROMAN HAD ENVISIONED them falling into each other's arms, celebrating their upcoming wedding by making love all night. Instead he was alone in his bed, and Kerrie was across the hall in the guest room. The short-lived engagement called off. So much for honesty and love. They were miles apart on some important issues, and there didn't seem a compromise both of them could live with that would span the gap. He'd never felt so miserable in his life. Sleep eluded him.

In the morning, it was all he could do to breathe every time he looked at her. Tiny bruises under her eyes told him that she hadn't slept, either. Her attitude was frosty. She spoke only when necessary. Frustration gnawed him. Normally his kitchen easily accommodated two people. Today it wasn't big enough for either of their egos.

She crossed to the kitchen counter and reached for the coffeepot, her arm brushing his. That was all it took. That tiny contact and he wanted her. He dragged his hand through his hair. Then gripped her by both upper arms and pulled her close. Desire was heating her eyes as it was heating his belly. "We're pathetic, Irish. We can't stay out of bed together, but we can't live together. Can't set aside our differences long enough to make it through one day together—unless it's to find a killer."

"I'm not having this conversation with you today. I want to see my daughters. That, at least, is one subject we can agree on."

He released her with disgust, most of it directed at himself.

THEY SET OUT in Roman's Blazer for Philip Waring's estate. They'd been driving for half an hour on 66 West now and were nearly to Middleburg, a charming and historic community where spectacular horse farms and wineries lived side by side.

Traffic was heavy and Roman had an inexplicable, nagging feeling that they should hurry. Maybe he just wanted less hostile company. Kerrie hadn't spoken to him since they'd left his town house, she just stared out her side window, but whether she was actually enjoying the passing countryside, he couldn't tell. Her mood was as dark as the clouds overhead.

His wasn't much better. He exited off 66 West and said, "Another ten minutes to Philip's." The cell phone rang. He'd left it in the cubbyhole between the bucket seats. He snatched it to his ear, driving with one hand. "Hello."

It was Green, calling from New Jersey. "What have you got, Chuck."

"The warehouse wasn't wired with any explosives, Donnello, but they did find something interesting."

"Oh?"

"A body."

"Another body? Why didn't you call about that last night?" He could have used a diversion. Something to get his mind off his heartache.

"Thought you'd like to know who the bird was before I called. The body was badly decomposed—been there about four months. Just got a positive ID a few minutes ago."

Roman's muscles tensed. "Who was it?"

"Dante Casale."

Roman felt as if he'd been blindsided. Casale dead for four months? If he wasn't heading up the campaign to kill Kerrie or the members of her family, that meant Tully Cage was. Why? What possible motive could he have? It didn't make any sense. "Let me think about this and I'll call you back."

"Donnello!" But Roman had disconnected and laid the telephone down. He brought Kerrie up to speed. She sat in silence, apparently processing the news. He could barely process it himself. Finally she said, "What is Tully's motive?"

It was the main question plaguing him, too. He was amazed how much alike they thought, how well they worked together. Why did she have to be so stubborn? Why couldn't she get her priorities in order?

Before he could answer her the telephone rang again. He lifted it to his ear. "Hello?"

"Are you on your way yet?" Philip asked.

"About eight more minutes." Roman passed a slow-moving vehicle pulling a horse trailer.

"Good, because a friend of Glynna and Kerrie's has turned up."

"What friend?" Roman's heart tripped. "Not Tully Cage?"

"Goodness, no. This is a woman. A neighbor from Seattle. She's down here visiting her daughter. We ran into them at a local restaurant last night. Quite a pleasant surprise for Glynna. Seem like nice women, even if the mother is a bit too fond of purple for my tastes."

He frowned. "Sophia Sommerville?"

"Oh, I see you know her, too. Grand. See you soon, then."

"Philip." Roman's nerves felt raw. "Tell Wong to keep his eyes peeled for a blond man with a crew cut. He has a scar through his left eyebrow and answers to the name Tully Cage."

There was a pause on Philip's end. "Is he Loverboy?"

"Yes. I'll fill you in when we get there."

"Fine, fine. We've just finished tea, and the twins are taking a nap." He yawned, then chuckled. "Sleepy myself. Maybe I should join them."

He hung up again and pulled his gaze from the road long enough to relay Philip's message about Sophia. Kerrie's eyebrows twitched. "What is she—"

The telephone rang a third time, interrupting her question. Roman said, "Donnello, here."

"You cut me off before you heard the rest of the report," Agent Green said, then he paused. "You know, I shouldn't have called you back. After reconsidering, well, it's probably nothing. It struck me as odd when I heard it, but I suppose it's not really unusual that those old warehouses on the wharfs would have cats prowling through them for rats.''

"Cats?"

"Yeah, Dante Casale's suit was feathered with orange-and-black cat hair.''

Roman shook his head and laughed. ''You're right, Chuck. I'm sure that hasn't anything to do the price of fish in New Jersey.''

As soon as he hung up, he recounted Chuck's news about the cat hair. He expected Kerrie would find it as funny as he did. When she didn't laugh, he glanced at her.

Her face was turned toward him, the color gone, her eyes wide with terror. "Professor Plum.''

His blood ran cold as the connections slammed together in his own mind. Somehow Sophia Sommerville was involved with Loverboy. And right now, she was with their daughters.

Like a death knell, Loverboy's words tolled inside Roman's head. *I'm one step ahead of you.*

Chapter Eighteen

"Sophia Sommerville." Roman slammed his foot on the gas pedal. The Blazer accelerated like a race car. He tossed Kerrie the cell phone. "Call Philip. Get Charlie on the line and tell him what's happening."

Her hands shook so hard she had to dial twice. The phone rang ten times. Twenty. "No answer."

The panic in her voice chilled his blood. He said, "Call 911."

A moment later, she was explaining the problem to an emergency dispatcher. "Tell them to hurry."

She disconnected, dropped the cell phone beside her and clenched her hands together to stop their trembling. "We sat right in her house and made our plans. She must've had some kind of recorder going."

"Or another bug. No wonder she left so accommodatingly." He veered recklessly around slower vehicles.

"It's unbelievable." Terror gripped her. "That house sat empty almost a year when she bought it. First thing she did was paint it purple. We thought she was whimsical, a bit eccentric."

"She was trying to get your attention."

"You said Philip and Mom ran into her at dinner last night." She felt a chasm of hysteria ripping through her brain and willed herself not to fall into it. "That's how she met Mom, she literally ran into her in Riley's Market—with her shopping cart.''

"Figures. When she didn't get the results she wanted from painting the house, she initiated the shopping cart incident.''

Kerrie's heart thundered. Roman glanced at her and she saw the fear tripping through her reflected in his eyes.

"To think I trusted her with the girls," she swore. A worse thought churned her stomach. "Now the girls trust her.''

Kerrie knew in that moment that she would never trust anyone easily again. Especially where her children were concerned. "Oh, dear God, please let them be all right.''

"They will be." They had to be. Roman drew a ragged breath. The Waring estate, smaller by many standards than most horse farms in the area, loomed ahead. High brick walls ringed the perimeter. The entrance was barred by a huge, white wrought iron gate, electrically controlled from within the house.

Roman punched in the security code. His fear leaped a notch higher. He clenched the steering wheel as the gate crawled open, then he stomped on the gas. The tires squealed on the tarmac.

Kerrie said, "How are Cage and Sophia connected? Is this about Tito Fabrizio or not?''

Roman's scalp felt two sizes too small for his head. "I'll bet she's Tito's widow. And Cage is a son-in-law.''

Kerrie gasped. "The daughter Philip mentioned, Tito's daughter?''

"Yes. Cindy Faber—unless I miss my guess.''

Trees lined the path to the house, blocking the view of the horse fields and barns in the near distance behind the mansion.

"Do you think Cage is her husband?''

"It's possible. Lucinda Fabrizio, Tito's youngest daughter, was supposedly widowed last year." Roman jerked the

Blazer to a stop on the circular apron, then leaned across Kerrie and dug a gun out of the glove box.

"No. No guns." She was surprised at her own vehemence. At her objection. But her daughters' well-being was priority number one. "Not around the girls."

"It may be the only way we can assure their safety until backup arrives."

She couldn't argue with his logic.

"I won't use it unless I have to. I promise." He tucked it into the waistband of his jeans at the small of his back. "Safety's on."

They ran to the house. The front door stood open. Roman hesitated, then stepped stealthily into the foyer. Kerrie copied his movements. Quiet permeated the house—as if it held its breath. "This way," Roman whispered, pointing toward an archway ahead and to the right.

Behind them the door slammed shut. Kerrie jerked around. Every muscle taut, readied for combat.

"Welcome." Cindy Faber, wearing an outfit similar to the one she'd worn at Mike Springer's two days earlier, leveled a gun at them. She was too far away for Kerrie to overpower her. "We're all in the living room. You know the way, Donnello. Lead on."

My girls. Let my girls be all right, resounded like a chant in Kerrie's head. But she knew she had to ignore it, or risk making this bad situation worse.

They entered a large oblong-shaped room. Vaguely aware that it reminded her of the house she'd grown up in—same colors, same furniture, same formal flavor—Kerrie froze. The girls weren't present. Her instant relief fled in blood-curdling panic. Sophia Sommerville was splashing gasoline from a small red can onto the carpet and curtains.

The stench burned Kerrie's nose. Where were the twins? Napping? Her gaze jumped to the three people sprawled on the furniture nearby—Charlie Wong sliding out of a high-backed arm chair, her mother and a man, presumably Philip Waring, lying slumped together on a deep purple Victorian sofa. They all looked asleep.

Her chest squeezed with pain. She wheeled on Cindy, oblivious to the gun. "What did you do to them?"

"Irish, don't."

Kerrie stepped back, glancing again at her mother and the two men. Were they alive? She saw no blood. Cindy hadn't shot them. What then? A tea service sat on the coffee table, cups abandoned. She frowned, stifling the overpowering urge to check on her mother. Drugged? Poisoned? She glared at Cindy. "What did you put in the tea?"

"Why don't you have some and see if you can guess?" Sophia set her gas can down and strode straight to Roman.

"I'm not drinking that," Kerrie snapped.

"Then you'll force me to put a bullet into this man's gorgeous head." Sophia patted Roman down, found and took his gun. "With his own revolver."

Kerrie's pulse wobbled. Damn. If Roman moved toward his gun, he'd surely be shot. Dear God, they had to find the children. What if they'd been drugged or poisoned, also? What was taking the police so long?

Cindy poured a cup of tea and held it out to Kerrie. "You heard my mother. Drink up."

Kerrie grasped hold of her slipping nerve and reached for the cup. With a jolt of memory, she realized why Cindy had looked familiar the other day at Mike Springer's house. Her large sable eyes were the same as those of the "man" whose table she'd rammed into at McRory's the day Glynna was nearly stabbed. Her throat tightened.

Sophia jammed the revolver against Roman's temple.

Kerrie took a sip of tepid tea. She'd expected it to taste bitter. It tasted like normal tea. Fear dampened her palms. Some poisons, she knew, were tasteless.

Roman said, "You don't expect to get away with this?"

"Of course, we do. Let the police search for a fluffy old fool named Sophia Sommerville and her ditzy daughter, Sally. No one will connect those two with Sophia and Lucinda Fabrizio, who have been on an extended tour of Europe this past year, following the deaths of their husbands within days of one another."

Roman moved away from the gun. "Why did Mike Springer go along with this operation?"

"Money." Cindy laughed, waving her gun at Kerrie, motioning her to drink up. "Mike was desperate. We handed him a fistful of moolah in exchange for a few hours of his precious time. All he had to do was pick up women from a classified ad. The state his finances were in, he jumped at it. But lately he was starting to wonder why the women he dated were all becoming victims of Loverboy."

"Is that why he was killed?" Roman asked.

"That, and because," Sophia spat out, "he was the one person more than himself whom that betrayer Casale loved."

"Where is Tully Cage—or whatever his real name is?"

"Muldoon's partner?" Cindy gaped at him as if she didn't understand the question.

"I'm right behind you, Donnello," Cage said.

Roman's heart stopped. He whipped around. Tully strode into the room from the foyer, revolver drawn.

Sophia yelped in surprise. Roman grabbed her, yanked the gun from her hand and pulled her to him, using her as a shield against Cage.

At the same moment, Kerrie threw the remaining contents of her teacup into Cindy's face. Cindy yowled. Kerrie threw a karate chop to her stomach. Cindy buckled and let go of her gun. Her knees hit the floor. A split second later, Kerrie had the gun trained on her partner.

"Drop your weapon, Cage," Roman said.

Cage just laughed at them. "Hey, man, I'm on your side. I'm here to help you."

"Just put the weapon down and kick it over here," Roman ordered.

Cage did as he was directed. "You're making a big mistake, man. Lucinda Fabrizio, alias Cindy Faber, is Loverboy. I'm just plain ol' Tully Cage from Hoboken."

Kerrie decided Roman could handle it and tucked her gun at the small of her back and hurried to her mother. She was breathing. As were Philip Waring and Charlie Wong. "I'll call an ambulance."

"I already did," Cage said. "Used the cell phone in your Blazer."

They could hear sirens at a great distance. Were the police responding to her 911 call? Or was Cage telling the truth? Kerrie couldn't wait around to find out. Nor could she do any more for her mother or the others. She had to find her children. "Philip said the twins were taking a nap. Where?"

"Upstairs," Roman said.

She raced to the stairs. Roman ached to go with her. Instead he thrust Sophia to the floor. Roughly. Then he concentrated on Cage. Roman eyed him skeptically. "If you're on our side, how'd you end up here?"

"I was watching Springer's house and saw her—" he pointed to Cindy who was slumped beside the sofa. "She parked down the street and sneaked in the back way. When she came out, she'd changed clothes. I called it in, told the night clerk I was following a perp. In all the excitement over Muldoon's house, the message never made it to the lieutenant's desk. I realized that when I called earlier today from the airport. Muldoon had enough to deal with. I figured there'd be time enough to fill you both in on what I was doing—if anything came of it."

"What happened in the beach house in Wildwood?" Roman asked.

"I waited until she went inside, then followed her and I hid in a closet. Mike Springer showed up almost immediately. But before I could prevent it, she slit his throat and took off. I had no way of notifying the police and couldn't risk sticking around to be questioned and lose track of her.

"The next thing I knew we were on a plane headed to Dulles. In Middleburg, she met up with Sophia. They arranged to 'bump' into Kerrie's mom and Mr. Waring last night. I've been hiding outside. I was coming around the end of the house when I saw you come inside. I sneaked inside and listened, then used your phone."

Roman considered Cage's story. It made sense. And Cindy had gaped at Roman oddly when he'd asked about Cage—as if she hadn't the slightest idea why he was asking. Sophia claimed Lucinda's husband did die a year ago. That wasn't a cover, that was their true alibi. He pressed his lips together contritely, deciding he'd wait until backup arrived to make a decision.

Cage swore softly and pointed to something behind Roman. "Fire."

Roman kept his eyes trained on Cage, certain it was a trick. A second later, he heard a roar. Too late, he realized Cindy Faber was no longer sitting by the couch. He spun around. Flames licked along the floor and up the drapes, spreading and leaping with terrifying speed. Cindy Faber had dropped a lighter. Now she ran in the opposite direction for the French doors. Roman shot her. She collapsed in a heap. Sophia screamed and scurried off the floor, rushing to her daughter.

Cage said, "Quick—get Kerrie and the kids outside. I'll take her mother. Then you can help me with the others."

Roman sprinted for the stairs.

Chapter Nineteen

Kerrie found the twins in the room closest to the stair landing. They lay against the pillows of the four-poster bed, cute as a pair of Kewpie dolls. Chubby pink cheeks. Fluffy hair. Bow-shaped lips. Their eyes closed. Were they sleeping? Her heart slammed her ribs. Or had they been drugged? Poisoned?

She flew to the bed, but reined in the urge to shake them awake. That might scare them. "Gabby?"

She held her breath, then said louder, "Maureen."

Gabby scrunched her face. Opened her eyes. Squirmed up off the pillow. "Mommy."

Maureen blinked, stretched and opened her eyes. She focused on Kerrie's face and grinned shyly. "Nappy aw done?"

Kerrie released a ragged breath. "Thank you, God."

They were bright eyed and eager. Just fine. Still, she would have the paramedics check them over as soon as they arrived. She threw her arms open wide. "Come here, my angels."

The girls kicked off the covers and snuggled into her embrace. From somewhere on the first floor, she heard a loud pop. Her nerves pinched. A gun?

Before she could speculate, she heard Roman shouting.

His voice came closer. She grabbed the girls off the bed. The door burst open. "Moman," Gabby said.

Maureen smiled at him.

A look of vast relief spread over his face at the sight of them. "Yes! Thank God, they're all right. Quick, Irish. We have to get out. The house is on fire."

He scooped up Gabby. Kerrie hoisted Maureen. They fled into the hall. As black smoke billowed up from the foyer, Roman covered Gabby's head with his coat and Kerrie covered Maureen's head with hers. They scrambled down the stairs. Cage emerged from the living room, Glynna in his arms. She was waking up. Struggling. Coughing.

"Put her in the Blazer," Roman ordered.

Cage deposited Glynna on the front passenger seat. Roman and Kerrie set the girls on the backseat and fastened their seat belts. Kerrie said, "I'll move it away from the house and call for a fire truck. Go get Philip."

But Cage was already returning with Philip when Roman reached the front door. Philip was also coming around. They set him down on the grass a good ten feet from the mansion, then ran back inside for Charlie.

Blaring sirens accompanied the arrival of the patrol car and ambulance. Kerrie backed the Blazer several feet down the driveway, clearing a path for them. Fear sat on her heart. Twice in two days, she'd been forced to watch the ravages of fire. Both times because of the same person. Where was Cindy Faber?

INSIDE THE HOUSE, Roman and Cage ducked low, covering their faces with their coats. They made their way to Charlie Wong. He was moaning. In the corner against the French doors, Roman caught the soft weeping of a distressed woman. "Sophia?"

She lifted her head. "Yes, here. We're over here. Please, help me with Lucinda."

Cage muttered, "I checked her vitals—Cindy is dead."

"Sophia!" Roman shouted over the crackling of the fire. It had grown into a fence separating them. "Cindy is gone. Get out. Go out the French doors. Now."

"You killed her, Donnello." Sophia's voice sounded disembodied. "You'll pay for this."

"Come on, Roman," Cage urged. "Before none of us can get out of here. The cavalry has arrived. They can take care of Sophia."

As they hauled Charlie through the front door, one of the two uniformed patrolmen stopped them. "Detective Muldoon says there's still a woman and her daughter inside. Whereabouts?"

Roman shook his head. "The daughter is dead. I shot her as she tried to escape. Her mother may have fled through the French doors on the other side of the house. She's an accessory in five murders in Seattle and an arson. Another two murders in New Jersey and this fire."

The patrolman commanded his partner to watch the front door and set off at a run for the corner of the mansion. Roman and Cage abandoned Charlie at the ambulance.

"Donnello!" Sophia's cry rang through the smoke. She appeared a second later, her hair singed and smoking, her face streaked black. She lifted her hand. Cage shouted, "She's got a gun."

A second later, Cage lurched back, knocking Roman off his feet. Then Cage stared down, looking surprised to see a large red blotch forming on his shirtfront. As he crumpled to the ground, Kerrie screamed.

The uniformed cop jumped Sophia, wrestled her to her knees and cuffed her. The *bleat-bleat* of a fire truck punctuated the morning air.

Roman leaped up, and brushed himself off. He spotted Kerrie, kneeling beside Cage. "Paramedic! Now!"

The emergency team hurried to Cage. "We've gotta stop this blood."

"Come on, Irish. Let them do their work." Roman pulled Kerrie to one side. She held herself stiff, trembling, watching the paramedics working on Tully. Her face was ashen, and tears slipped down her cheeks. Roman's heart was in his throat. He folded her into his arms.

She clung to him. "He saved our lives, Roman. We should have trusted him. We thought he was Loverboy. I'll never forgive myself."

Roman's gut was in knots. Cage had just taken a bullet meant for him. He wouldn't forgive himself, either. Kerrie said, "What if he doesn't make it?"

Roman held her tighter, issuing reassurances as Cage was loaded onto a stretcher and hurried into the ambulance. It didn't look good. He'd heard the paramedic say Cage's pulse was thready; he'd lost a lot of blood and he'd be lucky to make it the hospital.

THE NEXT TWO HOURS passed in a blur of activity. The fire department contained the blaze at the Waring estate to the living room, but smoke and water damage were extensive. Kerrie and Roman drove the "poison" victims to the hospital in Roman's Blazer. It turned out they were only suffering from a mild sedative. All three had been revived and released.

Charlie, his services no longer needed, took a taxi to his condo in Centreville. Still, Kerrie was frightened, edgy. Loverboy's reign of terror had ended and Philip's insurance would repair the mansion, but Tully Cage was in God's hands. He had made it to the hospital. Into surgery. And now they awaited the outcome. The twins were playing on the floor of the surgical waiting area with their bunnies and "Moman" whom they were now calling "Daddy." Kerrie paced back and forth across the room. As she passed the chairs where Philip and her mother were seated, it struck her that Roman's friend was a very good-looking man. Not boldly so, like Roman. Not plastic-handsome like Dr. Jon Vauter. But in an understated way that complemented her mother.

She wondered at that wayward thought. "Are you sure you're both all right?"

"I'm fine, Kerrie Carleen," Glynna assured her.

Philip nodded. "We're tougher than we look."

Her mother patted her hand. "You save your prayers for Tully."

"I am."

In unison, Philip and Glynna said, "He'll be fine."

They glanced at each another, grinned and linked the little fingers of their right hands. Philip leaned toward her mom. "What goes up the chimney?"

Glynna answered, "Smoke."

"What comes down the chimney?"

"Santa Claus."

They shut their eyes, then looked at each other and said, again in unison, "Let your wish and mine never be broken." They wrenched their fingers apart and laughed.

Amazement swirled through Kerrie. Philip was super-stitious. Her mother had found a soul mate, and if she wasn't mistaken, he was as smitten with her as she seemed to be with him.

Dr. Jon had never made her mother glow like this. Only her dad had done that. Kerrie smiled wistfully at the thought. Roman was right. She still had her memories.

She moved across the room and sank into a hard plastic chair. Roman scrambled up off the floor and came to her. He hunkered down on his heels, took both her hands in his and gazed at her pensively, seriously. "The past couple of hours were a reality check. For the first time in my life, I was scared and didn't enjoy it.''

She didn't know where this was going, but she'd also done a lot of soul-searching. She grinned wryly. ''Losing your edge, Donnello?''

''Falling in love, fatherhood, they'll do that to a man.''

She laughed softly and shook her head. ''We *are* pathetic.''

''No, we're just a breed apart from most. We've always gotten a kick out of danger—it's one of the reasons we both went into law enforcement. But we have more important priorities to consider now.'' His golden eyes glowed with love. ''I want to be a full-time father. I want to be your full-time husband. I don't want some other man spending his days and nights with any of my girls.''

Kerrie felt a tingle of warmth starting through her, felt the chill easing from her heart and she had an abiding sense that everything would turn out well after all. ''You know what you're saying?''

Roman nodded. ''Yes, Irish, I'm ready to talk compromise.''

Cage's surgeon entered the room.

Epilogue

Nine months later

"Tully Cage, you are a sight for sore eyes." Kerrie held open the door of her new house and ushered him inside. He looked wonderful. The bullet had gone clean through his chest missing every vital organ by millimeters. Somehow he'd survived despite the massive loss of blood. He claimed he'd lived to make Roman and her pay for thinking he was Loverboy.

Whatever had kept him alive was fine with Kerrie. He was a man she would always want on her side. His crew cut had grown out. His tawny hair was swept off his forehead. She'd never realized it before, but he slightly resembled the actor Don Johnson. "Ready to get back to work?"

"Tomorrow will be soon enough. Right now, I want to see my godchildren." He draped his arm around her shoulder and kissed her on the temple. "How's their mommy feeling?"

"A little fat, but otherwise, the doctor says I can start back to work next week."

"So soon? With all you've done in the last two days?"

"A few hours a day at first. Come on. Roman is in the great room."

She led him out of the entry, her heart content, her new

life and her new home more than she'd ever imagined they
would be. The foyer opened onto a spacious room furnished with desks and computers and filing cabinets. "This
is the business area. It's adjacent to the main living quar-
ters back there." She pointed to a set of closed double
doors. "We have six bedrooms upstairs."

"Seems you're doing your darndest to fill them." Cage
teased.

She grinned. The extent to which Roman and she had
compromised was a true measure of their love. They'd
both quit their jobs, bought five acres in Middleburg, Virginia, and built this two-story, colonial house with a huge
fenced backyard. "The business is gaining solid ground."

"I'm honored that you and Roman wanted me on the
team."

"We're the ones who are honored." The business was
Bodyguards, Inc., a security company Roman and she had
started shortly after their honeymoon. It had been Roman's
idea to run the business from home, so they could both be
both working and stay-at-home parents.

She crossed the office with Cage following. "Charlie
already has an assignment for you."

"Wong's been promoted to manager?"

"Just the past five days. Good thing he was between
assignments when I went into labor. He's the only one,
besides Roman and me, who knows office procedure."

She pulled the double doors open, revealing one large
room that comprised both a country-size kitchen and great
room. Another compromise was visible in the decor. Instead of black leather furniture, they had settled on forest
green leather furniture with burgundy accents and black
accessories. The adult comforts interspersed with a children's play area where toys abounded.

Roman sat in the middle of the deep cushioned, leather
sofa. His raven hair was mussed, falling seductively over

his forehead, his concentration on the newborn babies lying one on each of his thighs. His face showed utter rapture.

"Fatherhood looks good on you, Donnello," Cage said, his accent thick with emotion.

Roman lifted his face and beamed at Tully and Kerrie. She'd conceived on the night her house had been broken into. The one night they'd made love without protection. The odds of it happening twice in one lifetime were phenomenal. A fact that laid all of Roman's misgivings about his sterility permanently to rest. "It feels even better, my friend."

"So these are the new twins." Cage sounded ill at ease. He wiped his hands on his pant legs as he strode to Roman for a closer look.

"I wanted boys," Kerrie said.

"I wanted girls," Roman said.

"And you got one of each," Cage said. "Who do they look like?"

"I wanted them to look like Roman."

"I wanted them to look like Irish."

"I'd say you both prevailed. Their daddy's thick black hair and their mommy's stubborn chin."

The front door burst open to the unmistakable exuberance of Gabriella and Maureen, who came crashing into the great room a moment later. Glynna and Philip followed. They had married almost a month to the day after meeting, and still had the glow of newlyweds. For Kerrie, the best part was having her mother so near, only four minutes up the road.

"Mommy, we missed you!" Maureen said.

"Missed you!" Gabby nodded. "We rode Poppy Phil's pony."

Laughing, Kerrie stooped and rained hugs and kisses on her daughters. "Oh, I missed you, too, my darlings."

She raised back up and hugged her mother. "Mom, Philip, thank you so much for keeping them."

Glynna released her and smiled. "We love baby-sitting."

Philip nodded. "Anytime. They fill the house with joy."

Maureen said, "You's tummy's not fat."

Gabby said, "Did those baby get out of you's tummy?" The adults laughed.

"Yes, Gabby. Daddy has the new babies now. See." Kerrie pointed toward Roman. The girls were three years old and talked incessantly, but seeing their places on their daddy's lap usurped by two new babies, silenced them.

Roman laughed and beckoned them over to him to meet their brother and sister for the first time. They hurried to the couch and cuddled against him, one on each side. Seeing her husband surrounded by their children stole Kerrie's breath away. She thought her heart would burst with joy.

Roman glanced at Gabby, then Maureen, then at their son. "This is your new brother."

Gabby touched the baby's tiny hand. Her eyes widened as the baby grabbed hold of her finger. "Who's his name?"

Roman smiled. "Nick."

He repeated the process with their new daughter. This time it was Maureen who was closer. She didn't reach for the baby's hand, but hugged Roman's side tighter. "Who's shes name?"

"Diamond," Roman said.

An incredulous chuckle burst from Cage. "You named the twins Nick and Diamond?"

Kerrie ran her hand through her wild red hair and smirked at him. "What else would we name them?"